LET HER REST

A NORTHERN MICHIGAN ASYLUM NOVEL

J.R. ERICKSON

Copyright © 2020 J.R. Erickson
All rights reserved.
This is a work of fiction. Names, characters, places, and incidents either are the products of the author's imagination or are used fictitiously. Any resemblance to actual persons, living or dead, businesses, companies, events, or locales is entirely coincidental.

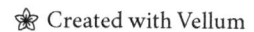

Created with Vellum

DEDICATION

For my Grandma Williams. Ninety looks good on you.

AUTHOR'S NOTE

Thanks so much for picking up a Northern Michigan Asylum Novel. I want to offer a disclaimer before you dive into the story. This is an entirely fictional novel. Although there was once a real place known as the Northern Michigan Asylum, which inspired me to write these books, it is in no way depicted within them.

In truth, nearly every book I have read about the asylum, later known as the Traverse City State Hospital, was positive. This holds true for the stories of many of the staff who worked there as well. I live in the Traverse City area and regularly visit the grounds of the former asylum. It's now known as the Village at Grand Traverse Commons. It was purchased in 2000 by Ray Minervini and the Minervini Group, who have been restoring it since that time. Today, it's a mixed-use space of boutiques, restaurants and condominiums. If you ever visit the area, I encourage you to visit The Village at Grand Traverse Commons. You can experience first-hand the asylums—both old and new—and walk the sprawling grounds.

1

"Jake... Jake! I'm talking to you!"

He looked up from his sodden corn flakes. "What? Sorry. I was thinking about the job today."

Allison sputtered and threw up her hands, getting one tangled in her unbrushed hair. "You're always thinking about the damned job. When do you think about us? Am I alone in this? If you came home, and I'd packed and left, would you even notice or just grab a beer and plop in front of the TV?"

"Allison, I'm not a drunk."

"Do you hear what I'm saying? Can you honestly be this dense? I'm not talking about you being drunk. I'm talking about you being absent from our life, from this room!"

Jake braced an elbow on the kitchen table and propped his chin on his fist. "I'm here, darlin', front and center. Go ahead." He considered a more genuine approach, but Christ if Allison didn't pull this shit every single morning.

She blinked at him, the tears working into her eyes, and he sighed and reached across the table. "Honey, I'm not trying to hurt your feelings. I have a lot on my mind. This job out on Rudolph is a doozy. I keep trying to figure how I'm going to get the 'dozer down that two-track. If I could just knock out that one oak… but man, she's a beaut. I don't blame Reggie for wanting to keep her."

Her tears vanished, and she ripped her hand from his, pushing back from the table and storming into the living room. Her footfalls pounded up the stairs and the bathroom door slammed.

Jake sighed, stood, and walked his bowl to the sink. He dumped the contents into the drain and flicked on the garbage disposal, flinching at the loud grinding sound as it chewed and swallowed the mush. In the window above the sink, he caught his reflection in the reddening glass as a morning glow crept over the trees. A blond fuzz covered his cheeks and chin. He hadn't shaved in a couple of weeks and he had been flirting with the idea of a beard, but with summer fast approaching, he'd likely scrap the idea.

He should have gone upstairs and made amends. Instead, Jake shoved his socked feet into his work boots, grabbed his thermos of coffee and walked into the brisk spring morning to his truck.

He backed down the driveway and Allison's silhouette filled the window in the master bedroom upstairs. He quickly flicked his gaze to the rearview mirror and reversed into the street.

When Jake pulled into the parking lot of his excavating business, he spotted Willis Dooby's truck and the little red Geo Ricardo Denaud had been driving since the transmission in his Dodge Ram had thrown up a death rattle two weeks before. The guys loved to heckle Ricardo, the nearly six-foot-five giant with a mop of black hair and muscles that made bodybuilders envious, for driving his wife's teeny-tiny two-door coupé.

Jake leaped from his truck, hitting his stride and all but forgetting about the tussle with Allison as he walked toward the two guys sitting on the tailgate of Willis's truck. They sipped coffee from flowery porcelain mugs that Jake's secretary

Barbara insisted on hanging from the little wooden mug tree next to the coffeepot in the office.

Despite Jake's best efforts to nudge her towards a more manly ambience, and repeated reminders that they were an excavating business, not a ladies' hat shop, Barbie had outfitted the office in framed photographs of Victorian ladies in frilly dresses, lamps with floral-patterned shades and candy dishes filled not with candy, but dried flowers and herbs.

"Barbie made some kind of apple dessert in there. Better get some before the Jones boys show up and devour it," Willis announced.

"Strudel," Ricardo corrected. "And here they come now."

The Jones boys, Allen and Jerry, squealed into the parking lot on two tires, causing shovels and rakes to crash inside the bed of their lifted pick-up. Their matching blond heads bobbed as the truck bounced back onto its wheels.

Two years into his forties, Jake no longer had the spitfire he saw in the Jones boys, but he liked to lean into the flame once in a while and remember.

Before Allen and Jerry could descend on the office, Jake hurried over, pushing through the glass door and into the pungent scent of orange rind, cinnamon and rose.

Barbie, clad in her usual jeans and brightly colored top—today a button-up blouse covered in pink flamingos—talked on the phone. She winked and gave him a wave. "Oh, come on now, Sampson, you old devil. You know I'm a married woman."

Barbie, a soft, round woman in her fifties, married for thirty years with three grown children she called daily, loved to flirt with the clients of Dig Deep Excavating. Jake could attribute half of his business to his secretary's wily phone skills.

"Sure thing," she continued. "Jerry and Allen will be there within the hour. Of course they'll bring the skid steer. No, you can't drive it, you scoundrel. You're not on our insurance, are you?" She released a throaty laugh. "Have a good day, Sampson. Oh, yes, I will. Thank you. Bye."

Jake scooped a chunk of strudel onto a china plate adorned in dainty purple flowers. "You better hide these plates before Jerry and Allen come in," he told her, sticking a forkful into his mouth.

She strained up in her chair and narrowed her eyes toward the window at the two young men who'd burst from their truck like jack-in-the-boxes. "Oh, no, I won't. Those boys know better than to get rowdy in here."

Jake smirked and gobbled up the pastry while leaning over Barbie to look at the desk-sized weekly calendar. "We finished Sampson's driveway last week. Why's he on the schedule again?"

"Oh, you know Sampson. He loves the driveway so much, he wants gravel clear back to his barn now."

Jake chuckled. "I'm pretty sure he just loves a reason to call and hit on you."

"Oh, you stop it, Jake Edwards. Sampson is just a baby."

"He's forty."

She fluttered her hand dismissively.

"Huntington, Stowers..." Jake read the names, double-checking which guys and which machines would need to go where on what days. "Can you call CAT and see if they've got a mini-excavator available for the septic system out at Hancock's place?"

Barbie made a note on a piece of yellow stationery topped by a spattering of red roses. "Yep, and Reggie called to say if you have to take down the oak, he'll allow it, though it will break his heart."

Jake frowned, imagining the tree with her giant trunk and gnarled branches. He shook his head. "I can't take her down. It'd break my heart too. Call him and tell him I need to push his project back until the end of the week. I need to brainstorm another way to get back there."

"And Dave Wilson wanted you to call him back with an estimate for a pole barn foundation behind his daughter's house."

The door flung open and Jerry and Allen rushed inside. They beelined for the coffee stand, not bothering with china plates. Scooping up the remaining strudel, they shoved it into their mouths, jabbing their forks at each other's bites as they polished off what remained in the pan.

Jake grinned at Barbie, who shook her head, barely concealing her look of satisfaction. Barbie regarded the Jones boys as she did her own sons. The motherly affection covered the entire crew, even Willis, who was a good five years older than her.

"And you know what else Sampson said?" she announced, cheeks glowing.

"That the door's unlocked, just come on up?" Jerry asked. His brother guffawed and gave him a high five.

Barbie shot them a scathing look. "No, thank you very much! He said the Rolling Stones are coming to the Palace of Auburn Hills this summer. Isn't that so exciting?"

"Barbie, you do realize it's 1996, right?" Allen asked.

"Unlike you boys, I keep track of the days of the week, yes," she said.

"And the Rolling Stones were hip in the 60s. Do you think Mick will be rolled onstage in a wheelchair?" Allen continued.

"Oh, you two just put a cork in it," she snapped.

Jake grinned. "Sounds great, Barbie. Better tell the old man to get you tickets for your birthday."

Jerry leaned in. "'But remember, you can't always get what you want,'" he sang.

Through the window, Jake watched a black sedan pull into the muddy back lot.

"That wash job was a waste of five bucks," Allen commented, also watching the car.

A tall, slender woman dressed entirely in black stepped from the car. Large black glasses covered the top half of her face. A plait of dark hair fell to the center of her back. She walked briskly as if to retreat from the chill, though the spring morning was fast approaching sixty degrees.

Allen whistled. "Got a new hottie on the line?" he asked Jake.

"Bite your tongue," Barbie snapped. "Jake is with Allison. Of course he doesn't—" But she didn't finish her statement as the woman brushed into the office, her nose wrinkling with distaste as her eyes flicked to a glass bowl of potpourri. Barbie bristled.

The woman paused and gazed around the room, removing her glasses to reveal large almond-shaped green eyes. Her shirt beneath her black coat was white, silky-looking, and spotted in little Scottie dogs. After noting each face, she fixed on Jake. "Jacob Dunn?"

Jake gave a little start and glanced toward the Jones boys. The name Dunn startled him. He hadn't heard it in thirty years.

"Jacob?" Jerry snickered, elbowing his brother.

"How can we help you, ma'am?" Barbie asked, stepping from behind her large desk and slightly blocking Jake, her mama bear instincts kicking in.

The woman blinked at Barbie, and then stepped to the side, fixing her eyes on Jake. "You are him, aren't you?"

"Uh, no, sorry. Jake Edwards, not Dunn." He thrust out his hand, but she didn't take it.

Her own hands, narrow, bony and covered in silver rings, stayed at her sides. "I'm Petra Collins. Do you remember me?"

Jake stared at her, puzzled. He doubted he could have forgotten her. The name alone should have rung a few bells, but he drew a blank. "No, I'm sorry. Did you ask about some excavating work or—?" He gestured emptily. Or what, he didn't know.

She looked at Barbie and then Allen and Jerry. "It's probably best if we speak in private. Do you have an office?"

She was very forward and Barbie stiffened at the suggestion

that Jake would have anything to say to this woman that he couldn't say within her earshot.

"Sure, yeah. Follow me." He gave Barbie an appeasing look and opened a door into the inner office.

Bids and rolled prints covered his desk except for a small space in the front where he scratched out property diagrams, estimated costs, and sometimes doodled as he planned out projects in his head. It didn't have the homey feel that Barbie had created in the outer office. The walls were white and bare. The only item of décor was a lamp pushed to the corner of the desk as paper filled its original spot.

"Oh," he said, realizing the office contained only one chair, his own. He dipped back into Barbie's office and grabbed a chair, dragging it into the room and avoiding Barbie's curious gaze and the matching smirks on Jerry and Allen. "Here, have a seat," he told Petra.

Jake hurried around to his own chair, feeling oddly nervous. He disliked sitting in the stark little room with the stranger, a woman he'd easily have noticed at a bar, but who in the confines of his office made him uneasy.

Petra sat in the chair and folded her hands in her lap, studying him. "Your eyes are the same," she told him.

He blushed and fidgeted in his chair, steepling his hands on the desk and then pulling them down to tap his thighs. She wasn't hitting on him, but the way she'd spoken revealed an intimacy that implied they'd known one another for a very long time. "How do I know you, Petra? I'm not usually one to forget a face."

Petra smiled, but there was no mirth in the expression. "Thirty years ago, this wasn't my face. I had a little girl's face."

Jake frowned. "We knew each other as children?"

Jake had few memories from his childhood. The black hole of trauma, one of his ex-girlfriends had called it while simultaneously nudging him into couples therapy. He'd quit the therapy and the girlfriend after one session.

"I didn't expect you to remember me," she admitted. "Maybe my name. I never forgot you, though. You and Maribelle. You were the only friends I had in those days."

Jake frowned and his heart seemed to lurch at the name, Maribelle, though that too brought nothing in the form of memories. "Did we meet in Alpena?" he asked.

Jake remembered little of life in Alpena. All of his memories seemed to exist after the age of ten when he'd found himself living in Frankenmuth with his adoptive parents, Faye and Lennon.

Petra shook her head. "We met at the Northern Michigan Asylum for the Insane," she said.

Jake cracked a smile. "Is that a joke?"

Petra wasn't smiling. "No, it's not. You don't remember being at the asylum?" She frowned as she spoke, and he saw suspicion, perhaps even fear, in her eyes.

2

Jake sighed and leaned back in his chair. "What's the deal, lady? Did Allison put you up to this because she's pissed at me?"

Petra's face darkened. "You were at the Northern Michigan Asylum for the Insane in 1966. You were a patient there, as was I and Maribelle."

Jake offered her a sardonic grin. "You've got to be fucking kidding me. Sorry for my ungentlemanly vocabulary, but Petra, I've got a crew kicking dirt in the parking lot and three jobs that need to start in ten minutes. I'm not sure why you're here, and I've got a sense I can thank my old lady for it, but you'll have to excuse me."

Jake stood and brushed past the woman. He had half a mind to get Allison on the phone and tell her what he thought about her shitty joke, but that would only delay his morning.

He saluted Barbie, which she'd give him hell for later. Usually he pecked her on the cheek and told her to have a good day.

In the lot, he called out to the guys. "Jerry, you're with Willis on the Sampson job. Ric, I need you to take the dump truck to Marly's Gravel and pick up ten yards of road gravel. Allen and I will meet you on Rinehart Road." Jake grabbed a folded map from his truck and showed Ric where the property was at.

As Allen climbed into the passenger side of his pickup, Petra emerged from the office. She had not put her glasses back on and she looked troubled, her stony expression replaced with confusion.

∽

DESPITE HIS BEST efforts to forget her, the woman's words plagued him.

He climbed into the excavator and lifted the bucket against a tree, pushing until the tree crashed forward, where Allen started on it with the chainsaw.

After an hour of ruminating, Jake told the guys he was making a coffee run and drove to the gas station on Miller Road. Allison worked as an accountant and wouldn't be home. He walked to a payphone and fed it a quarter before punching in the numbers of her office.

"Premier Accounting," a nasally voice told him.

"Hi, Regina, it's Jake. Is Allison around?"

Regina's voice dropped. "Sure is, Jake, but she had a scowl on her this morning. I know you didn't forget your anniversary."

Jake frowned, tallied up the months in his mind. Had they already been dating for a year? "Shit," he muttered.

"You have some serious making up to do," she whispered in her conspiratorial way that made Jake's ears throb. Whenever he listened to Regina speak, he felt sympathy for her husband of ten years.

"Yeah, I guess I do. Can you put her on the phone, please?"

"Sure thing," Regina told him. "And P.S., she loves that Italian place downtown with the red awning and the dim little booths all lit with candles. In case you needed some direction."

"Sure, thanks."

"Hello?" Allison's voice sounded more weary than angry when she got on the phone.

"I'm sorry, Al. I didn't realize..."

She sighed. "You never do."

"Dinner tonight. Okay? We'll celebrate." He said the words, but something else almost slipped out: *This isn't working. I think we should part ways...* He hadn't thought of them before that moment, but there they were, sticky in the back of his throat.

He wanted out. It wasn't Allison. She was great. Pretty, independent, with a supportive family, and plans to one day open her own accounting business. It was Jake and the way something in him shriveled when she cooed over babies and cried at weddings. To Allison, a one-year anniversary meant there was more to come, a ring and a house and babies. She was an old-fashioned girl, and she expected Jake to step up to the plate.

"Okay. I can't believe you forgot, Jake. I wrote it on your calendar and circled it with a big heart," she grumbled.

Jake pictured the calendar hanging next to his cupboards in the kitchen. He looked at it every day, but he hadn't noticed her not-so-subtle reminder.

"Listen, Allison. Did you, uh..." He tried to think of how to form the question that wouldn't sound like an accusation. "Do you know a woman named Petra?"

"Petra?" Her tone told him the answer was no. "No. There's Patricia, the woman who does my hair."

"What does she look like?" he asked, though he doubted Petra and Patricia were the same woman.

"Short, skinny with big blonde curly hair." She paused. "Why?" she asked innocently, but he heard the note of suspicion underneath it.

"Nothing, no reason. Barbie had a message from a woman named Petra at the shop this morning. I thought you might know her."

"Nope. So, dinner tonight. Did you make reservations?"

"Yeah," he lied. "Six at that little Italian place you like downtown."

Allison laughed, and he could imagine her smile brightening her entire face and the surrounding office. "I'll have to go home and change and do my hair. I just threw it into a ponytail this morning. But I could come by your house and we can ride together."

"Sure, that's great. Bye, Al."

"I love you," she told him.

"Love you too." He hung up the phone and fished another quarter out of his pocket.

He called Barbie and asked her to set up dinner reservations for that evening.

Halfway back to his truck, he turned on his heel and walked back to the phone, lifting the receiver and hitting 0 for the operator.

"Directory assistance," a woman answered.

"Hi. I'm trying to reach Petra Collins."

"Hold, please."

He listened to sleepy piano music for nearly two minutes.

"Sorry. I don't have a Petra Collins in the directory."

∼

Jake worked the rest of the day, but his mind strayed frequently to Petra Collins. It was nearly five when Jake returned to his office. With limited time to rush home and get ready for dinner, he hurried inside.

When he pushed into the office, Barbie rattled off a list of messages he only half-listened to.

"Sure, yeah. Thanks, Barbie. I'm in a pinch for time. We can go over it in the morning." He ducked into his office and leaned over his desk to flick off the light.

In the center of the bare wood, as if someone had cleared a space for it, sat a black business card with silver writing. He read the name Petra Collins, and beneath that he saw a phone number and an email address.

Jake paused, his legs still trying to carry him out the door in a hurry. He snatched up his phone and punched in the number.

It rang four times, and he expected an answering machine, but listened instead to silence.

"Hello?" Jake asked. Someone had picked up. The sound of breath, almost imperceptible, whispered across the line. "Petra? This is Jake Edwards. Hello?"

The person at the other end said nothing, and a chill spilled down Jake's spine. He held the phone away and stared at it, oddly fearful that the person on the other end might see him. Tempted to drop the phone back into the cradle, he held it above the base for several seconds and then lifted it back to his ear. For six seconds, and then ten, twenty, he listened to the hushed sound of breath.

As he listened, the breath grew deeper, huskier and then seemed to get caught in a whoosh as if the caller had stepped into a windstorm.

Deep in the sound, Jake's name emerged, but not from Petra's mouth. A young girl released the sound, a call somewhere between a sob and a scream. "JAAAAAAAAAAKE!"

The door to his office banged open, and Jake screamed, flinging the phone across the room where it smacked the wall and landed on the brown carpet.

Barbie shrieked and dropped the bundle of pencils she'd been clutching in her hand. Her bosom heaved as she stared at him and then at the phone stretching from his desk to the floor across the room. "Jake! What in the world? I just sharpened those pencils. I could have killed us both."

Jake swallowed and crouched, gathering Barbie's pencils before plucking the phone from the floor.

"Why did you throw the phone? Did you and Allison have a fight?"

He shook his head and returned the phone to his desk before handing the pencils back to Barbie.

"Those are for you. I figured the ones in here were probably all dull from your endless scribbling." She smiled and patted his back. "You okay, honey?"

"Yeah, I'm fine. I... uh, got one of those fax machines. That sound." He shuddered.

Barbie nodded knowingly. "Like a hot poker to the ear" she agreed. "I don't understand why people can't dedicate separate numbers to fax machines. It can't be good for the brain to get one of those pitches right into the eardrum."

Jake got in his truck, engine idling. Barbie locked up and walked to her car. He waved goodbye as she drove from the parking lot.

Buckling his seatbelt and trying not to look at the clock—twenty to six pm—he shifted into reverse and rolled backwards. Barely thinking, he slammed on the brake and put the truck back in park, punching his seatbelt open and turning off the engine. He trotted back to the office, unlocked the door and slipped inside.

When he dialed Petra's number a second time, a man's breathless voice answered the phone.

"Hello?" the man shrilled, and Jake grimaced.

"Hi. Is Petra there?"

"Oh, God," the man moaned.

"Hello?" Jake asked. The word was all wrong, but in that

moment sweat had broken out beneath his arms and a balloon of dread had expanded in his chest, eating up the room his lungs needed.

"There's blood everywhere," the man cried and his voice sounded high again, terrified, on the verge of panic.

3

Jake blinked at his desk. Sweat slithered down his sides and lodged in the waistband of his pants.

"Is this a joke?" He repeated the same words he'd spoken to Petra that morning, but he knew it wasn't a joke.

The man on the other end of the line wheezed for breath. "Oh, Petra. Oh, God, no. I have to... I have to get help. Help us!" he shouted into the phone.

Jake cringed and pulled the phone away, his own panic wriggling behind his eyes. "The police," Jake said, trying to keep his voice calm. "You need to call the police."

"Oh, God," the man repeated.

"Tell me the address. Where are you? What's the address?" Jake demanded, some shred of common sense finding a foothold in his brain.

"It's on my feet," the man groaned. "There's blood on my feet."

"Hey!" Jake snapped. "Listen to me. What is the address?"

"It's... 933 Laramie..." The man's breath sounded choppy. "I... what do I do?"

"In Saginaw? What city?"

"It's..." Only breath for several seconds, breath with a high squeak like the man was squeezing the oxygen between his teeth. "Bay City. 933 Laramie in Bay City. Side B. It's a duplex."

"Okay. I'm calling the police," Jake told him. "They might need to call back. Stay by the phone."

Fingers shaking, Jake hung up and dialed 911.

"What's your emergency?" a woman asked.

"Hi, umm... my name's Jake. I just tried calling a woman in Bay City and a man answered the phone and said there's blood everywhere. I'm not there, but he needs help."

"What's the address, please?"

∼

IGNORING THE SPEED LIMIT, Jake made the drive from Saginaw to Bay City in fifteen minutes.

The duplex occupied a short rectangular ranch on a suburban street on the southwest edge of Bay City. The connected homes were mirror images except Side B had dark curtains covering the front window and a standard black mailbox. Side A's curtains were bright yellow and its white mailbox was painted with little blue swirls.

Two police cars, lights flashing, occupied the driveway. An ambulance idled at the curb.

Jake parked on the street. In his rearview, more flashing lights appeared. Two more police cars pulled into the driveway.

The only man not in uniform on the property was tall and thin with dark curly hair. His eyes were wide, his mouth open and his face pallid. He held his hands pressed as if in prayer against his chest. An officer spoke to him, but the man's lips barely moved. He'd been the man on the phone, Jake was sure of it.

Jake didn't have to approach the scene. He hadn't seen

anything, but he had called it in and... he wanted to know if the woman he'd met that morning lay dead inside the duplex.

As he walked toward the duplex, two officers strung yellow tape across the recently mowed lawn. The day smelled of cut grass.

One officer glanced up at him, pausing and squaring off as if he expected Jake to rush the tape. Other people trickled from their houses and gathered on the lawns down the street.

"I'm the one who called," Jake said, gesturing at the house. "The police. I called them."

The cop lifted an eyebrow. "You'll need to talk with the detective. I'm here to secure the scene and that's it."

∼

JAKE APPROACHED THE TALL, anxious looking man he assumed he'd spoken to earlier. The man had wound his hands through his button-down shirt, which he'd tugged loose from his white jeans. The shirt was loud and covered in blue and pink stripes.

"I spoke with you on the phone. I'm the one who called the police." Jake told him.

He blinked at Jake, and then slowly nodded. "Yeah," he whispered. "Okay. I wondered if I'd imagined it. If I'd called myself." He released a nervous laugh.

"I'm Jake," Jake extended his hand.

The man shook it limply. "I'm Norm," he mumbled, gazing at the dark window on the right side of the duplex.

"Was she in there?" Jake nodded at the duplex where he could see a jumble of uniformed cops crowding the doorway.

Norm frowned and bit his lip. He shook his head slowly. "I don't know. I walked in and there was..." He closed his eyes and winced. "Blood on the carpet, the walls. At first I thought she was painting, which is insane. But then I smelled it." He took his hands from his shirt and undid the bottom button before immediately threading it back through the hole. He did it a second time and a third.

Jake found his eyes drawn to the white button slipping in and out of the fabric. "But you didn't find her? The woman herself?"

Norm's eyes stayed fixed on the house. He shook his head.

"Have they brought out a stretcher or anything?" Jake asked.

"No," Norm breathed. He looked away from the house, his gray eyes settling on Jake. They'd momentarily cleared. "How did you know that she needed help?"

Jake shook his head. "I didn't. I called her and you picked..." He paused, realizing that that had been the second time. The first time he'd called, someone else had picked up.

He'd forgotten all about it.

Jake tried to phrase his next question in a non-accusing way. "How long were you in there, Norm? Like ten minutes or more?"

Norm's eyes widened. "Oh, God, no. No. Two minutes maybe. I mean I walked in, called out for Petra, saw the blood and the phone rang." Norm snapped his fingers. "It felt like minutes, but maybe it was seconds."

"So you only answered the phone once?" Jake asked.

Norm nodded, eyes drifting back to the duplex.

"Could she have just like... cut herself and driven to the hospital?" Jake asked, throwing out one of a series of theories he'd developed on the drive to Bay City.

Norm released his shirt and moved one hand to his mouth, where he pulled at the skin on his chin and cheeks. "There was so much blood," he murmured.

"Is her car here? Was it in the garage?"

Norm nodded. "We share a garage. I got home from work, and her car was in there, so I assumed she was home. I just walked right in. I always do."

"Were you dating or—"

Norm snorted. "No. I'm not Petra's type. Not most women's type, I guess."

Silently they watched as uniforms went in and out of the duplex. Ants scurrying, Jake thought. No stretcher covered in a white sheet emerged.

After a while, the ambulance lights flickered to dark, and the vehicle pulled away, struggling down the congested street that hours earlier had been void of life.

Eventually a short, brawny man in brown slacks and a mismatched gray blazer approached them. "Norman Groesbeck?" The man locked small, brown eyes on Norm.

He carried himself with an air of authority, and Norm straightened at the sight of him. Jake felt himself doing the same, firming his legs and rolling his shoulders back as if he were a soldier and his lieutenant had just called him to attention.

"Yes, I'm Norman Groesbeck," Norm said, offering a shaky hand.

The man shook it gruffly. "I'm Detective Bryant. I'd like you to accompany me to the station to answer a few questions."

Norm's face paled, and he glanced nervously at Jake. "Of course, yes, anything to help." His voice had taken on the high-pitched tone Jake had noted earlier. "Umm…" Norm gestured at Jake. "This is Jake. He called the police. He called you guys."

Jake frowned, aware that Norm wanted to shift some focus away from himself and onto Jake. He wondered suddenly if the man standing beside him was involved in Petra's disappearance.

Jake stuck out his hand. "Jake Edwards."

The detective gripped his hand, watching Jake with interest. "You phoned it in? Do you live nearby?"

Jake shook his head. "I live in Saginaw. I called Petra and Norm answered the telephone. He was panicking, I guess. He'd just walked into the apartment—"

"And seen all the blood," Norm cut in, voice tiptoeing notes that seemed higher than most men could muster. "Blood on the walls and the couch and her white shoes. The high-heeled ones with little bows." Norm's face twisted, and he made crying sounds, though no tears fell from his eyes.

The shoe comment struck Jake as strange and he could see it had a similar effect on the detective.

"Maybe both of you could join me at the station? The sooner we get statements, the sooner we can find the missing woman."

"Okay, sure," Jake agreed. He thought of dinner. Allison meticulously placing bobby pins in her hair. He hadn't called her to cancel. She'd be sitting at the kitchen table, watching the clock, hurt turning to anger.

~

DETECTIVE BRYANT DISAPPEARED down the hall with a shivering Norm, whose teeth had been chattering despite the warmth in the police station.

Jake felt suddenly as if he'd fallen into a strange movie. Had he called Petra only moments after Norm attacked her? If Norm had hurt Petra, what had he done with her body?

A young woman sat behind a bulletproof window. She slid the glass open and offered him a wave. "Can I get ya a coffee? Or some water?" she asked.

"Coffee would be great," Jake told her, though he knew drinking coffee after five would leave him running through his mind and to the john all night.

When she pushed through the door a moment later, Jake saw she was tiny, barely five feet tall. She handed him the Styrofoam cup of coffee and pulled two creams from her jeans pocket.

"Not to judge a book by its cover, but you seem awfully out of place here," Jake told her, taking the coffee.

She grinned. "My dad's Detective Bryant. I'm an intern for

the summer. He hoped I'd choose something safer like teaching grade school, but cops are in my blood."

Jake widened his eyes. "You're going to be a cop?"

"A detective. But everyone starts somewhere. I'm Adrian," she told him.

"How old are you, Adrian?" Jake asked.

"How old do I look?" She winked at him and backed toward the door.

He chuckled. "My mother told me if a woman asks that question, I should pretend I didn't hear her and compliment her hair instead."

Adrian laughed. "Considering I didn't wash my hair today, if you compliment it, I'll suspect you're lying."

"I'd peg you at twenty."

"Twenty-two," she corrected.

"Just a baby," he said, sipping the coffee. It was thick and grimy, but the heat soothed him as it flowed into his stomach.

"Hardly." She pushed backwards through the door and took up her post behind the glass window.

He sipped his coffee and watched her on the phone. Fresh-faced with not an ounce of makeup, she wore her hair secured in a topknot, though he imagined if she shook it loose it'd be long and wavy—a color his mother would have labeled something quirky like coriander. She'd called Jake's hair candied ginger.

The clock read seven-forty p.m. He thought of Allison and a sliver of guilt wedged between his ribs. He hadn't called her.

He tried not to picture her sitting at home with her hair and face done, mascara lines dripping down her cheeks. Allison was a good girl. Pretty, nice, and ready to get married and settle down. Not to mention her clock was ticking and her sister had just given birth to her fourth baby, a girl they'd named Allison after her beloved sister. Allison's family expected Jake to do right by their daughter, but lately he'd known more and more that he and Allison weren't destined for the long haul.

"Jake?"

Jake looked up to find Detective Bryant watching him from the doorway.

"Where's Norm?" Jake asked.

"In the back with my partner," he said curtly. "Follow me."

4

Adrian offered him a thumbs-up as he followed Bryant into a small box-like room with thin blue carpeting and four white walls. A video camera hung in the room's corner.

"Are you taping this?" Jake asked.

"Yep. That okay with you?" the detective asked, but Jake sensed if he said no, the polite edge in Bryant's voice would fast disappear.

"Sure, fine with me." Jake sat in a stiff metal chair and crossed his legs at the ankle.

Bryant sat on the opposite side of a small rectangular table that was bolted to the floor. "Full name, please?" Bryant asked, pen poised above a blank page.

"Jake Fritz Edwards."

"Can you give me a timeline of your day, starting with what time you woke up this morning until right now?"

Jake squinted and thought back to the morning, which felt as if it had been days earlier. "I woke up at six am. That's what time my alarm went off, same time every morning. Made coffee, took a shower. Woke up Allison at six-thirty."

"Who's Allison?"

"My girlfriend."

Bryant nodded. "Go on."

"I had some cornflakes and left for the shop at six fifty."

"The shop?"

"Yeah. I own Dig Deep Excavating."

Bryant cocked an eyebrow but said nothing. Jake realized how the name Dig Deep Excavating must sound to a detective searching for a missing woman.

"At the office, I chatted with a couple of my guys and then Barbie, my secretary. Before seven-thirty, a woman pulled into the parking lot. It was Petra Collins."

Bryant paused and studied Jake. "How do you know Petra Collins?"

Jake swallowed, palms beginning to sweat beneath him. He extracted his hands and clasped them in his lap. He wasn't guilty, not in the slightest, but something about the small room and the detective's steady gaze made him uneasy. "I don't. I'd never seen her before she walked into my office this morning."

"Was she inquiring about excavating services?"

Jake shook his head and wiped his hands on his jeans. "She said we knew each other when we were kids. She'd tracked me down and wanted to know if I remembered her."

Bryant clicked his pen and made a note on the notepad. "Let me get this straight. You'd never met Petra Collins before she appeared at your place of business this morning claiming that you knew each other as children?"

"Yeah, exactly," Jake told him.

"Did she offer any reason for looking you up now? For showing up at your office so early in the morning?"

"No, not really." Jake thought about Petra's comments about the asylum and stuffed the words down. He could only imagine this man's expression if he thought Jake had once been institutionalized, and he hadn't! But once the thought was in the man's mind, well, there was no taking it back.

"What exactly did she say to you, Mr. Edwards? Or Jake. Can I call you Jake?"

"Yeah, sure. Umm... she said my eyes looked the same."

"Your eyes?"

Jake chuckled and shrugged. "Yeah, pretty much. Honestly, I didn't take her seriously because I thought my girlfriend Allison was playing some kind of prank. I'd forgotten our one-year anniversary..." He trailed off. The excuse sounded flimsy.

"What kind of prank? I mean, it's not exactly funny. Or cruel. Sending someone in to claim they knew you as a child?"

Jake placed his hands palm up on the desk. "Yeah, it doesn't make much sense, but my head had already kicked into work mode and I wasn't paying her much mind. I brushed her off and left for the job. When I got back to my office around five, I saw she'd left her card on my desk. I called her."

"What time was that?"

"Right around five, but that was the first call."

"You called twice?"

"Yeah. The first time, someone answered but didn't say anything. I just heard breath." Jake recalled the memory of the child's voice, far off, strange. He had to have imagined it.

"So you called, and a person answered and simply breathed into the phone?"

"Yeah. I decided to head home. Packed up for the day and got in my truck and then... I went back in and called a second time. I'm not sure why. It was about fifteen minutes between the two calls. When I called the second time, Norm answered. He was screaming about blood. I told him to hang up and stay near the phone. I called the police."

"And then you drove to Petra's home? If you'd never met the woman, how could you have known her address?"

"I got it from Norm so I could call the police. I didn't know his name was Norm then. I just knew he'd walked in and saw blood and he seemed to be in shock. I didn't think he could make the call himself. He was hysterical."

"I see." Bryant wrote a few lines and then flipped the page in his notebook as if he didn't want Jake to see what he'd scribbled. "Tell me about your call with Norm. What did he say?"

Jake closed his eyes and tried to remember. "He… umm… he kept saying 'Oh, God' and 'There's blood.' Maybe he said 'There's blood everywhere.' I thought it was a joke. Kind of like I had with Petra that morning. I realized pretty quick it wasn't a joke. Norm sounded really upset. I told him to call for help, but he didn't seem to get what I was saying, so I told him to hang up and I'd call them. I asked for Petra's address and he told me. Then I hung up and called 911."

Bryant nodded and clasped his hands on the desk. "Had you ever spoken with Norm before?"

"No."

"And what is your impression of his tone? Did he sound angry?"

"No," Jake said. "He sounded scared and upset."

"Did it sound like he was moving around at all? Cleaning things? Moving things?"

Jake shook his head. "I couldn't hear it if he was."

Bryant didn't speak for several seconds.

"Do you think it was Norm? That Norm did something to Petra?" Jake asked.

Bryant focused on Jake. "Do you?"

"Shit, I don't know. I don't know Norm or Petra from Adam. I only met them both today. I just… I mean, did you find her? Or…"

"We did not find her, no. As for whether Norm had something to do with her disappearance, it's too early to know."

"This is nuts." Jake leaned forward and braced his elbows on his knees, pushing his hands into his mess of hair. He sat up and looked the detective in the eye. "What now?"

Bryant gazed at Jake for several long seconds and then flipped the page in his notebook and slid the blank page toward him. "Write down your full name, phone number and home address. If we have more questions, we'll be in touch."

～

THE HOUSE WAS dark when Jake returned. Allison's silver Probe was not parked in the driveway. She had stayed at her own apartment or, equally likely, gone to her parents, where she and her mother would have drunk coffee late into the night and trash-talked Jake. He deserved it.

The house was quiet except for the tick-tock of the kitchen clock. Quiet and dark and a little eerie.

Shuddering, he flipped on the entryway lights and continued lighting his way as he walked down the hall and into the living room.

He rarely watched television before bed, but he turned it on and punched seven for the news. A commercial displayed a game of beach volleyball with a bucket of icy-cold beer in the foreground.

Instead of sitting, he returned to the refrigerator for a beer, smiling at the thought of Lennon, who would have said, "See? Advertising. They got ya again."

He returned to the couch, sipped his beer, and watched another commercial. This one displayed a woman rushing down a flight of stairs, across a park and into a busy courthouse, all without getting a run in ultra-sheer pantyhose.

The news came on. A weather man, in a brown suit, and gestured at the days ahead, mostly sunny skies, maybe a chance of rain on Tuesday.

If the weather was on, the major news had come and gone.

He'd missed whatever had been covered about Petra. And something had been covered because when he'd left for the police station, several news vans had crowded the street.

He sighed, left his three-quarters-full can of beer on the coffee table and walked up to bed.

5

Charlie parked on the curb in front of her new house, giddy to the point of shaking.

A Queen Anne Victorian, the listing had read. *Welcome to Wilder's Grove in the heart of picturesque Frankenunmuth, Michigan. A home with historical charm, a huge wraparound front porch and ornate front entry doors. Host parties in the grand formal living room. Prepare meals in the remodeled rustic farmhouse kitchen. You'll love the floor-to-ceiling built-ins, original hardwood floors, vintage fireplace mantels, stained-glass windows and wrought-iron banisters and railings.* Charlie had read the listing half a dozen times before she even saw the house.

She stepped from the car. It was everything she could do not to run to the porch and hug the railing.

Instead, not yet ready to scare all her neighbors away, she padded across the lawn and grabbed the 'For Sale' sign from the soft earth. She carried it to the garage and laughed out loud as she extracted the ring of brass keys from her pocket. Each key held a little colored label. 'Garage,' 'Master,' 'Study,' 'Shed.'

Sliding the garage key into the lock, she slipped into the cool interior and inhaled. It wasn't a smell most people would relish, but in that moment, Charlie savored everything—the stale odor, the dust floating in the sunlight filtering through the windows, and even the mouse traps she could see in every corner, which she intended to throw away. The last thing she wanted was to come in and find a poor mouse, neck broken, struggling against the little wooden platform.

She set the sign down on the long work bench that occupied one wall of the garage. As she returned to the house, she made a mental note of what she needed. A few chairs for the deck and maybe a little table for glasses of ice tea, a cat to deal with the pesky mice she wouldn't be trapping or feeding poison, and flowers for the large empty pots that flanked the wooden stairs leading up to the porch.

Before she slid the master key into the front door lock, she turned and gazed at the lawn, at the start of her new life.

Across the street, an older woman stood hunched over her porch rail, gesturing. "Howie, come on. Come here, sweetie," she called out.

Charlie followed the woman's gaze to a little black dog in the front yard. The dog watched Charlie, staring at her with such intensity she shivered.

The old woman looked up, eyes locking on Charlie's. Charlie raised her hand to wave, but the woman didn't respond. She scurried down the porch, snatched the dog into her arms and ran back to her house, nearly tripping as she crossed the threshold and disappeared inside.

Charlie dropped her hand. "Okay then, nice to meet you too, cranky lady across the street."

She wouldn't let one irritable old woman dash her excitement. Charlie unlocked the door and stepped into her new house.

The front hall, long wood floors gleaming, smelled of lemon disinfectant. Kate had left a welcome basket on the marble-topped buffet table in the foyer. It contained a bottle of red wine, a box of truffles and a card that read 'Congratulations' in big gold letters. Charlie flipped the card over.

Best of luck in your new home, Charlie! Yours truly, Kate.

Kate was her real estate agent, a bit of luck that Charlie saw as fate. She'd met Kate the morning she filed for divorce from Jared as she sat alone on a park bench, crying into the newspaper and likely startling the mothers of the children racing along the wooden play structure.

Kate had sat down next to her, reached into her purse and drawn out a plastic bag of tissues and a box of truffles, the same kind that now sat in her welcome basket. "Here," Kate had said. "There's no problem that can't be quashed by a truffle."

Charlie had laughed for the first time in days, eaten a chocolate, and proceeded to tell Kate her life story, though they'd only met twenty seconds before.

Eventually Kate gave a bit of her own story. She was a realtor visiting her sister in Pontiac. She was from Arizona. No kids, no husband. Been there, done that, she'd said. Not the kids —well, not her own. Two stepkids who'd hated her from the word 'go' and a husband who spent his money on dog races and strippers.

Charlie's marriage too had failed, though it wasn't a spending problem that had done them in. The last miscarriage had done it. Two dead babies in as many years. Each time she watched the blood swirl down the toilet, Charlie lost a piece of herself.

In the end, she wasn't the same woman Jared had married, and he told her as much shortly before taking up with another woman at the healthcare company he worked for. She might have forgiven the indiscretion had the woman not left a pair of her pink-and-blue polka dot panties on Charlie's bureau to find after a twelve-hour shift at the hospital.

Jared had made a half-hearted attempt to keep her, but the spark between them had long since died out. She'd packed her stuff and moved into a studio apartment that she'd furnished with items from a thrift store. She'd been living there for three months when she'd met Kate that fateful April morning.

Five weeks later and she'd bought a big old Queen Anne Victorian house and moved seventy miles north to Frankenmuth, home of the world's largest Christmas store, to start a new life.

The previous owners had moved abruptly and left most of their furnishings behind. Charlie had been all too willing to accept the house as is. After all, she'd left all the furniture she'd bought with Jared behind. Try as she might, she couldn't shake the image of him screwing his mistress on the table, on the heather-gray sofa, in the log bed they'd bought at an Amish furniture store on their honeymoon.

The long rustic farmhouse table in her new house had benches on either side. It was far too big for a single woman living alone, but she loved it. Charlie set the basket on the table and lay down on a bench, stretching out her legs and kicking off her white slip-on tennis shoes. She gazed at the white beams crisscrossing the ceiling. A white paddle fan hung from the ceiling and turned in slow lazy circles.

The kitchen cupboards were white, the floor a dark wood marred with scratches from a century of use. It was a sunny, light kitchen with windows and double glass sliding doors opening on to the back deck.

Kate had told Charlie that the house had been built in the early 1900s and renovated several times, though much of its original architecture remained. Prior owners had updated the kitchen to more of a farmhouse style, simple and open, but the rest of the house held to its original ornate character with crown molding, thick carpet and wood floors. The living room and master bedroom both included working fireplaces. In total, the house contained four bedrooms, three bathrooms, a living room, kitchen, laundry room, study and half a dozen closets.

Charlie could never have imagined affording it on her nurse's salary, but Kate had told her it was a steal. The prior owners wanted to unload it. Charlie put an offer in on a whim, never expecting to get the house. The owners had accepted within twenty-four hours.

Now Charlie sat up and drew in a big breath. Boxes filled her car and waited for her to begin the unpacking. Her entire life fit into the backseat and trunk of her twilight-blue Ford Taurus.

She carried boxes inside and set them in the foyer, pausing every few minutes to marvel at the space. A tiny seed of fear rolled in her belly. Could she afford the house? The mortgage was one thing, but what of the utility bills in the winter? What if a pipe burst or the septic tank overflowed? What if the great deal had a scary underlying reason like black mold?

"Stop it," she muttered.

Charlie paused in the hall and glanced in the mirror, adjusting the red headband she'd slid over her unwashed hair to keep it out of her face. An eyelash clung to her cheek and she leaned closer to her reflection, plucking it off. As she blew it off her fingers, another image in the mirror caught her eye.

A woman stood in the corner of the foyer, dark hair and dark clothes and worst of all dark eyes, black and angry, watching her.

Charlie screamed and spun around, snatching a candlestick from the foyer table and raising it above her head.

No woman stood in the corner. Only the coat rack and Charlie's hooded black coat.

Charlie's breath hitched as she tried to force her body to accept what her eyes knew. A trick of the mind, a cruel prank by her own psyche.

"It's a coat," she laughed as she shakily returned the candlestick to the table, eyes still locked on the corner.

She walked over and ruffled the coats. Nothing but air. No

one had stepped behind them, no feet poked from beneath them.

On the sidewalk out front, two little girls paused on their bikes. They both gazed up at Wilder's Grove before squealing as if with fear and pedaling away.

Charlie smiled and shook her head.

"Kids."

6

Jake parked in front of Allison's office and, before he could talk himself out of it, stepped from the truck and hurried through the glass door.

Regina, the wife of the head accountant and one of Allison's best friends, pursed her lips and gave him a curt nod when he walked in.

"Is Allison–?" He gestured toward Allison's office.

"Yep," she said coolly.

He knocked on Allison's door and then pushed it open.

She sat at her desk, hair down and curled with a curling iron, her makeup expertly applied. She wore a low-cut black top and a gold necklace with a butterfly charm in the center.

He knew why she'd put so much effort into her appearance that morning, which made his intended words sticky in his throat. Not because he wanted her. But because she expected him to grovel, apologize and beg for her to come back.

She said nothing, only shot him a scathing look and returned to punching keys in the large electronic calculator that clacked and beeped as she worked.

"I'm sorry about last night," he said, sitting in the chair opposite her desk.

"Hmph," she scoffed.

"Allison. This isn't working."

A little frown creased her brow, and her typing stopped. She turned to face him, her eyes misting.

"I'm so sorry, Al. I am. I never wanted to hurt you. I just don't think…"

Tears rolled over her cheeks. The cool demeanor vanished in an instant.

"Shit, I'm sorry. I'm so sorry." He walked around the desk and knelt before her, taking her hands and squeezing them against his chest.

He truly didn't want to hurt her. It tore him apart to see her cry, but it was time. It had been time for months.

She shook her head. "But… I thought… You said you loved me," she sputtered. Her hands shook as she pulled them away from him. "You stood me up last night and now you're breaking up with me?"

Jake looked up at her. "I didn't stand you up on purpose last night. Some stuff happened. It was… out of my control. But I realized I've known for a while we're not… we're not a good fit."

Her face contorted as if he'd punched her, and she pushed her high heels into the floor, rolling her chair back on the plastic mat, putting distance between them.

"You led me on," she whispered. "You knew I wanted to get married. How could you, Jake?" The tears came harder now, faster.

Regina stuck her head through the door. "Is everything okay?"

Allison looked at her and shook her head.

"Maybe I better go. I'm sorry, Al. I'm…" But he didn't finish. He brushed past Kim, who hurried into the room as he left.

When he climbed into his truck, he cranked the key and slammed on the gas. The truck shot forward. He wanted to get away, though he couldn't outrun the look in her eyes, the guilt pressing in around him.

He drove straight to the job and didn't mention the break-up to the guys.

The next eight hours passed with barely a thought of Allison.

∽

HE RETURNED HOME from work to find Allison had emptied the house of her things. She didn't live with him, but she'd left bits of herself when she stayed over—a silky pink robe on the back of the bathroom door, a pair of knee-high red suede boots in the front hallway, a scattering of romance novels, chapsticks and makeup.

She'd even taken the three photographs she'd stuck to his refrigerator with little heart-shaped magnets. They had taken two on Mackinac Island the previous fall when she'd talked him into taking a weekend off work and going north. The third had been Allison alone, wearing a fluffy purple bridesmaid dress as she sat on the edge of a fountain. He'd missed her friend's wedding to shore up a seawall in front of a mansion that was slowly slipping into Lake Michigan. But that had been the early days of their relationship when such transgressions had been forgivable.

Her key sat alone in the center of his kitchen table.

The rooms held an emptiness without her. The halls were dark and cold. When he sat on his couch in the living room a tiny puff of despair seemed to release with the dust motes that floated in the late afternoon sun. He'd never been good at being alone, and yet he'd never been good at being a partner.

He tried to watch the game, gave up, and walked into the kitchen where he'd spread a print for a clearing job on his counter. The owners, wealthy thanks to the husband's recent sale of an insurance business in Farmington Hills, wanted to return to northern Michigan. Foundations needed to be dug for a house, a guest house, a pole barn. But first, weeks of tree-clearing and grading the land.

It was the perfect distraction from Allison, but as he scratched his pencil across the gridded page, he thought not of his now ex-girlfriend, but the woman who'd arrived at his office two days before.

Petra.

Her name filled his head, pressed against the hard contours of his skull and refused to be contained.

"Petra." He spoke her name as if to relieve the pressure, but it didn't help.

"Shit," he muttered, realizing he hadn't just said it, he'd written her name on his print. He erased the name.

He'd watched the news each evening after work, but the reporters only offered brief snippets. *The search continues for missing woman Petra Collins...* They didn't offer details on her life. No crying boyfriend or hysterical mother pleaded for her safe return. It got under his skin. The lack of friends or family parading across the screen and demanding justice.

The evening before, Norm had done an interview—eyes dripping, hands tugging at his button-down shirt, this one as outrageous as the one he'd been wearing the day Jake met him. It was pink and dotted in tiny black flamingos.

Jake took the stairs two at a time to the second floor. The jeans he'd been wearing two days earlier lay crumpled next to the hamper. Allison had given him hell about that more than once.

"Right next to the laundry basket, Jake? Really?" she'd demand, but in a sweet voice before she plucked the garments from the floor and crammed them inside.

They were the kinds of comments that usually made him feel better after a break-up. This time he only felt guilty.

He dug into the back pocket of his pants and found Norm's phone number written on a Post-It note with a grinning cat hanging from a tree branch on the top. 'Hang in there,' a voice bubble by the cat said.

Jake grabbed the cordless phone from the stand next to his bed and dialed Norm's number. It rang once, and the man picked up.

"Hello?" His voice had the same high-pitched, though slightly less hysterical, edge Jake had heard the first day they'd spoken.

"Norm?"

"Yes?"

"It's Jake. We met the other day."

"Oh, Jake." Norm's voice lowered a bit as if some helium had rushed out of him. "I thought you might be the police. They've called me half a dozen times. They think I had something to do with Petra's disappearance."

"Really?" Jake feigned surprise. He'd had the same thought. "Listen, I'm feeling kind of plagued by this whole thing with Petra. Would you be up for meeting me so we can talk?"

"Yes, please," Norm answered quickly. "Me too. And nobody gets it. Petra was my best friend. I would have talked about this stuff with her and now... Oh, God. I can't even say it."

"You name the place and I'll come to you," Jake told him.

"Hmm... Oh, I've got it. Petra and I love this martini bar in downtown Bay City called the Pink Drink. Meet me there at seven?"

"See ya then," Jake agreed.

∽

THE PINK DRINK was a corner bar with a neon-pink sign

depicting a lit pink martini with a laughing woman perched on the edge of the glass. The bar was mostly dead on Thursday night, though a group of likely coworkers occupied one table wearing suits and stilettos.

Norm was already there, perched on a high chrome barstool and sipping from a pink martini not unlike the one on the sign.

Jake paused next to him.

"The pink lady is the best," Norm said, nodding at his drink. "Petra and I always order them."

Jake grinned and shook his head. "No martinis for me. What do you have on draft?" he asked the bartender.

The man, who really looked more like a boy and couldn't be much older than twenty-one, rattled the list off from memory.

"I'll take an MGD," Jake told him.

The bartender filled a frosted glass and pushed it across the bar.

"Maybe we better grab a table?" Jake suggested, inclining his head toward the empty tables deeper into the bar.

Norm looked ready to disagree and then seemed to understand. "Oh, yeah, good idea. Privacy." He grabbed his martini and followed Jake to a little table next to a mirrored wall.

"Do the police have any idea what happened to her?" Jake asked, skipping the small talk.

Norm sipped his drink and shook his head. "Not that they've told me. They talk to me like I did something to her. One minute, the nice detective calls—Jasper is his name. And then an hour later the mean one calls—Bryant. They're trying to confuse me, but my story's not changing. I got home from work on Tuesday at five o'clock. I walked into my apartment, took off my shoes and left my keys on the counter and then walked across the garage to Petra's. We usually watch *Friends* in her apartment because she has a nicer TV. I opened her door and..." He trailed off, blinking down at his cup as if he still couldn't make sense of what he'd seen. "I thought it was paint," he whispered.

"When did you realize it was blood?" Jake asked.

Norm frowned. "I... I smelled it."

"Do you have any idea what might have happened, Norm? Was Petra having issues with anyone? Did anyone have it out for her?"

Norm sipped his drink. "Petra could be a little edgy. She had a hard life. You know?"

Jake shook his head. "No, not really. I met Petra on Tuesday. She came into my office."

"Oh, yeah. I forgot." Norm sighed. "Well, Petra didn't grow up with the *Little House on the Prairie* kind of life. She said her family was more like the Munsters and even they were too nice."

Well, that explained the lack of family presence on the news. "They're not around then?"

"Oh, God, no," Norm exclaimed. "Not at all. Petra hasn't spoken to her parents since she was a teenager. She grew up somewhere in the middle." Norm held up his right hand as many Michiganders did and pointed toward his palm. "A real dump, I guess. She had a brother and a sister. But the mom had a lot of boyfriends. Petra's dad split when she was young. The boyfriends..." Norm frowned. "They abused her. Touched her and stuff, probably worse than that. When Petra told, they sent her away. Eventually she ran away, but..." Norm shrugged. "You don't get over that. You know?"

Jake paled. "She was molested?"

"Yeah, and I feel like that's a nice way of saying what happened to her. She didn't tell me the details. I don't blame her. But she did some work with a psychiatrist, and, over the last few months, she's been working with a hypnotherapist, trying to heal the past."

Jake frowned. "Is there any chance she confronted some of that family? Maybe threatened legal action for what they did?"

Norm's eyes widened. "I didn't even think of that."

"You're a lot closer to the situation than I am. Sometimes an outside perspective helps."

"She might have. I mean a year ago, I would have said no way. She hated those people and never wanted to see them as long as she lived, but, well… The last few months, she's been angry. She used to be just sad and hurt. I mean angry too, but not the kind of angry that would go after someone."

"Did you tell the police all this?"

Norm shook his head. "They didn't ask. All their questions have been about me. I mean, they asked if she had a boyfriend or anything."

"Did she have a boyfriend?"

Norm shook his head. "Not for a long time. She dated a guy last year, but it ended after a few months. Before she moved into the duplex, she'd lived with a guy for a few years, but he'd get drunk and hit her. He was a real asshole. He showed up one time a few months after she moved in. He smashed her car with a baseball bat. She ran to my door crying, and I let her in. We became best friends that night."

"Whoa, that's crazy. Maybe it was that guy."

"He's in prison. Got arrested about five months after he came to the apartment. He hit his new girlfriend with his truck. She lived, but she was in bad shape. They convicted him of attempted murder."

"Good grief," Jake murmured.

"Yeah, it's really not fair. I mean, Petra's entire life has been hard and now…" Norm pressed his lips together and started to cry. He wiped at his tears with his sleeve. "Sorry. I'm just… I'm afraid something terrible has happened to her."

"Where does she work, Norm? Does she have other friends?"

Norm waved at the bartender and pointed at his glass. The young man nodded and gave him a thumbs-up.

"I tip him good," Norm confided. "Normally they won't deliver right to your table, but since Petra and I are regulars…" He didn't finish the statement. "She works at a boutique clothing store downtown. It's called Jessica's. They sell high-end stuff, clothes and shoes and scarves. The owner, Jessica Larson, has already offered a five-thousand-dollar reward for any information that leads to her whereabouts."

"Retail?" Jake said, rather surprised. Petra hadn't struck him as a saleswoman.

Norm laughed. "She helps Jessica as a buyer. Once in a while she works in the store, but she's a little cool with strangers, you know? But she has a great eye. Jessica's in her sixties, mostly retired now, so she relies on Petra for most of the new buys. Next to me, Jessica is the only person who really knows Petra, I'd say. Petra doesn't have many friends."

"Norm," Jake started, pausing when the bartender delivered his drink.

"Thanks, Sky," Norm told him, patting the guy's hand.

Jake's eye lingered on the touch, and he wondered if Norm was gay. He honestly didn't have a clue.

"His name is Skyler," Norm told him after the bartender left. "Such a brilliant name. I've asked my mom several times why in the world she had to name me Norman when she could have opted for something fantastic like Skyler or Thorn."

"Thorn?" Jake frowned.

Norm laughed. "Yeah, that was Petra's reaction too."

"Did Petra mention me at all?" Jake asked. "Or a girl named Maribelle?"

Norm sputtered, a mist of pink martini spraying from his nose onto the table. "Oh, ouch." He stuffed a napkin into his nose. "Damn, that burns." He clenched his eye shut, pulling the napkin away a moment later and wiping the table. "How do you know about Maribelle?"

Jake shook his head. "I don't. When Petra stopped by my office, she said we'd known each other as kids—me, her, and a girl named Maribelle."

Norm put two fingers to his lips as if shocked by Jake's revelation. "Maribelle is... Well, she's Petra's ghost."

7

"Her what?"

"Her ghost." Norm leaned across the table, dropping his voice. "That's why Petra started seeing the hypnotherapist. Last year we went to a psychic medium. You know, one of those people who speaks to the dead. The lady told her she had repressed memories related to the ghost."

"Okay, I'm not following. What do you mean, ghost? Like she was seeing a spirit?"

Norm nodded, wide eyes locked on Jake's. "She'd been dreaming about Maribelle for years, but then she started to see her and hear her. She'd wake up in the morning and find all her cupboards open. Her jewelry would go missing and turn up in the freezer or tucked in one of her shoes."

Jake took a swig of his beer, which had sat mostly untouched. "Did you believe it?"

"I saw it with my own eyes. I mean, not Maribelle, but… well, something. I was at her apartment one night, and the door just flung open. No wind, and it opened hard, like someone had kicked it, but there was no one there."

Jake shivered. "Why does she think it's this girl Maribelle?"

The record in the neon jukebox that sat in the corner changed. Simon and Garfunkel's song, *The Sound of Silence*, began to play.

Hello, darkness, my old friend,
  I've come to talk with you again
  because a vision softly creeping
  left its seeds while I was sleeping.

"She's here," Norm said.

Jake chuckled and took a long drain on his beer. "I gotta piss," he announced, and stood abruptly, hurrying for the men's room.

The sign on the door read 'Gents' in hot pink calligraphy. He pushed into the dim interior, lit only by blue and pink halogen bulbs. Drunk, he might not have minded the bar, but sober and semi-spooked, the neon lights left him feeling like he was in the Eagles' *Hotel California*.

He peed, avoided looking in the mirror for superstitious reasons he didn't care to acknowledge, and strode back to the table.

Norm hummed along to the song, eyes drifting among the tables as if expecting to see someone he knew.

"It's weird to be here without her," he confessed when Jake sat down. "I only ever came here with Petra. When she first moved in, my hangout was Pete's Bar over on Main Street. It's a dive, but they have a popcorn machine and a great happy hour. Petra said, 'No way we're drinking in a joint like that.' That's the sort of place she met Vince in; he was the beater. She said if we wanted to level up our mates, we had to pick better drinking spots. A lot of business folks come here." Norm inclined his head toward the table of suits.

They'd visibly relaxed. One man in the group had removed his tie and it lay crumpled on the table. A woman in red heels had slipped them off and tucked her legs beneath her. It reminded Jake of Allison and his heart briefly spasmed behind his ribs.

"What do you do, Norm? For work?"

"Clean. I have my own company. Norm Tidies Up. I've been doing it for ages now, started right after high school. My mom says I'm fastidious." He beamed. "Anyway, her friends started hiring me to clean before family gatherings and word got around. Now I have a little office with cleaning supplies and a van. How about you, Jake? You strike me as a man who works with his hands." Norm eyed Jake's hands.

Jake gazed at them as well. "Yeah, true enough. I own an excavating company."

"Strong," Norm murmured.

Jake couldn't quite pinpoint the tone. Somewhere between envy and desire.

"You remind me of an older Zack Morris," Norm told him.

"Should I know who that is?"

Norm gazed moonily toward the bartender. "*Saved by the Bell.* Probably not your kind of show, but Petra and I like to watch it. We decided everyone fits the looks or personality of a sitcom character. You've got the looks of Zack, but the personality of Slater, I'd say."

"Norm, how did Petra find the hypnotherapist?"

"He found her." Norm leaned across the table as if revealing an extraordinary secret. "It was the strangest thing. We were here at the Pink Drink having our usual Friday night cocktails, and he just stopped by our table and handed her his card. He said something compelled him to come over and give it to her. It affected her. It really did. I mean she was in recovery working with a psychiatrist on all her issues and it seemed... well, it seemed like destiny or something kind of magical. She talked about it for days afterward and then finally she went there and met with him."

"I think I'd like to talk to him," Jake said, watching the woman who'd slipped off her red shoes stand in nyloned feet to sway to *Let's Stay Together* by Al Green.

"Oh, I love this song," Norm sighed, bobbing his head to the song.

"How can I find the hypnotherapist, Norm?" Jake asked.

"'Lovin' you forever is what I need...'" he crooned.

"Norm," Jake said again, tempted to clap his hands to get the man's attention.

Norm sighed, dreamy-eyed. "Such a great song. Okay, I'm back. The hypnotist. Hmm... You know, I'm not sure. I don't even know his name. Petra just called him 'the hypno.'"

"Was he here in Bay City? How many hypnotherapists can there be? Maybe I'll just start calling all of them listed in the phone book."

They finished their drinks and walked out into the warm evening. Jake paused at Norm's car and held out his hand. "Thanks for meeting me tonight, Norm."

"No, thanks for meeting me."

Jake glanced into Norm's little four-door Saturn. A pile of mail sat on the passenger seat. A shiny silver credit card stuck out from the pile and as Jake studied it, the name on the card materialized.

P-E-T-R-A.

He frowned and leaned closer. "Norm..."

Norm followed his gaze and his eyes widened. "Oh, Jeez. It's not what it looks like. I mean, it's Petra's card, but she gave it to me to pick up her dry-cleaning last week."

Jake straightened back up, shoving his hands into his pockets. "I'd find that receipt, Norm. Have a good night."

8

"New job, new house, new life," Charlie said, clinking her coffee mug against Beverly's.

Bev made a face. "New town, probably a new best friend," she grumbled.

"Never a new best friend," Charlie promised. She took a sip of her wine. "I need new wine glasses though." She held up her coffee mug, a tiny chip missing from the lip. It said, 'I have no life, I'm in nursing school.'

"I would have forgiven you if you threw that away," Bev told her.

Charlie looked shocked and held the mug against her chest. "Never. I love this mug. Someday, I will take a class that teaches me how to repair beloved chipped coffee mugs. I think it would be a great small business venture when I retire."

Bev cocked an eyebrow. "Let's hope you've won the lottery by then."

Charlie nodded. "Guess I'll have to start buying tickets if that's my retirement plan."

Beverly stood and walked away from the chaise lounge she'd been draped across. "I can't believe you got such a good deal on this house. And the furniture, too. I mean, these side tables alone... This is solid wood." She ran her hand over the smooth surface.

"Crazy, isn't it? The last six weeks have been a blur."

Bev continued around the room, touching tasseled lamp shades and trailing her fingers along the backs of silk-upholstered chairs. "They're beautiful, but a little..."

"Outdated?"

"Eerie."

Charlie chuckled and surveyed the furnishings. They were old, but everything looked pristine, as if much of it hadn't been lived in at all. The chairs didn't contain discolored patches where people had sat for years knitting scarves or reading books. "I think one of the previous owners must have been a collector. This furniture hasn't been here for a hundred years. It would be worn."

"Yeah. Maybe that's the eerie thing about it. It's like stepping into a museum. Where are the smudge prints? The little rips from overuse? The evidence of life?"

Charlie shrugged. "I'm getting a cat. There will be tears in no time."

Bev made a horrified face. "No," she groaned. "Let me consult my *Steps to Becoming a Crazy Cat Lady Handbook*." She pretended to flip pages in an invisible book. "Step one, buy a big empty house. Step two, start filling it with cats."

Charlie threw a pillow at her friend.

Bev caught it. "Uh-oh. Step three, decorate big house with tasseled pillows." She threw the pillow back and laughed. "I'm kidding, I swear." She sat next to Charlie on the couch and squeezed her hand. "I'm happy you're finally getting a cat after Jared pretending to be deathly allergic for a decade. You deserve a decent companion."

"He was allergic," Charlie said, leaning her head on Bev's shoulder.

"Maybe," Bev agreed. "But I still think we should have filled his SUV with cat hair just to make sure. And as a little payback for his shittiness this last year."

"Refill?" Charlie asked, standing and grabbing Bev's empty mug from the coffee table.

"Heck, yeah. I brought two bottles and I won't consider this evening a success unless we drink both of them. But don't change the subject on me. Speaking of Jared the Gigolo, have you talked to him since you moved in?"

Charlie walked into the kitchen and filled both of their mugs with Riesling. "No. I'll have to call him eventually. He's still getting half my mail at his house, but..." Charlie didn't need to explain. Bev understood why Charlie hadn't called.

"Are you excited for tomorrow night?" Bev asked.

Charlie bit her lip and nodded slowly. "Excited and nervous."

"The first night's always hard. But you're a great nurse, Charlie. They'll be thanking their lucky stars you showed up by the time your shift ends."

"Yeah, hopefully. I hated leaving Pontiac General though. I even miss that grumpy night nurse, Velma."

"Velma," Bev groaned. "Can you imagine seeing her with those arthritic hands coming in with a needle? I'd have run screaming into the night."

Charlie laughed. "She didn't shake. Meaner than a hornet, sure, but she had a steady hand."

Bev shrugged. "What do I know? I'm a flight attendant."

~

Despite some initial anxiety, Charlie's first night at her new hospital went smoothly.

"Uh-oh, another lamb to the slaughter," a handsome nurse in turquoise scrubs announced when Charlie appeared at the nurses' station. He had close-cropped black hair, dark eyes, and a quick foxlike smile.

Charlie had worn her gray scrubs, freshly laundered in her brand-new washing machine, but immediately noticed all the other nurses on the ward in shades of green, turquoise or bright blue.

"Don't mind him," the middle-aged nurse at the computer told her, shooing the man away.

He winked at Charlie and then trotted down the hall to help a man who'd appeared at his door holding his bed pan. "Bert, you're not supposed to get out of bed. Remember?" the man called.

"You must be Charlie," the woman said, standing. Charlie offered her hand, and the nurse shook her head. "Nasty case of influenza blew through here last week. We're not shaking hands."

Charlie pulled her hand back down.

"I'm Jane, the charge nurse tonight, and we've got a call-in, so I need you on the floor, but first I've got to give you the standard manuals. It looks like you filled out all of your paperwork out at your orientation?"

"Yep," Charlie agreed.

"Well, we could use you, that's for sure. We don't have many nurses with years of experience in the ICU. Warren, the nurse you just met, came over from pulmonary last year. Marilyn—don't even think about calling her Mary—has been puttering around this hospital for a hundred years, it seems, but only came to the ICU a few months back when one of our nurses left on maternity leave. You know the drill. They come and go."

Charlie nodded and took the booklet. She'd worked in the ICU for seven years after a stint in the maternity ward and a few months in the emergency room. ICU had been her fit. Ultimately, she liked feeling needed, which had become especially important when things started to fall apart in her marriage. Her husband had made it abundantly clear he didn't need her for anything, not even sex. The patients in the ICU were another story. They'd become her sanctuary during the darkest times.

~

"Mrs. Cline lives in a nursing home," Warren explained, opening a door to a patient's room, "but she broke her hip and ankle last week, which triggered a stroke. She had a rough few days, but seems to be on the other side now." Warren walked into a room where a woman lay in bed, staring unblinking at the ceiling.

"Is she awake?" Charlie asked.

"Hard to say. She lapses into these states once in a while. It creeped me out the first few times, but I've gotten used to it."

The woman blinked and turned her head toward Warren, a tired smile cracking her lips. "I'd like a Popsicle," she said.

"Sorry, Mrs. Cline. Remember, no treats at night. How about a cup of water?"

"I could get her some ice," Charlie offered.

The woman's eyes slid from Warren to Charlie and her face darkened, her eyes going wide. Charlie could see the red capillaries that had burst in her eyes from the stroke.

"Run," the woman mumbled, and then she said it louder. "You're in danger. Get out!" She started to wail and thrash. She clenched her eyes shut and shoved her papery hands over her face.

Charlie looked at Warren, who looked as shocked she felt. She backed out of the room and closed the door. For another minute, she listened to the woman's shrieks.

When Warren stepped out, Charlie saw red welts on his arms where the woman had scratched him.

"Holy crap. Is she okay?" Charlie asked.

Warren looked irritated. "Crazy old bat," he muttered, rubbing his arm.

"Has she ever done that before?"

"Not on my watch. Probably day nurses fucking up her meds. Total idiots." He stomped off down the hall in the direction of the supply room, likely to disinfect the scratches on his wrists.

Charlie stood in the hall, leaning close to the door. She no longer heard the woman and didn't dare step back inside to check on her.

The rest of her shift unfolded without incident, but the look in the woman's eyes trailed her throughout the night.

9

Jake didn't have to look far to find the hypnotist. The man's card poked from the door of Dig Deep Excavating the following morning.

Trent Henderson, Hypnotherapist. A phone number and email were printed beneath the name.

Jake turned the card over and read the scribbled writing.

'I hoped to speak with you about Petra Collins. Please call.'

Jake flicked on the office lights and hit start on the coffee pot that Barbie had set up the day before. He walked to his inner office and picked up the phone, dialing Trent's number.

"Trent Henderson," a man said.

"Hi, Trent. This is Jake Edwards. I just arrived at my office and found your card."

The man pulled in a little breath. "Jake, hello. I heard about Petra and called Norm late last night. He told me how to get in touch with you. Can you meet me today, Jake?"

"Today? Well…"

The outer office door opened and Barbie bustled in, her hands full with a tray of plastic-wrapped muffins.

"Petra and I spoke extensively about you, Jake," the man

continued. "And her situation may have arisen from those very conversations."

"Sure, yeah. I can come to you this afternoon. Where's your office?"

"I'll pencil you in for three o'clock. My office is at 218 Industrial Street, Suite C in Bay City. Can you find that?"

"Sure. Yeah." Jake jotted down the address and hung up the phone.

"Good morning, Jake. Apple cinnamon muffins this morning," Barbie told him.

"I'm good. Thanks, Barbie."

⁓

THAT AFTERNOON, Jake drove down Industrial Street, rather surprised the man would have a hypnotherapy office in a warehouse district. Most of the buildings were large metal or brick structures. Their parking lots included heavy equipment, stacks of tires and a range of machinery.

218 Industrial Street was a large cinder block building with five offices in a row. Suite C did not have a sign, but on the door, Jake saw a small gold placard that stated 'Trent Henderson, Hypnotherapist.'

Jake pushed the glass door open to reveal a square waiting room with two chairs and a coffee table scattered with magazines. There was no reception desk and little artwork or décor. A single painting hung on one wall, featuring a beachscape with rolling waves and a colored sailboat in the distance—hotel room art.

A man opened an interior door, smiling and waving at Jake as he talked on a cordless phone. "Lucy, it's best if we do your next session in the morning. Okay, Friday at nine. See you then."

Trent looked to be well into his sixties with silver hair and pale, milky skin. His hazel eyes were light and a little weird-looking. Jake stared at him for a moment, struck by his unnerving eyes and the sudden sense that he'd met the man somewhere before.

Trent gazed back at him, lifting an eyebrow. "Jake Edwards, I presume?" he asked, holding out a hand.

Jake shook it.

"And I'm Trent Henderson. Call me Trent."

Jake followed Trent into a large square office decorated in characteristic shrink. A ceramic statue of a head sat on a shelf, the skull mapped into sections, each with labels like 'immortality' and 'self-esteem.'

Jake nodded at it. "I've seen those before. What are they for?"

Trent put his hand on the statue. "It's a phrenology bust based on the theories of Franz Joseph Gall, who believed the contours of the skull could reveal critical aspects of the self. Debunked science for the most part." Trent shook his head and laughed. "But I like to keep an open mind."

Jake shifted his attention from the head to the chaise lounge in the center of the room. The only other furnishings were a plain desk, void of papers, and two wooden chairs.

"No need to hop on the couch just yet," Trent told him with a wink. He grabbed a chair from behind the desk and wheeled it out. "Have a seat."

Jake sat and studied the books on the man's shelf. He read a few of the spines. *Man and His Symbols*, *The Ego and the Id*.

When he turned back, Trent studied him and Jake felt as if the man were silently appraising him.

"So," Jake started. "You heard what happened to Petra?"

Trent's face fell, and he shook his head. "Terrible. But she hasn't been found, so we mustn't lose hope."

"You said you and she talked about me?"

Trent nodded. "Oh, yes. In fact, I was rather delighted to hear she'd found you. I'd joined in the search with her, you see.

What a mystery. And I dare say nothing damages a person like repressed memories."

Jake scratched at the back of his head.

"Would you be willing to talk to me, Jake? About your time at the asylum with Petra?" Trent's eyes were bright with anticipation.

Jake picked at a bit of varnish peeling from the arm of the chair, stopping when he saw Trent's eyes drift to his fidgeting hands.

"Well, that's the thing," Jake admitted. "I don't remember being at the asylum with Petra. When she came into my office, I thought it was a joke."

Trent studied him and Jake wondered if he questioned Jake's story.

"Curious," Trent said finally. He stood and went to his desk, reaching into a drawer and pulling out several photographs. He handed them to Jake.

Jake studied the images. "This is the asylum?" he asked, though he knew the answer. The truth tugged at him, a child's memories trapped in some dark corner of his mind.

The third photograph revealed children, arms linked, and he blinked stupidly down at their faces. He saw himself there, tucked between the two little girls. It was the same boy who gazed up at him from the pictures in Faye's photo albums, but when he looked at her photos, he had memories to go with them. This image, like the pictures of the asylum, brought only that nagging flutter of something…

"That is you, isn't it?"

Jake nodded. And he recognized Petra too from her almond-shaped eyes, though her hair had been lighter in childhood. The girl on the other side must be Maribelle, and the quiver of knowing trembled through him. He could almost feel her arm snaked through his. He thought she might have pinched him playfully right before the picture had been taken. Her hair was glossy and black, long and draped over each shoulder, parted in the middle of her head. Two round eyes, dark brown, peered out from her pale face. Both girls were pretty. Jake stood nearly the same height as Petra, but six inches taller than Maribelle.

"Yeah," he sighed after several seconds. "It's me. I don't remember it, but it's me."

"Would you be open to going under a bit? Hypnosis isn't losing consciousness. Think of it as bypassing the conscious to access the subconscious."

Jake shrugged. "Sure," he said, "though I wouldn't hope for much."

～

"Jake, go ahead and close your eyes and focus on the breath. Bring your awareness into your breath. Breathe deeply into the diaphragm. Draw breath in, deeper. Now slowly release it. As you listen to my voice, allow your breath to deepen, your exhales to lengthen. Notice your eyelids getting heavy, so heavy you can't possibly open them. The body is getting heavier too. With each exhale, you're sinking deeper into the couch."

Jake concentrated on the backs of his eyelids. Not that he could see anything, but he imagined words written there. 'Stay Awake' in bright white letters.

～

Jake opened his eyes, blinking at the white drywall ceiling pocked with water marks. It took him a moment to get his bearings, but then he turned his head.

Trent Henderson sat in his wooden chair, gazing at Jake curiously, his hands folded in his lap. "You were there, Jake. You were at the asylum."

Jake's eyes widened. "Huh? Did I say something?" He had

no memory of telling Trent anything. He assumed he'd fallen asleep.

A little smile played on Trent's lips. "It's all still in there." Trent tapped a finger on his temple.

Jake sat up, slightly confused, but gradually piecing together what the man was trying to say.

The smile reappeared on Trent's face. He reached to the floor, picking up a plastic voice recorder. "Just give me a second to rewind."

Jake watched the tiny cassette in the tape and listened to the droning whiz as it wound the black tape backwards.

Trent hit play.

TRENT: Jake, go ahead and close your eyes and focus on the breath. Bring your awareness into your breath. Breathe deeply into the diaphragm...

The relaxation guidance went on for another several minutes.

TRENT: Now you are not asleep, Jake. You are very much awake, merely in a trance, in the realm of the subconscious. Tell me, Jake, what is it you see there?

When Jake heard his voice, he gave a start and stared incredulously at the tape. He sounded like a young boy.

JAKE: It's so big. The buildings are as high as the sky. Maribelle," he called out. "That's Maribelle. She's my best friend. Oh, and Petra. Petra, come with me and Maribelle, we're going to the canteen for chocolate milk.

TRENT: Tell me about the buildings, Jake. What's inside of the buildings?

JAKE: Crazy people.

TRENT: Are the buildings a mental institution?

JAKE: Maribelle calls it a looney bin.

TRENT: And why are you there, Jake?

JAKE: I live here. We all live here. I'm a bad kid. That's why they sent me here.

TRENT: Really? And the doctors let them do that?

Jake heard a rustling sound in the tape recorder.

"You were squirming a bit here," Trent told Jake now.

JAKE: They said it's because of Horace. My friend, Horace.

TRENT: And who is Horace?"

JAKE: He's dead. He's been dead for a long time.

TRENT: I see. And your parents knew you had a friend who was dead?

JAKE: My mother. I don't have a father. I don't tell people about Horace now. Except Maribelle. Maribelle knows because she saw me talking to him.

TRENT: Can Maribelle see Horace?

JAKE: No, nobody can see him. Except, well, the lady in the woods. She sees him, but she's dead too.

TRENT: Tell me about the lady in the woods.

Jake stared at the recorder, eyebrows pulled together, waiting for the next words and simultaneously afraid to hear them.

But Jake the child didn't answer. A muffled sound like crying began and then tapered off to silence.

"I lost you here," Trent said, stopping the tape. "This is clearly a traumatic memory that your child self didn't want to reveal."

Jake sat up and rubbed his hands down his cheeks.

"If you'd like we can try again, Jake. Take a few minutes' breather and—"

"No," Jake barked. He stood abruptly and staggered when a surge of light-headedness washed over him. He steadied as Trent held out a balancing arm. "No, it's okay. I just stood up too fast. I have to go, Trent. I appreciate your help."

He started toward the outer office and then remembered the detective. He pulled his billfold from the back pocket of his jeans and extracted Bryant's card. Jake copied Detective Bryant's name and phone number onto a sticky note and handed it to Trent. "Detective Bryant. He's working Petra's case."

"I'll call him right away," Trent said, folding the paper in half and slipping it into the breast pocket of his shirt.

Jake started toward the door, Trent following behind him. As he stepped into the parking lot, Trent stopped him.

"Jake, listen, I'd like you to come back. There's more to uncover here and"—he chuckled dryly—"with the sincere hope of not sounding like a crackpot, I wonder if the secrets hidden in your and Petra's memories might hold the key to her disappearance."

Jake didn't bother to hide his unease at the suggestion. He stuffed his hands in the pockets of his jeans and shook his head. "I'm swamped right now. And, just so we're clear, I don't buy into all that." He gestured dismissively at the study, but found it difficult to meet Trent's eye.

Trent smiled warmly and stepped back into the office. "You have my number, Jake."

∼

JAKE RAN a red light and nearly collided with a station wagon full of teenagers when they pulled out in front of him on a country road.

"Damn it," he bellowed, slamming his foot on the brake and gripping the steering wheel like his truck might go airborne.

A boy in the backseat of the station wagon offered Jake a grin and a one-hand salute while the girl sitting beside him flipped Jake the finger.

"Nasty little punks," Jake shouted, though they couldn't hear him, and to his own ears he sounded old and crotchety.

He drove slowly the rest of the way to the shop, waiting the customary four seconds at every stop sign and not even bothering to turn on the radio for fear the distraction would send him careening into a ditch. He wanted the distraction, though, wanted it bad as his head pumped his own words, spoken in a child's voice, back to him like a noxious gas meant to turn his brain into mashed potatoes.

When he parked, he jumped from the cab and hurried inside, startling Barbie, who stood in the corner watering a ficus tree she'd insisted added fresh air to the office. "Lord Almighty, Jake, you near gave me a heart attack."

"Sorry, Barbie," he mumbled, glancing at his office and suddenly unwilling to go inside. "What's new on the books? Anything?"

Barbie poured the last of the water into the black soil and tucked the watering can behind the ceramic pot. "Since this morning?" She looked at him sideways as if she might need to check his temperature.

"Sure. I thought maybe..." But the names of the clients had suddenly slipped his mind and he couldn't think of a single one to fill in the blank that followed. "Uh, I just thought maybe some new business came in is all."

He ignored her motherly concern and shuffled over to her desk where the calendar sat. He glanced at the names of his crew, studying each job he'd dispatched them to that morning, but his usual vigor to join them eluded him. Equally dissatisfying was the thought of working on bids, servicing the equipment, or any of the other daily tasks that he usually reveled in.

"Are you okay, Jake?" Barbie asked, putting one hand on her hip to let him know he'd best not lie to her.

"Yeah, just a little off. Maybe I'll call it a day."

She tried to conceal her surprise, but Barbie rarely hid anything and it didn't come naturally to her. "Should I call Dr. Barlett? Get you in for a physical?"

Barbie had been making his doctor appointments for years. It had been a sore point with more than a handful of previous girlfriends, including Allison. *Barbie's been around longer,* he once told Allison, which had earned him an evening of the silent treatment.

"No. Just a little headache."

Barbie nodded. She wanted to ask about Allison, it was plain on her face, but bit her tongue. He hadn't announced his break-up with Allison, but Barbie's best friend was Allison's cousin. It would have gotten back to her the day it happened.

"You do that." She patted his shoulder. "And how about I bring some lentil soup by later and check on ya?"

Jake shook his head. "I've been craving a meatball sub from Bella's," he lied.

"Mmm," she said. "And maybe get a little side salad too."

"I just might. Call me if anything pops up," he told her and strode back into the parking lot.

He drove home and walked into the house on heavy legs. The exhaustion had hit him like a hammer to the back of his eyes. A mile away from home, his headache had gone full-blown, the first glimmer of a migraine strobing its ugly lights across his vision.

Faye had also suffered migraines, so severe at times she vomited and spent days in a gloomy room, a cold washcloth on her forehead and Lennon and Jake tiptoeing in the hallways outside.

When Jake started getting migraines, despite no history of having them before, the doctor believed they were sympathetic headaches brought on by Faye's own painful episodes. It didn't really matter what lay at the heart of the headaches. After they started, they never stopped, though like Faye's they only wreaked havoc a few times a year. For Faye, they appeared around her mother's birthday—her mother had died tragically when Faye was a young woman. The migraines also popped up for Faye during times of high stress, like when Jake got kicked out of school for putting cherry bombs in the boys' toilets.

Jake's, on the contrary, had no obvious trigger. Chocolate,

sugar, too much television—he'd heard a plethora of diagnoses by doctors over the years, but none seemed to ring true.

This one, however, was obvious enough. In the previous three days, he'd broken up with his girlfriend, become embroiled in a missing person's case and discovered some secret history about an asylum he had no recollection of ever being a patient at.

When he made it into the front hall, he dumped his keys and wallet, missing the black trunk he used as an entryway table. The keys clattered on the wood floor. Not bothering with any lights, he crawled on hands and knees up the stairs, gritting his teeth at the pulsing ache digging deep into the soft tissue of his brain. He was tempted to smash his head against the wall, though knew it wouldn't do any good.

He staggered into his room and hastily thrust the curtains across the window before collapsing onto the bed. He stuffed two pillows over his head to block out the remaining light and settled in for the miserable hours to come.

And come they did, but not filled with the emptiness of sleep. A decade of memories marched through his head. His mother, often angry or sad, scolding him, crushing him with looks of disgust, sometimes fear. A plain little house filled with silence. So quiet you could hear a mouse scurry across the attic floor above.

10

He woke to the far-off ringing of the telephone. Groping for his bedside alarm clock, his hand hit the lamp and nearly sent it crashing.

"Fugh..." he mumbled, still groggy, the darkness in the room only deepening his stupor.

His hand closed on the plastic box and he lifted it, squinted: six-thirty a.m. He'd slept for over fourteen hours.

Jake staggered out of bed, steadied his hand on the wall when the tipsy little vertigo tried to spill him sideways, and then walked, hand sliding on the wall until he was sturdy. He clomped down the stairs and snatched up the phone as it released another shrill cry.

"Hu-llo." He sounded drunk or drugged.

"Jake?" a man's high voice asked on the other end.

"Norb? Norm... yeah, it's Jake."

"Are you okay? You sound..."

"I'm okay," Jake reassured him, flicking on the hall lights. The brightness burst through his eyes and into his brain like an electric shock. He was grateful to find it didn't hurt. The migraine had passed. "I just woke up."

"Oh, dagnabbit. I was afraid of that. I figured you for an early riser. Sorry, Jake, should I call back?"

"No, it's fine. You probably saved me from rolling in an hour late to my own business. I went down with a migraine yesterday, and apparently I needed some sleep."

"Golly. Yeah, those are nasty, huh? I don't get them myself but Petra got them all the time. She bought blackout curtains for her bedroom."

"Yeah. I should pick some up. What's up, Norm? I'm going to have to hit the shower and the coffee soon to get on top of this late start."

"Oh, sure, yeah, okay. I'm calling because I remembered something I wanted to pass along. I already left a message with Detective Bryant. He acted like I was blowing smoke up his ass. They want me for this, Jake. I know they do. I didn't sleep a wink last night. Just lay in my bed rolling through it all—that damn blood—and then every time a branch blew, I about jumped out of bed. I don't own a gun, not allowed to technically, but I kept the biggest kitchen knife I got right under my pillow. Course then I was scared if I fell asleep, I'd somehow stab my own cheek." He released a strangled laugh, and Jake heard the tremors in his voice he'd missed in his earlier fugue.

"What is it you remembered, Norm? Something to do with Petra?"

"Yeah, yeppers. Petra thought she'd found a doctor from the asylum she'd been at as a kid. I don't know why he was important, but she'd been searching for him and a few days before she went missing, she made a comment about finding him."

"Hmm... What was his name?"

Norm snorted. "I don't know. I'm not sure she ever told me. Do you think it's a lead, Jake? Maybe he's the guy..."

Jake shook his head. "I don't know, Norm. I've got to get some coffee in me. I'll call you back this evening after work. Yeah?"

"Sure, that'd be great, Jake. Really, I appreciate it. I feel all alone here. Petra was my best friend, and I'm sure the cops are trying to pin this on me—"

"Norm—"

"They love a guy like me for stuff like this. God forbid they do any real detective work—"

"Norm," Jake said, louder.

"Sorry, yeah. Okay, call me later."

"Bye, Norm."

Jake hung up the phone and hurried to his kitchen. He'd have to forgo the shower this morning. He brewed a pot of extra-strong coffee and poured a mug three quarters full and then added a shot of cold water so he could slurp it down fast. He shrugged off yesterday's clothes in the laundry room, pulled on a pair of jeans and a Dig Deep t-shirt out of the dryer before filling a thermos and jumping in his truck.

His crew was already at the shop, and he smiled to see them loading the day's equipment. They could function without him. It was a reassuring notion, and he was especially grateful for Willis Dooby, the man who'd been best friends with Lennon and had mentored Jake as he started the business. He'd been an equipment operator himself for thirty years. Rather than retirement, he'd taken on the role of Jake's foreman and he'd begun grooming Ricardo for the job when age would finally push him off the equipment and behind a desk, or, better yet, into an easy chair. Jake dreaded the day that he no longer drove into the shop to see Willis, with his silver hair and beard, a toothpick sticking from the corner of his mouth, his replacement for cigarettes that he'd quit more than two decades before.

In some ways, Willis had taken the place of Lennon after his death and Jake knew he'd mourn the passing of Willis as deeply as he'd felt the loss of Faye and Lennon.

Jake parked and hopped out to a cascade of whoops and calls

from Allen and Jerry. "Just under the wire, boss," Jerry yelled. "My watch says six fifty-five."

"When did you learn to tell time?" Ricardo called to him.

Jerry undid his pants and mooned Ricardo, who covered his eyes and groaned.

"You better hope Barbie didn't see that," Jake laughed as he hurried for the office.

Barbie hadn't seen it. She stood in the inner office beside Jake's desk. When she heard him walk in, she spun around, her face as white as plaster.

"What?" he asked, stopping.

She blinked at him and then put a hand to her heart as if he'd startled her—which, from the look on her face, he had, but that wasn't all.

"Barbie?"

"Jake..." She shook her head and then stepped aside so he could see his desk.

Something lay there, a balled-up bit of fabric streaked with dark stains.

As he studied it, the funny little pattern took shape. White fabric spotted in little Scottie dogs. It was the shirt Petra had been wearing the day she'd walked into the office.

11

He looked at Barbie, whose face was ashen. She recognized the shirt too.

"Did you touch it?" he asked.

She shook her head.

"I better call the police."

"The police?" Barbie took a step backward.

"The woman, Petra. Do you remember her? The one who came in the other day?"

"Of course."

"Well, she disappeared that night. She, um… I don't know, but there was blood in her apartment."

"Blood." Barbie said the word breathlessly. Her eyes had returned to the shirt.

Jake reached for his phone and then paused, gazing at the dark receiver. "I better use your phone. Come on. Let's close this door." He waited for Barbie to step out of the office and shut the door behind them.

He pulled Detective Bryant's card from his wallet and dialed the man's number. It rang several times and Bryant's message clicked on.

"This is Detective Bryant with the Bay City Police. If this is an emergency, please hang up and dial 911. For a call back, leave a detailed message and your phone number."

"This is Jake Edwards. I've come into my office this morning to find something pretty disturbing. It looks like the shirt Petra was wearing the day she disappeared and it looks like it might have blood on it. You'd best come out here and bring someone to collect it."

After Jake hung up, he turned to Barbie. "Was anyone in here this morning?"

Barbie shook her head. "Just the boys, but no one went in your office. The door's been closed. I just went in there to get the print for the Gillespie job."

"Shit," he muttered. A few months earlier, Willis had told him he should think about installing security cameras around the property. A few other construction companies had been vandalized around town. Probably kids playing a prank, but they'd done some serious damage to a few tractors. Despite his friend's advice, he'd never bothered with the cameras.

"Who would put such a thing in your office?" Barbie asked. Her hands were trained on the edge of her desk as if to keep her from falling to her knees.

"Sit down, Barbie," he told her, nodding at her chair. The last thing he needed was Barbie having a stroke.

She sat and balled her hands together against her large bosom.

"I don't know who could have done it. It's crazy." He rubbed his eyes and turned in a slow circle, scanning the office for anything out of place. He walked to each window and studied the locks, all secured. "You locked up last night?" he asked Barbie.

"Yes, same as always."

He nodded.

They didn't keep any cash in the office. If a burglar broke in, the most he could help himself to was Barbie's ancient desktop computer and a handful of Dig Deep pens. For that reason, security had not exactly been a top priority. Anyone with a mind to do it could credit-card the door open.

"I better send the guys off and I'll hang around." He was halfway out the door when Barbie's phone rang.

She released a shrill cry and put a hand over her heart.

"I'll get it," he told her, taking two long strides back into the room and snatching up the phone. "Dig Deep Excavating."

"Jake? This is Detective Bryant returning your call."

"I thought so. Did you listen to my message? There's a piece of clothing here in my office—"

"I heard it," Bryant cut him off. "I'm leaving here in ten minutes. What's your location?"

Jake told the detective the company's address.

Outside, he put Willis in charge of the crew.

"Everything okay?" Willis asked when Jake handed him the business credit card to gas up the trucks.

Jake frowned. "I don't know. Some weird shit is going on. Maybe we can grab a beer after work."

"Lilith is making boiled dinner tonight. You bring the beer."

"It's a plan," Jake told him.

He didn't return to the office but walked around the dirt parking lot. He studied the tire tracks, but it had been dry for nearly a week. There weren't many tracks to see.

Two hours later, Detective Bryant, Barbie and Jake sat alone in the outer office. A crime scene investigator was still in Jake's office, dusting for fingerprints. Two additional officers were outside walking the property and looking for anything unusual.

Bryant focused on Barbie. "Jake says you found the shirt?"

Barbie nodded and then stood. "Detective, can I get you a cup of coffee? Or a lemon poppy seed muffin? Baked fresh last night?"

"No, thanks."

"It's okay, Barbie," Jake said, trying to hide his exasperation. "Just sit down."

Barbie sat and fiddled with pink silk tassels sticking from her daily devotional. She opened the book every day and sat it on the corner of her desk as if hoping the guys coming through the office might absorb some grace by proximity.

"Start at the beginning, Barbie. What time did you come in this morning?"

Barbie glanced at the clock, thinking back. "I arrived at six-fifteen, a little earlier than my usual time because it's my post office day and I wanted to get the mail done before the boys came through."

"What time do you usually arrive?" Bryant asked.

"Closer to six-thirty, sometimes six forty-five. And I was a little surprised because Jake wasn't here yet. He's early most days. Six- fifteen himself," she said.

"Or six," he corrected.

"Or six," she agreed. "I unlocked the office, started the coffee and put out my muffins." She pointed at a platter of muffins sitting on the table. "Around quarter to seven the boys started coming in. I almost called Jake, but he left with a headache yesterday and I thought he might have been struck with a bug." She looked at Jake sympathetically.

"You were ill yesterday?" Bryant directed his question at Jake.

"Migraine," Jake explained.

Bryant said nothing but turned back to Barbie. "And then what?" he prodded.

"I said good morning to the boys. They grabbed muffins and coffee and found out where they were headed today. Then I went into Jake's office because Willis needed the print since Jake wasn't here. He's running the excavator today and needed to see where the drain field is at the Gillespie house. That's where they're at today."

"Is your office usually locked?" Bryant asked Jake, gesturing at the closed door.

Jake shook his head. "We lock the main door there, but, well… it's not exactly a fortress around here."

"So you walked into Jake's office and then…?" Bryant asked Barbie.

"And then I turned on the light and started toward the rolled-up prints in the corner. I bent down to grab the print and then…" She glanced at Jake as if afraid to say more. "And then I saw the shirt."

"Do you usually go into Jake's office in the morning?" the detective asked.

"Not usually, no. Jake arrives before me, so…"

"And the shirt wasn't there when you left yesterday evening?" He gazed at Barbie.

Her eyes darted to Jake, and she shook her head. "No, I mean I don't know because I didn't go in there. Jake left around four-thirty. His door to the office was closed. I locked up and went home around six."

"And Jake, you didn't see the shirt in your office yesterday?"

Jake stared at him. "Of course not. I called the minute I saw it this morning."

"Who has access to the office?"

Barbie looked at Jake, but he answered first. "My crew, but they rarely go into my office. Willis, my foreman, does occasionally to grab a print, but that's it."

"Did you see anyone enter Jake's office yesterday?" Bryant asked Barbie.

"No one," she said.

"And were you at your desk all day? Could someone have come in and you missed them?"

"I highly doubt it," she said. "I used the bathroom a few times, but I stayed in for lunch. Had a sandwich at my desk yesterday. If I leave during the day, I lock the office behind me."

"Who else has a key?"

"Me and Barbie," Jake said.

"And the fox," Barbie added.

"Oh, shit, yeah." Jake felt color rising into his neck.

"The fox?" Bryant glanced between them.

"It's a hollow ceramic fox out by the shed. It has a key to the workshop and a key to the office tucked inside," Jake explained. "But only we know about it. I mean us"—he pointed at Barbie and himself—"and my crew."

"And anyone else who's worked for you previously?" Bryant asked, sighing.

"Well, yeah. But I'm not exactly running a big operation here. I can list on two hands every guy who's ever worked here."

"No hands necessary," Bryant told him, flipping to a blank page in his notebook. "I'll need their names and phone numbers right here."

Bryant stood and knocked on the interior office door. The technician opened it.

"We've got a ceramic fox outside that will need to be dusted for fingerprints and two keys inside."

"Right-o."

Fifteen minutes later, the tech stuck his head into the office from outside. "I've got one key inside the ceramic fox." In his gloved hand he held a single key.

"Double shit," Jake muttered, and as he'd done before he flashed on Allison. She wasn't a vindictive woman, and she wasn't a prankster, but when Petra had first appeared at his office, his first thought had been that Allison had put her up to it. Could she be behind the blouse? It made zero sense, but she also knew about the keys.

"Who's on your mind right now?" Bryant asked him.

"Huh? Oh, nobody."

"Hold on there. I can see in your face you think you might know who grabbed the key, so say the name. The more transparent you are at the beginning, the faster we'll figure this out."

Jake glanced at Barbie, embarrassed. "Um... well, I broke up with my girlfriend Allison a few days ago."

Barbie's mouth dropped open. "Jake! Allison would never—"

Bryant quieted her with a look.

"No, she wouldn't," Jake agreed. "She's not mean-spirited. And plus, how could she have gotten Petra's shirt? It doesn't make any sense."

"Allison what?" Bryant asked, pen poised above the paper.

He wished he'd kept his big mouth shut. Barbie stared at him venomously as he spelled out Allison's full name and phone number.

"Did she know Petra? Have any reason to suspect you were having an affair?"

Barbie's eyes widened.

"No, God, no. We weren't. I told you. I just met Petra the day she stopped in here..."

Bryant nodded, but glanced at Barbie. "How well do you know Allison?"

"Very well indeed," Barbie snapped.

Bryant shifted his attention back to Jake. "Are you aware that Norm Groesbeck is a felon?"

Jake looked up, startled. "A felon? No. For what? What did he do?"

The detective didn't immediately answer but watched Jake as if trying to sense a lie.

Jake sighed, exasperated.

"Check forgery."

Jake tried to hide the absurd laugh that bubbled up from his gut. "Check forgery? And that's got you looking at him for murder? I mean, that's what this is, right? You're assuming Petra was murdered?"

"Do you think she was murdered?" the detective demanded.

Jake tried to keep the annoyed look from his face but was unsuccessful. "I think a monkey given the facts would veer towards that. Blood all over her apartment and she's been missing for days."

"You seem awfully sure."

"I'm not sure. I'd love there to be some other explanation, but I tend toward logic."

"What would you think of Norm's ability to kill Petra if I told you he was stealing from her?"

"Was he?"

The detective didn't answer.

Jake knew how this worked. Police could lie. They could say anything they wanted to get someone to incriminate themselves. Jake thought of Petra's card in Norm's car. If he murdered her, why would he leave it sitting there for the whole world to see?

12

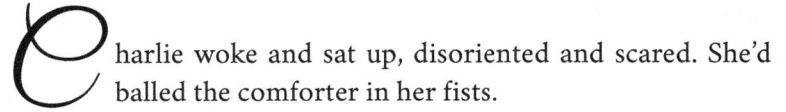

Charlie woke and sat up, disoriented and scared. She'd balled the comforter in her fists.

Holding still, trying to slow her uneven gulps for air, she listened. Something had woken her, some strange sound piloting through the darkness and warning her to wake up and be prepared.

Heart thumping, she slid to the edge of the bed and put her feet to the floor, shivering at how cold the wood felt beneath her. She made a mental note to buy slippers, and the thought instantly calmed her. How great a threat could exist if her mind had already shifted to purchasing slippers?

Smiling, a tactic her mother had taught her instantly calmed the nervous system, she stood and walked across the room. She hadn't learned the creaks of her new house yet, and one floorboard released an agonized groan as she stepped on it.

Through the window, the yard stood empty, illuminated by a bulb over the garage door. The entire neighborhood slept. The only movement was a cat several houses down prowling the bushes near the street.

The warmth of the bed beckoned to her, but she wouldn't sleep until she investigated the rest of the house.

It had become a habit after her marriage had ended and she'd found herself living alone for the first time in her adult life. It had been one of the hardest adjustments, waking in the darkness, scared, lonely, her mind racing with what-ifs. Women who lived alone sometimes got attacked. One of her closest friends at the hospital during those days had been a young nurse who'd worked in the emergency room. She'd told Charlie more than a few horror stories about women coming in who'd been raped, beaten, nearly strangled, woken in the night by a stranger or, worse, someone they knew.

Charlie shivered and grabbed her black fleece robe from the hook on the back of the door. She eased the door open and listened.

Quietly, she stole into the hallway and pressed against the wall, sliding her feet over the wood floor to make as little noise as possible. She hadn't heard anything to alert her to someone in the house, but on the slim chance there was, she wanted the element of surprise.

The staircase curved down, flanked by a white bannister. Charlie slid her hands, sweaty, along the rail as she crept down the stairs. At the curve, she gazed into the entryway and the front door. The door was closed, the space empty, but she didn't feel relieved yet.

She walked slowly down the stairs and paused again, listening. No sounds.

Sticking to the wall, she crept along the front entrance hall, peering into each room, looking at windows to ensure none of them stood ajar. Everything appeared as she'd left it. At the kitchen, something seemed out of place—an object protruding into the dark space. She stared at it for a long time before mustering the courage to flick on the lights.

The bright overhead bulbs illuminated the kitchen and

revealed the oddity: a cupboard door open too wide, revealing a single row of glasses and two empty shelves.

Had she left it open? She honestly couldn't remember, but it hardly seemed like something an intruder would do.

"Hello?" she called out anyway, in part to allow her own voice to break the heavy silence. No one responded.

Charlie closed the cupboard door and started back toward the doorway. As she reached for the light switch, another anomaly caught her eye. A single set of silverware sat on the kitchen table, a fork, a knife and spoon neatly lined up.

Fear streaked down her spine and before she could rationalize, she sprinted toward the front door, wrenched it open and ran onto the darkened porch. She shrieked when she collided with a man in a nylon coat, flailing her arms and realizing it was not a man but the flag that hung from the front porch bannister. She shoved it away and ran to her car, jumping inside and locking the doors.

"Shit," she moaned.

She hadn't brought her car keys. They hung from the little metal hooks inside the door.

Still, she felt safer in her car. If someone came out of her house, they'd have to make a lot of noise to break into her car. She could honk the horn. Maybe they hadn't seen her flee the house at all. They'd assume she ran down the street, went to a neighbor's for help.

She reclined her seat so she could not be easily seen, putting the seat all the way back.

Staring at the gray ceiling in her car, she felt those familiar pangs of loneliness and terror. Tears rippled up through her chest and throat, towards her eyes, but she didn't let them come.

"Mom, I need you to send the angels. Okay?" She closed her eyes as her mother had taught her so many years ago and imagined beings of light, huge feathery wings opening behind them, floating from the sky. They settled around the car. Some sat on the hood, one in the seat beside her. Their brilliant light would vanquish the darkest souls away.

Teeth clenched, eyes closed, she thought only of the angels until exhaustion crept in and carried her into sleep.

⁓

WHEN SHE AWOKE, the early light of dawn had washed away the slippery night shadows. The house looked innocent, empty of whatever violent fantasies Charlie had imagined hid in its rooms the night before.

She stepped from her car and a man several houses down offered her a half wave as he walked to the end of his driveway and bent down to grab his newspaper. A small black and white dog followed close at his heels.

Despite her relief at daylight, she still paused at the front door and peered into the foyer. Everything was as it had been.

Grabbing her keys from the hook in case she had to race to her car a second time, she crept into the house, pausing every step to listen.

At the kitchen, the morning light revealed the utensils still sat untouched on the table. She hadn't put them there. She was sure of it, and the strangeness took her back to the final days with Jared—the days when he'd tried to hide his affair by convincing Charlie that she'd gone nuts. Those were her panties, he'd insisted. Didn't she remember? He'd bought them for her on Valentine's Day. Of course he'd been home before two a.m. She must have read the clock wrong when he'd slid into bed beside her the night before. The list went on, the dozens of transgressions he'd cloaked by insisting she'd had a memory lapse.

Charlie paused at the table and touched her fingers to the silverware. It made no sense. And yet perhaps she had taken them out unconsciously the day before. She'd ordered a pizza earlier in the evening. Perhaps unthinking, she'd taken out the silverware and placed them on the table.

She returned them to the drawer and then set about checking the house yet again for intruders. The house was sizeable, nearly three thousand square feet. She checked beneath beds, tugged on windows to make sure they were latched and finally treated herself to a long hot shower when she felt confident no hooded man crouched in a shadowy corner of her house.

She put her hair in a towel and pulled on the black robe before returning to the kitchen to grab the phone book the realtor had tucked into a drawer.

Charlie called the local paper and put in an ad for a roommate. She'd already been considering it before she'd even put an offer in on the large Queen Anne house. It was too big for one person.

∾

"Uh-oh, silverware with a mind of its own? You better come home!" Bev insisted.

Charlie rolled her eyes and carried the cordless phone into the bathroom, the mirror still fogged, to grab her flip-flops. "It was obviously me, but Bev, I spent half the night in my car." She chuckled.

As the morning had progressed, the fears of the previous night had faded until they were merely a shadow of what they'd been. Now she felt foolish and grateful the man down the road hadn't noticed she was sleeping in her car.

"New house jitters," Bev explained. "When Rodney and I moved into our place, I had nightmares for a week. I walked into the wall like three times when I got up to pee in the middle of the night. Your head's just got to get used to the big classy place you're calling home now."

Charlie smiled and sat on the edge of her bed gazing around the room.

It was a classy house. The ceiling in every room had crown molding. Waist-high trim divided the dark wallpaper on the lower wall from the bright white paint on the upper.

It was also a steal and rather than squander the money she'd received in the divorce settlement, she'd searched for a place to invest it that would offer not only a return, but a doorway into a new life.

"Yeah. It's a whole new level of living alone. I mean, I lived alone in the apartment in Pontiac, but apartments are different, you know? Although honestly I got spooked a few times there as well."

"I remember," Bev told her.

And she probably did, since Charlie had shown up at Bev and Rodney's one night at midnight, still clad in her pajamas, and asked to sleep over. It hadn't been strange silverware that night, but a nasty fight between a boyfriend and girlfriend in the apartment next door. Their screams had turned into thumps against the wall. Charlie had called the police and then quietly crept out of the apartment building to her car and driven to her friend's house.

"Yeah, anything's got to be better than living next door to the War of the Roses."

Charlie laughed. They'd named the couple the Roses after they'd watched the movie The War of the Roses, which starred Michael Douglas and Kathleen Turner as a couple who became so entrenched in a bitter divorce they eventually killed each other. "Ooh, let's do a girls' night this weekend and watch it. Yeah? You can come stay the night. If anyone comes in to move my silverware around, I'll have backup."

Bev giggled. "Let me check with Rodney. He was going on

about some ferryboat poker tour that his friends want us to go on. Not my idea of a good time, but so long as the wine is flowing, I'll survive."

"Oh, all right." Charlie feigned disappointment. "But we'd better do it soon or I'm liable to have a roommate and then our girls' night will include a third."

"How do you know you're not going to have some hunk knock at your door looking for a place? I'm thinking like Tom Cruise, circa *Top Gun*. He's looking for a woman to tame his wild side."

"Thanks, but no thanks," Charlie told her, walking to her window still clad in her robe. "The last thing I need is a bad boy with a chip on his shoulder. I'm hoping for someone more like Tom Hanks circa *Sleepless in Seattle*. Wholesome, a little heartbroken. A guy who's happy to stay in on a Friday night, eat popcorn and watch television."

Bev groaned. "Charlie, you're single again. Don't ruin my chances of hearing stories about sweaty one-night stands with hard-bodied strangers so you can have some softie who lives in sweatpants and chews with his mouth open."

Charlie laughed, watching the quiet street and wondering if she should say hi to her neighbors, maybe make them care packages. She shook her head, realizing that was usually what the neighbor did, not the newcomer. "One-night stands are not in my vocabulary. Plus, in case you've forgotten, I'm a nurse. I have two words for you: venereal disease."

"Listen, don't ruin my fantasies with your filthy medical terms."

"All right, Bev, but I've got to put this phone down and get some clothes on before my neighbors notice I'm standing in front of my window half-naked."

"You're standing in front of your window naked? Ooh la la."

"In a robe. Goodbye."

"Love you, bye-bye. Oh, and don't forget to nail the utensil drawer shut tonight."

"Very funny." Charlie ended the call and went to the closet.

She'd hung up all her clothes the day before. Sliding shirts to the side, she searched for the gray cashmere sweater her mother had sent her for Christmas the previous year. It was nowhere to be found, though she distinctly remembered hanging it up.

"Where are you?" she asked, stepping into the closet and pulling shirts apart.

The phone rang on the bed behind her.

"Shoot." She grabbed a different sweater, a simple black knit, and thrust it over her head, yanking on a pair of jeans as the phone rang a third time.

She lifted the receiver and pressed it to her ear. " Hello?" she asked breathlessly.

"Hi," a woman's voice said. "I'm calling about the ad for a roommate."

Charlie frowned. She'd just called the paper that morning. They couldn't have possibly run the ad that day.

"Umm... how did you hear about it?"

Silence.

"Go away," a woman's voice, this one much more gravelly than the first, whispered.

"Is this a prank?" Charlie asked, pressing the phone too hard against her ear. She loosened her grip.

"Hello? Hello?" the original woman's voice said again. "Is anyone there?"

"Yeah. I'm here. How did you hear about the room?"

"My brother works at the paper," the woman said. "He called me after you submitted the ad. I've been looking for a place."

"Oh, okay. Did someone else just get on your line?"

"I'm not sure what you mean?"

"Well, I heard another person's voice on the phone."

"Really?" The woman sounded genuinely surprised. "Maybe the lines got crossed. You sort of tuned out for a minute, so…"

"Yeah," Charlie agreed. "That must have been it. Well, anyway, when would you like to come see the house? I've got to print an application, but I can meet today."

"Oh, wow, that'd be wonderful. I moved back in with my parents after I graduated and I've been desperate to get out." She laughed. "I can come by this afternoon. What's the address?"

"It's 319 Elmwood Drive. It's called Wilder's Grove."

"Wilder's Grove?" the woman blurted.

"Yep, do you know it? It's the big Queen Anne house right on the corner."

The woman didn't answer for a moment.

"Hello?" Charlie asked.

"Sorry, yeah, I know it. Umm… I don't think this afternoon will work after all. I'll give you a call back. Thanks."

Before Charlie could respond, the woman hung up.

Charlie hit off on her phone and dropped the cordless back onto the bed. "Well, that was kind of rude," she told the room. "But you know what? It's sunny today and I have a brand-new waffle maker waiting to get broken in."

She ran a brush through her hair. Wet, it hung past her shoulders. She'd been cutting it in the pixie style for years. Jared had preferred short hair, but since the separation and eventual divorce, she'd grown it long for the first time since she'd been in college. Reaching back, she ran her fingers through it several times, enjoying the sensation of finger-brushing the damp strands as they stretched long. When it dried, it would be slightly wavy, messier.

Once in a while she straightened it, but for work it stayed in a ponytail at the base of her neck and at home she left it unruly because she could. It was one of the many little gratitudes she'd focused on after life with Jared ended. She didn't have to style her hair or put on makeup. She never had to wake up to a comment about her morning breath or a mention that she was wearing sweats again.

"Good riddance, Jared," she yelled, her voice echoing in the high room.

She stared at herself in the mirror, mostly clear of the condensation. Her wide-set green-blue eyes looked back at her. Her slightly wide nose and her even wider full-lipped mouth made her face full. Men paid attention to her, though not in the way they looked at the perfectly symmetrical ladies with the perky noses and rosebud mouths. More than one boyfriend had described her as unique, which in her younger days had seemed like an insult. Only age had given her a shred of wisdom to appreciate her differences.

Turning away, she flipped off the light and smiled at the day ahead.

13

"Jake." Lilith beamed when she opened the door to find him on her front step.

Jake held up a six-pack of beer and a bouquet of daisies.

"You didn't have to do that," she told him, taking the flowers and kissing his cheek. "Willis is out back, honey."

Jake walked through the house and out the glass patio doors. Willis sat in a lawn chair, flipping through a newspaper. "Jake." He waved at the younger man. "Pull up a chair, good man."

Jake handed Willis a beer and kept one for himself before settling into a matching lawn chair.

"Tell me about this bloody shirt madness. Barbie said that woman who came into the shop the other day disappeared."

Jake opened his beer and took a long drink. "Yeah. My head feels ready to explode trying to make sense of it all. The shirt… just took it to a whole new level of bizarre."

Jake gave Willis a quick rundown on calling Petra's house several days before and getting a frantic Norm.

"And they still haven't found her?" Willis asked.

"I don't think so. I've been watching the news. Plus, Norm would have called me."

"How could her shit have gotten in there? You weren't messing around with this girl, were ya?"

Jake shot him an incredulous look, but Willis was unfazed. "Don't get your jockstrap in a twist. I'm not trying to imply anything. I saw the woman. She looked about your type and—"

"And what? Now I'm a womanizer and a homicidal maniac?"

A flush rose into Willis's neck, but he didn't back down. "I'm just saying things happen for a reason. Is the girl trying to get back at you for breaking her heart by staging some big scene?"

"I'd count my lucky stars if it were that simple."

"You suspect something bad happened to her?"

"Something bad did happen to her. Her neighbor found blood all over her apartment. Why her shirt ended up in my office is beyond me, but it scares me half to death."

Willis frowned. "You seem pretty stressed, Jake."

"Wouldn't you be?"

"Yes, I would. What concerns me is how stressed you've been for months, long before this woman went missing. What's it all for?" Willis stuck his index finger beneath the tab on his can of beer and snapped it forward. A mist shot into the air above the can and a burst of white froth peeked through the dark hole before sinking back down. Willis didn't take a drink, but balanced the can on his knee and steadied his gaze on Jake, waiting for an answer.

It was a Lennon question. The man had always known to go deep. No chat about the Detroit Lions' latest failure or the coming rain storm, he wanted to know the driving urge beneath it all. Had he lived, he would have asked the same question of Jake far sooner than Willis was asking it now.

"What do you mean?" Jake asked, swallowing a mouthful of

his own beer and letting out a subdued belch. "Excuse me," he murmured, eyes drifting toward the screen door where Lilith might have heard him.

Willis didn't elaborate. He just waited.

"The business? The work?" Jake asked.

"Sure," Willis said. "All of it. The twelve-hour days, the bigger bids and bigger jobs. What's it for? Just the thrill of it? The money?" Willis paused and took a drink. "I've been to your house. You live like a college kid. A futon for a couch. Folding chairs in the kitchen. No roots, no commitment."

Lilith stepped through the screen door, a stack of plates in her hands, silverware resting on top. She set the patio table and paused by Willis to kiss the top of his head. He squeezed her backside, and she squealed, flicking one of his ears. "Behave yourself, Willis Dooby," she laughed.

Jake and Willis watched her retreat into the house.

"Barbie told me you broke up with Allison," Willis said.

Jake sighed and tugged the collar of his shirt down, wishing he'd gone home to shower and change after work, He suddenly felt grimy, like he wanted to crawl out of his own skin.

"Al and I weren't right for each other," he said, a blush rising into his neck.

Lennon and Faye had been his parents, but Willis had been around a lot. He'd dole out a lot of advice and he and Lennon could give you a look that made you want to shrivel up and slink into a rat hole. It wasn't mean-spirited. Both men operated within a code of virtue that much of the modern world had forgotten existed. Do right by everyone, not simply the people you love, but everyone.

Jake liked to believe he'd developed his own moral decency, but he had not acted honorably in his relationship with Allison, in any of his relationships. He pretended not to know what they wanted as if his ignorance made it all okay.

"That might be true," Willis said. "But things being right and making them right are two different things. If I believe I'm destined to win the lottery, I'll see the winning numbers in everything I do. Billboards, gas receipts, heat indexes. If I believe it's a farce, I'll see lackeys lining up at the counter, throwing their money into a furnace and dying poor. Whatever I believe, or maybe I should say whatever I want to believe, is what I'll see."

"You think I wanted things to not be right with Allison?"

"I think you told yourself a story about things not being right with Allison that didn't have a thing to do with Allison. It's a story you've been telling for a long time. Remember Kim, that little curly-headed blonde you dated a few years back?"

Jake sighed. "Yes, and it was more like ten years back."

Willis waved a dismissive hand. "Kim had a smile that lit the room on fire! And Lennon loved her. Remember? They used to argue over the crossword puzzle. 'I'm telling you it's 'darkness,'' she yelled that one time. Remember, at Wilder's Grove? We were all sitting out back having a barbecue and they'd been bickering over that crossword for half an hour."

Jake laughed, thinking back to the sparkle in Lennon's eyes as he'd argued with Kim. "'The more of this there is, the less you see,'" Jake said, shaking his head. "Lennon kept saying it was 'seawater.'"

Willis burst into another peal of laughter and nearly knocked his can to the ground. "'Seawater,'" he guffawed. "He knew damn well she was right, but he loved to rile her up."

"He sure did," Jake agreed, and the laughter ebbed away as something else slipped in.

His stomach cramped at the memory of ending things with Kim. She'd been standing outside a bulldozer he rented in the pouring rain. Her cowboy boots were mud-splattered and the brown splotches were creeping toward her jeans. The rain hid the tears but not the plumes of anger and grief high in her cheeks. He hadn't called her in two weeks, just fallen off the face of the earth, but she'd seen him the night before. He hadn't seen her, hadn't had a clue she was even nearby as he escorted another young woman, whose name he couldn't even remember now, to the theater on Main Street to see *Top Gun*.

She'd confronted him on a job site the next day. Her eyes had the blued, hollowed look of a sleepless night. Easygoing Kim with the beautiful smile who could drive excavators and dozers and dump trucks. That was how he'd met her, at an equipment auction with Lennon. She'd been the closest thing there'd ever been to a 'one,' but he'd never much believed in finding the one. Other people did, sure, but not Jake. He flew solo. It was less complicated.

"If you could hand-pick from every woman in the world, you couldn't have chosen better than Kim. You were crazy about each other, and then one day she was just gone. Just never came around again."

"What's your point, Willis?"

Willis took another sip of beer and leaned forward in his chair, balancing his elbows on his knees. "My point, Jake, is that compatibility isn't the issue here. It's this bad ending story you're always rehearsing in your head."

"Willis, I hate to burst your bubble, but there are no happy endings. I've yet to meet anyone who fit the mold of happily ever after."

"How about Faye and Lennon?"

"Oh, yeah." Jake released a sarcastic laugh. "They fell madly in love, built a wonderful life, save for never being able to have children, though they managed to adopt some homeless kid, so that was magical. Then Faye got cancer and Lennon followed a few years later with a heart attack. Call Disney. They're going to want to write this one down."

Willis frowned and Jake almost expected him to lash out, scold Jake for demeaning Faye and Lennon's life. But in true

Willis form, much like the man who'd been his best friend, whose coffin he'd helped carry six years earlier, he simply leaned back and fixed those studious blue eyes on Jake's face. "The ending isn't the point, my friend. There are endings to everything. It's the stuff in the middle that counts."

∼

THE FOLLOWING AFTERNOON, Jake met with Trent for a second time.

"Carl Jung wrote extensively about the shadow. Let's explore that a bit, shall we?" Trent said.

"The shadow?" Jake asked.

"Yes, the repressed self, the darker self. We all have our dark half, Jake. Oftentimes our trauma lives there. So, tell me about your dark side."

Jake laughed. "I'm transparent. Vanilla, one girlfriend called me. What you see is what you get."

"Oh, I highly doubt that. I'd like you to recall a memory of shame. Tell me the first thing that comes to mind."

Jake frowned. Trent was feeling more like a shrink than a hypnotist, but what did he have to lose?

"Shame," he murmured. "Uh, well, I cut holes in one of Faye's blankets one time to scare my buddy who was staying the night. Turns out her mother had given her the blanket." He remembered Faye's hurt expression and how Lennon had told Jake if he wanted to scare his friend, he should have just skipped brushing his hair that day.

"Okay, let's go deeper. What else, Jake? Something that even to this day feels hard to embody, hard to look at?"

Jake blinked at his hands, the memory of his friend's face on New Year's eve when they were nineteen rising into his thoughts. "I... ugh. I slept with my best friend's girlfriend on New Year's Eve when I was nineteen. I was plastered, and she came on to me. They'd gotten in a fight earlier and he took off." Jake shook his head, color rising into his neck.

Their friendship had never recovered from the betrayal. That fall, his friend had moved to California for school, and Jake had never seen him again.

"Good, very good. I see you fidgeting. That tells me we're getting to the shadow. Go on, keep it going."

Jake bit his cheek and thought of Allison. But it wasn't only Allison, a string of Allisons he'd led on, knowing full well they wanted to get married and have children. "Al, Jenny, Corina, Harriet, Kim, Stacey."

"Who are they?"

"Just women. Women I've dated who I guess I duped into believing we had futures."

"They wanted a commitment, and you did not?"

Jake nodded.

"Did you tell them that?"

Jake sighed. "I don't know. I thought I did, but their shock when I broke things off tells another story."

"A fear of commitment is not an issue that arises in adulthood out of the ether. Some clinicians believe it starts with attachment issues in childhood. It might also be related to some kind of earlier trauma. Let's go back in time, into the dark space of forgotten time. What trauma lives there? What shame?"

Jake closed his eyes, thought of those sprawling asylum buildings and tried to place himself in their halls, their rooms.

"Lie back, Jake. Let's go under a bit. Shall we?"

He drifted, dreaming maybe, though he couldn't remember the dream. Trent's voice registered.

"When I count back from ten, you'll be back in the present moment, here in the room. Ten, nine, eight, seven..." Trent said one and Jake opened his eyes.

"Did I fall asleep?" Jake murmured, sitting up.

Trent shook his head. "No, but you did go into a hypnotic state. Shall we replay the session?"

"Sure," Jake said, rubbing his eyes.

Trent turned on the tape recorder to Jake's whispered voice.

JAKE: Sshhh… we can't tell anyone, Maribelle. We'll die for this.

14

*J*ake stiffened at the words, sitting all the way forward and leaning his head closer to the tape recorder.

JAKE: No, I'll put it in my bag. It's safer here.

"What are you referring to here, Jake? Any idea?"

Jake struggled to find the link. It had to be there. The child version of Jake remembered it all and yet the man might as well have been walled off in a cement room. He couldn't access that kid's memories. No matter how he tried, he couldn't get there.

He leaned back on the couch and closed his eyes. "If I'd ended up in Boston or New York, in a world where street kids actually existed, my life would have turned out differently—badly, I guess. But I was ten years old. I bought a ticket to Frankenmuth, Michigan. The Christmas city. Petra told us about it. A city that looked like Munchkinland from *The Wizard of Oz*, that's how she described it."

"And what of your life before the asylum?"

Jake stiffened. The night of the migraine, a tidal wave of memories had come rushing back, hard little memories that made him want to get drunk. He didn't want to remember the years before the asylum.

"You never thought about where you came from? What you were running away from?" Trent continued.

Jake scratched his chin, the shadow of days without a shave thickening into the coarse hair that Allison complained scratched her chin when they kissed. "I don't know. I must have, but... I can't remember. Those years are a blur. I remember sleeping in a shed by this big old house downtown. It was beautiful with a wraparound porch and wicker furniture. My second night in town, they had a dinner party with a grand piano on the deck. I sat in a park down the street and listened. It was a fairytale. There were twinkle lights strung from the trees and I could smell the food. They left some of it out on plates. They'd been drinking, and they went home or went to bed and I gorged myself on steak and salad and cheesecake. Then I walked into the shed and fell asleep on a tarp in the corner.

"Faye found me the next morning. She didn't scream or anything. I woke to the light coming in from the open door. Lennon came out a few minutes later."

"Faye and Lennon?"

Jake smiled and shrugged. "It was a storybook life. They were in their sixties and had never had children. They tried to find my home. They asked me a lot of questions and made calls, but they never turned me over to the police. I think they sensed that if they returned me to my family, it wouldn't be good for me."

"Did you tell them where you were from? Did you remember?"

Jake frowned. "I didn't tell them. I... I don't even know if I remember now. That time is such a blur. And what's crazy is I never thought about it. Where I'd come from. It's like it all just disappeared. Lennon had a successful excavation company. He taught me to run the dozers and excavators, the skid steers, the mulchers. Everything. They enrolled me in school. Faye was an artist. She sketched and painted and sold her artwork at a little studio in town."

"Sounds idyllic."

"What are the chances of that?" Jake wondered. "Ending up in a place like that? And why did everything before slip away? Something must have happened the night we escaped the asylum. Maybe I fell and hit my head. But it's coming. The memories of the time before the institution. I was born in a home for unwed mothers. I never knew my father. My mom never spoke of him. No one in my family did. They were strict Catholics, my mother and my grandparents."

Trent nodded as if encouraging him to go on.

"They all saw me as… a burden, or worse, a curse maybe, because of the spirits."

"Tell me about the spirits," Trent urged.

"In Mass one Sunday, I stood up and blurted, 'Annie's dead!' Everyone balked—how could I say such a terrible thing?—but then they went home and she was dead. No known reason, but I knew something exploded in her head. It was an aneurysm. We were both five. She was my only living friend and she'd appeared to me in the church, just standing quiet next to the pew, blood running from her ears.

"I was inconsolable but no one really tried to console me either. I spent more and more time outside. And then Horace started to appear. I'd be sitting on the footbridge over Pear Creek and I'd see his face in the water gazing back at me."

Unlike other sessions, Jake did not drift into oblivion as he spoke. Instead, he seemed to have walked into the back corner of an unlit room. He sat in a little wooden chair and watched the memories play across a screen.

"I tried to keep my mouth shut about Horace, about the others, but I was a kid. I couldn't sometimes."

"When did they commit you?"

In his mind, Jake stood from the chair, walked to an old-fashioned film projector and wound the tape.

He was transported back thirty years.

Back to the austere little kitchen with the white hard plastic table always shining. His grandmother slapped his hands with a switch that hung by the door if he rested his hands or elbows on the table.

"I was sitting at the table eating my oatmeal when a woman walked in and took the opposite chair. Her skin was black and curdled. I screamed and threw the bowl at her. It smashed on the chair, but there was no one there. I started to cry and tried to explain. At the noise, they all ran in, Grandma and Grandpa and my mother.

"'It was Genevieve,' I told them, though I didn't know the woman. I'd never met her. My grandmother stalked from the room, but some look passed between her and my grandfather. I believe they'd had an affair, he and this woman. Now she was dead from cancer.

"The next day my mother and grandfather drove me to the asylum."

"Let's follow that thread. Try to tell me, now that you're fully conscious and still back in those memories, what you remember about the asylum."

In the dark room, Jake fiddled with the tape, but it had begun to swing faster and faster. The images on the screen blurred and then the hard roll of film cracked off from the projector and rolled across the floor.

On the couch, Jake opened his eyes. "I can't. It's gone. I'm here..."

"It's a lot to remember, Jake. I think we ought to wrap up for today. Let's not overwhelm the psyche."

As Jake stepped out the door, Trent followed him.

"Jake, sometimes when you open the door, you can't exactly close it. Understand? We're out of hypnosis now, but things might start to come back. Call me if you remember anything significant, anything about Petra or Maribelle. And my suggestion to you is to come back every day, every other day at the least. Allow the mind to reveal its secrets so you can begin to heal and move forward."

∽

JAKE DROVE HOME and hurried into his house and up the stairs. He pulled the loop that drew down the folding staircase into the attic. The ladder groaned beneath his weight and he made a mental note to check the bolts in the coming weeks. He rarely went into the attic. It held the remnants of life with Faye and Lennon, the things he'd been unable to part with.

Faye had made an album for his high school graduation. He carried it downstairs to the kitchen table, leaving the attic ladder down.

Jake looked at a photograph of his first birthday at the house, a birthday they'd created because he couldn't remember his own. The day he'd arrived had been July twelfth. And ever since then his birthday had been on July twelfth. But now he knew. He'd been a fall baby, born the night before Halloween. Devil's Night, some people called it, or Mischief Night—pagan ideas that his mother's family had insisted were the work of the devil.

Faye and Lennon had presented Jake with a shiny blue ten-speed bicycle. It had a metal basket so he could start a paper route, which he did that very summer. His life with Faye and Lennon had been a dream. Never once had he passed the morning hours with his knees aching from the hard wood of the prayer bench as his stomach hungered painfully for the plain oatmeal his grandfather would prepare after they'd offered up their sins and begged forgiveness.

"O, my God, I am heartily sorry for having offended thee

and I detest all my sins, because I dread the loss of heaven and the pains of hell..."

The prayer trod through his head, heavy and loud, and he wanted to shake it out, return to the shadowy bliss of his ignorance. But had he been ignorant? Or had he willfully forgotten them? Blanked his mind to ensure he would stay with Faye and Lennon, forsaken his own blood for a life of comfort.

Faye and Lennon had thrown him birthday parties, and Faye's sister, who owned a bakery, had made him beautiful delicious cakes—any flavor he wanted. One year he'd chosen red velvet after he'd seen an advertisement claiming it was the most decadent cake on earth. It had been a rich dark red color and heaped with sweet cream cheese frosting. He'd eaten three slices and gone to bed with a stomachache.

That had happened a few times in the early years with Faye and Lennon. He'd eaten until he was sick. He'd overheard Faye and Lennon talking one night and they'd worried he might be ill. But no, he realized, he'd merely been acting out because of the years of refusal. No sugar in his oatmeal, no sweets, no candy.

His favorite of all the birthdays had been the year Faye and Lennon took him for a weekend to the Grand Hotel on Mackinac Island. He still remembered eating roasted peanuts from a paper bag as he and Lennon leaned over the side of the ferry, watching the choppy Lake Michigan waters as they crossed to the island.

What had become of his mother? The thought made his stomach churn. He tried to place the terrible gloom that overcame him at her memory and he realized it was guilt. Guilt that he had escaped their unhappy little life. Guilt that he'd forgotten her, and something else too, that same old familiar longing. A longing for a mother like other mothers who hugged their children and kissed their booboos rather than surveying the scrapes and bruises with a look of veiled accusation.

The mother he'd found in Faye.

He stood abruptly and slammed the album closed. Grabbing his keys, he trotted to his pick-up and jumped behind the wheel, cranking the radio up loud. A Garth Brooks song came on, *The Thunder Rolls*, and though he didn't know the words, he hummed loud to quiet the sounds in his head.

He drove into town and pulled to a stop in front of Kenny's, a bar with five big-screen televisions always playing the latest games. Faye and Lennon had loved Michigan State University, both being alumni, and their enthusiasm had rubbed off on Jake. Every year he followed the MSU basketball and football teams, usually at Kenny's Bar, watching with Willis or a handful of other guys from his crew. Once in a while Allison had joined him.

As he sat at the bar, the thought of Allison caused a tremor in his chest, but he wouldn't call her. It was the natural thing. It happened after most of the break-ups, an inevitable dip in his resolve, a desire to spend the night with her, wake up to her asleep on the pillow beside him.

"Hey, Jake. Done for the day already?" Kenny asked.

"Cut out early for some appointments. I'll take a Miller."

"Comin' right up. Hey, I just saw your girl across the way there. Must be making her hair look nice for you." He gestured toward the street.

Jake had forgotten that. Allison's hairdresser worked at Shear Sensations just across the road. He hadn't even noticed her little silver Probe parked there by the curb.

Kenny set the beer in front of him and Jake swallowed it in three gulps. "I'll take another," he said.

Kenny refilled him without a pause.

Four beers later, Jake had all but forgotten about Allison across the street when the door to Kenny's Bar opened and in she walked.

He glanced at her and smiled, big and hopeful. He had a buzz going, and she looked good, her hair blown long and straight. She wore snug jeans and a low-cut purple top. A silver necklace lay against her chest and she'd put on her big silver hoop earrings.

"Hi," she said, pausing next to him. "Can I sit down?"

"Yeah, sure. Please." He stood and pulled out a barstool, all his good sense fading when he smelled her vanilla lotion.

She ordered a rum and Coke.

"Hair looks good, Al," Kenny told her, sliding her the drink.

"Put it on my tab," Jake told him.

"Well, duh," Kenny laughed, turning away to serve two guys at the opposite end of the bar.

They ended up back at her apartment, their kissing frenzied as they tugged off each other's clothes. He picked her up and carried her to the bed.

15

Charlie made Belgian waffles in the bona fide cast-iron wafflemaker that had come with the house. When they were finished, which took nearly an hour because she burnt the first batch beyond recognition, she added fresh cream, strawberries and syrup to her waffles and carried them to the porch. She sat in an iron chair, made comfy by bright turquoise and red cushions, and propped her feet on the porch rail.

As she gazed at the other yards in the street, she mentally ticked off things she still needed to get: a bird feeder and seed, a spray nozzle for the long green hose coiled at the side of the house, wine glasses, a welcome mat for the front porch, and a soapdish for the upstairs bathroom.

As she moved down the list, two little girls skipped along the sidewalk across the street from her house. One of them stopped, jerking the other girl's arm back and then leaning in and whispering in her hair. The second girl swiveled her head to stare at the house.

Charlie lifted her hand and waved, but neither girl waved back. The second little girl looked terrified and the first had a sort of frightened glee written in her features.

Charlie stood up, intent on meeting the neighborhood kids. As she stepped to the stairs, the second little girl shrieked and ran off down the sidewalk. The first girl followed. At the end of the block, they paused, glanced back at Charlie and then broke again into a run.

~

CHARLIE GRABBED a cart and steered into the first aisle, which displayed the store's summer shelves—colorful lemonade pitchers, tall plastic cups decorated in fish and bright, tropical plastic placemats. Optimistically, Charlie grabbed a four-piece set of bright orange and yellow plastic plates and silverware. Bev and her husband would come over and who knew, maybe she'd make some new friends at the hospital and do cookouts in the summer.

In the bird seed aisle, she spotted a little yellow bird feeder shaped like a house. It came with a stake that could be screwed into the ground. She added it to her cart along with several bags of bird seed and bright red hummingbird feeder.

As she left the bird aisle, she passed pet food and turned down, gazing at bags of cat food, each displaying a cat jumping in the air or lazing in the sun. She picked up a bag of cat food, a litter box, a bag of litter and two food bowls.

"I hope you're not luring the birds to feed the cat," a voice said from behind her.

She jumped and dropped the cans of wet food she'd picked up, which crashed to the linoleum floor and rolled away.

Warren, the handsome nurse she'd met in the ICU several nights before, stood behind her. "Sorry," he laughed, chasing down the can that had rolled to the end of the aisle.

Charlie grinned and took the cans from his hands. "It shouldn't be easy to surprise someone in a grocery store, but there it is." She dropped the cans in her cart. "But to answer your question, no. I'm not feeding the birds to fatten them up for the cat." She blushed. "I don't even have a cat!"

He eyed her cart and lifted an eyebrow. "Well, now this is weird."

"I'm going to get one," she said quickly. "I just decided like ten seconds ago, so…" She motioned at the cart.

"If you don't have one, that means you're not yet a crazy cat lady then?"

"Nope, not yet. But a girl can hope."

He chuckled. "I'm a dog man myself. Rodolpho"—he held up the bag of dog food he'd tucked under one arm—"he's my German Shepherd. Doubles as a security system so I figure his food is a small price to pay."

"Huh. I probably should be looking at a dog then."

"Where are you at? Jane said you just moved here. End up in a dodgy area?"

She frowned. "Actually, no. I'm in Wilder's Grove in Frankenmuth. It's a really nice area, but single woman living alone and all that. I love dogs, I just can't commit. Twelve-hour days at work and everything."

"That's what crates are for," he said, reaching into her cart and picking through the contents. "I can tell you right now what's missing here. A good bottle of Cabernet, a couple of ribeyes, some asparagus and potato salad."

She wrinkled her forehead. "I'm pretty sure none of those items are on my list."

"I'll get them and meet you at your place in, say…" He looked at his watch. "Two hours. And I'll help you put up this bird feeder, so your invisible cat has dessert after all that bland cat food." He patted the little yellow bird feeder.

Charlie almost said no. She wasn't ready for a smooth-talking guy to start doing little fix-its around the house. Avalanches could start from a pebble after all, but she imagined Bev in her head and the woman was all but screaming,

'Charlie, say yes. Do something fun, let your guard down. Live!'

Charlie smiled, studied Warren's face with his square jaw and his glittery brown eyes and nodded. "Okay, sure. That would be all right."

He hoisted the bag of dog food into his other arm. "Well, try to contain your excitement, why don't you?"

She smiled and reached into her purse, pulling out a little notepad Bev had given her during their Happy Divorce Day celebration. A cartoon of an angry old woman was etched across the top. She held a rake next to a thought bubble that said 'Take No Shit.'

"This is the only paper I have," Charlie admitted, mildly embarrassed by the stationery. She wrote down her address and phone number and handed it to him.

He laughed and tucked it into his pocket. "I like a woman with a sense of humor," he told her with a wink. He turned and started away, swiveling back for a final look. "See you tonight."

"Yeah, see ya then." She waved at him and then felt foolish since he was only six feet away from her. Her face warm, she turned her cart the opposite way and headed for the rugs.

∼

FROM THE MEIJER STORE, she drove to the Humane Society and had to keep from selecting five cats to take home. She hadn't owned a pet since she'd been a girl, in the brief days when her family unit was whole, before her father left and her mother's hair started to show premature grays.

As she walked along the rows of cages, their occupants meowing and reaching padded feet between the bars or rubbing their knobby foreheads against the metal, she spotted two distinct little paws. They were white and large, each punctuated by an extra thumb. The cat lay stretched on his belly, paws through the grate. She ran a finger over his furry hand and he stood and did the customary 'pet me' roll. She opened the cage and before she could reach in to pet him he jumped out, clutching her shoulder as she caught him.

"It looks like he's picked you," the attendant who'd been scooping litter at the opposite end told her.

"He?" Charlie asked.

"Yep. He. One of six. Four girls, two boys. His brother died the day after they arrived, unfortunately. The whole lot had been left in a cardboard box out in front of some old guy's farm. The farmer kept one girl, but he couldn't handle the pack. We bottle-fed them for a month. He's a lover, that one. Skin and bones when he came in, so we named him Bones, but now that you're his mommy, you get to choose his name."

Charlie gazed at the cat, entirely white except for two gray ears and a gray spot on his chest that looked rather like a heart.

"Bones?" she asked him.

He nuzzled his head against her chin.

∼

AT HOME, Charlie freed Bones from his cardboard cat carrier before filling a litter box and setting up a bowl of food and water in the laundry room. Bones sniffed the litter and the food before wandering into the hall. She followed him for several minutes, watching him hesitantly step into each room, pausing to sniff the furniture. He attacked a pair of her sneakers, flopping sideways and tangling the shoestrings in his claws.

She returned to the kitchen and unpacked her stuff. Bones followed her dutifully from room to room as she put things away. When she opened a coat closet, he stepped inside.

"Don't get lost in there," she told him, sliding a pack of batteries onto the shelf above the clothes.

The cat hissed and rushed out of the closet, his tail blown up and bristly. He ran smack into the wall and then scrambled down the hallway and into the living room.

"Jeez-o-Petes, Bones," she huffed, her own pulse racing in response to his fright.

She pushed the coats open and looked into the back of the closet, half expecting a raccoon or opossum crouched in the corner. The space stood empty except for a small dust pan and broom leaning against the wall.

∽

WARREN KNOCKED on her front door a little after five.

He'd changed his clothes, slipping out of the tracksuit he'd worn earlier in lieu of dark jeans and form-fitting black t-shirt. She smelled his cologne and tried not to wrinkle her nose. He wore Cool Water, the same overpowering scent Jared had switched to shortly after he started his affair, though she hadn't known it at the time. Now the scent was forever ingrained in her brain as the odor of cheaters.

He grinned, paper bags of groceries filling his arms. "Out of my way, hottie. I need to get these groceries to a table. One of the bags is about to break." He shuffled past her, glancing into rooms until he spotted the kitchen. He dropped the bags on the table. "This place is epic. You live here alone?"

Charlie nodded, some part of her wanting to walk backwards until she reached the cat food aisle and tell Warren he couldn't come over that night. She didn't know this man and now he stood in her kitchen reeking of her ex-husband's cologne and looking at her in that too-comfortable way certain men looked at women, like they were all there for the taking.

From the cupboard, she extracted two of her brand-new wine glasses and set them on the counter. "Yeah. It was a great deal. I'm looking for a roommate though. It's pretty big for one person."

He emptied the bags and then set about opening drawers. "Knife?" he asked finally.

She'd tucked her wooden block of knives in the closet that morning after the previous night's creepiness had worn off. She pulled them out and Warren selected the largest one.

"Cutting board?" he asked.

She grabbed the wooden board and handed it to him, feeling out of place in her own kitchen. He took up the space, not only his physical body but his presence. It was a quality that Jared had shared, a quality she'd liked in the early years when he walked into a room, larger than life, his laugh drawing stares.

"Oh, umm... I forgot a bag of bird seed in my car. I'll be right back."

"Do your thing, babe," he told her. "Oh, but pour us a glass of wine first? My hands are covered in raw meat."

She uncorked the wine and poured them each a glass, carrying hers with her.

In the hall, a little creature popped from beneath the wooden bench by the door.

"Bones, are you trying to scare me?" she asked, squatting down to pick up the wriggling kitty. She kissed his head and let him jump from her arms. When she opened the door, he followed her onto the porch, walking along the rail and sniffing each post.

"Okay, you can come out, but stay on that porch," she told him, knowing he'd do whatever he damn well pleased.

She had left a bag of bird seed in her car, though she hadn't needed it at that moment, just the fresh air, some relief from the cloud of Cool Water. She grabbed the bag and set it on the porch and sat on the top step.

Bones walked over and crawled into her lap, pawing her thigh.

"Steaks are breathing. Let's get that bird feeder set up, shall we?" Warren announced, walking from the house. He grabbed the feeder from the porch and held it, studying the base. "Perfect, it's got a screw base. Easy peasy."

He didn't ask her where she wanted it, just strode across the yard and jammed the pointed end into the earth and spun it down.

"Bird seed?" he asked, returning to the porch.

Charlie had stood and started to grab the bag, but he beat her to it.

"I've got this," he insisted, tearing the bag open. "I don't want you to break a fingernail or hurt those pretty hands." He filled up the feeder and tossed the bag of seed back on the porch.

"Thanks," she mumbled, drinking the rest of her wine.

He looked at her empty glass and smirked. "Looks like we're going to have some fun tonight."

Charlie forced a smile and went back into the kitchen for a refill. She didn't need a second glass, but a sliver of anxiety had slipped in and started to wedge open.

She heard a clattering near the shed and walked to the side of the house. Warren wheeled a barbecue grill from the shed. "Look what I found," he called.

"Great!" she told him, following him to the cement patio behind the house. A fire pit sat in its center. He parked the grill and then returned to the garage for lighter fluid and coals.

It was an odd sensation swirling inside of her. He was doing the thing she'd so appreciated in Jared, the take-charge, get-it-done thing, but a part of her hated it. Hated how he moved in and out of her new home as if he knew it better than she did, as if he belonged there more than Charlie herself.

He struck a match and dropped it into the grate. An orange ball of flame whooshed out, engulfing his face. Warren screamed and stumbled back.

Charlie dropped her glass of wine on the grass and ran to grab a bucket of water she'd been using the day before to water plants. She ran toward him and flung the water into his face.

He fell back and landed hard on his butt on the stone patio. "Urgh, what the hell?" he grunted.

"Oh, my gosh. Are you okay?"

His face was not burned, but his eyebrows looked singed. Water dripped from his jaw. He stood and stomped into the house. Charlie followed him. He snatched a rag from the counter and swiped his face. "What the hell! Did you pour gasoline in the damn thing? Women. Seriously? Common sense is in short supply in your group."

Charlie stared at him, his red face and hands clenched into fists.

A sudden urge to pick up the mallet he'd been hammering the steaks with overcame her. She stepped closer to the table and then stopped, swallowing her rage.

"I think you'd better leave, Warren," she said through gritted teeth.

He stared at her as if he could hardly believe her nerve. "You nearly set me on fire and now you want me to leave? I think I'd like to eat my dinner first."

"Take your food and get out," she snarled.

"You are a piece of work. You know that? No wonder you're divorced. The guy must have finally got some sense kicked into him." Warren stomped out the door and grabbed the plate of steaks next to the grill. He marched around the house, climbed into his car and backed out of the driveway so fast his tires squealed when he turned onto the road.

∾

The following day, Charlie showered, put on clean scrubs, downed two cups of black coffee and ate a piece of dry toast. She tried not to think of her evening with Warren from the day before, but it flitted into her mind again and again.

"Hi there, Bones," she told the six-toed kitty as he swirled between her feet, rubbing his face against her shins. She sat on the floor and cuddled him, nuzzling her face in his fluff of white fur

As she walked to her car, she noticed little odd lumps in the grass beneath the bird house that Warren had installed the day before. She walked closer, frowning, and then stopped cold.

Birds lay beneath the bird feeder. She counted five, all dead, some with their spindly legs stuck into the air.

Charlie put a hand to her mouth and backed away. She ran back to the house and grabbed the bag of bird seed she'd put in the laundry room. Was it rancid? She hurried to the other bird feeders, which contained bird seed. Not a single dead bird near any of them.

And then she thought of Warren and her stomach rolled. Had he come back in the night and poisoned the bird seed to punish her for turning him away?

"That's crazy," she whispered. So crazy she couldn't rightly believe it, and yet... She hurried back to the front porch and gazed at the side of the house where the bird house stood. A cardinal flew down and landed on the little wooden ledge.

"No," she shrieked, running into the yard and waving her arms.

The red bird took flight and disappeared into the trees.

Charlie looked down the street, hoping none of her neighbors had seen her. She sprinted back to the house and grabbed a garbage bag, returning to the feeder and emptying the contents. She added the open bag of bird food to the trash bag as well and then set about emptying every feeder. She didn't want to risk it. Other animals ate the bird seed too, squirrels and chipmunks. The thought of returning home after a twelve-hour shift to a yard full of dead animals was more than she could bear.

She put the garbage bags in the metal trashcan by the back door and glanced at her watch.

"Shit, shit, shit." She was going to be late.

She locked the door and ran to her car, backing into the driveway too fast and then slamming her brakes. What if a little kid had been in the road? She wouldn't have seen...

"Calm down, Charlie," she said, letting the car drift back now, checking the rearview and sideview mirrors. The street was empty. She drove down the road slowly, not allowing her foot to jam on the gas until she was safely out of her neighborhood.

16

The sun roused Jake from sleep. Allison lay beside him, breath steady, her newly cut and styled hair matted against the pillow. She looked soft and peaceful, the opposite of how Jake felt. He was a snake, a weasel.

"Fuck," he breathed.

Now he'd done it. Gone home with her, taken her to bed, and gotten her head all mixed up.

Years earlier, before he'd ever had sex for the first time, Lennon had sat him down and given him a long talk about the fragility of women's hearts. Jake had tried to heed his advice, but a certain recklessness had always run through him. In his early twenties, one of his friends had nicknamed him 'Love 'Em and Leave 'Em'. More often than not, he'd lived up to the label.

He wanted to get up, throw on his clothes and leave, but when Allison woke, she'd be hurt. He lay back down, assuming he'd not sleep, but after several minutes of listening to her breath, he too slipped into the void.

"I MADE YOU BREAKFAST," Allison told him, waking him with a kiss.

He opened his eyes.

She had restored her hair to the previous day's glossy straightness. She'd put on her makeup, but not yet her clothes. She wore her pearl-colored silk robe that stopped just above her knees. Desire swarmed through him, and he hardened beneath the sheet. Before she could notice he rolled to his side and closed his eyes.

She rubbed his back. "You were talking in your sleep. I've never heard you do that before."

Jake stared at the wall. The word 'jackass' played like a broken record in his head.

"I'll be out in a few minutes," he promised.

He waited until the sensation subsided and then he got dressed and found her in the apartment's little kitchen.

She'd scrambled eggs with cheese and peppers. A pot of coffee sat on the table along with a plate of toast.

"Thanks, Al," he told her, kissing her cheek and sitting down in a chair.

She scooped their eggs and sat across from him. "So..." she started.

He shoved a bite of eggs in his mouth and forced himself to swallow.

She hadn't completed the sentence, but when he looked up, the question hung between them. He knew the answer was likely apparent in his eyes.

She blinked and frowned. "We're not getting back together. Are we?" She steadied her voice, but the tremor ran just below the surface.

"Al, I'm just... I'm not the guy. I'm not."

She stood fast, her chair jerking back and teetering. It didn't tip. Her eyes went to the coffee and for a horrifying second he thought she might throw the cup in his face, scald him for his bad behavior. He would have deserved it.

She didn't. A whimper slipped from her lips, and she ran from the kitchen, slamming the bathroom door so hard the walls shook.

He waited a few minutes and then walked to the door, knocking softly. "I'm sorry, Allison. Last night, I made a mistake and…"

She whipped the door open, her carefully applied makeup destroyed by her tears. "Fuck you, Jake!" She picked up a bottle of perfume and threw it at him. He ducked, and it hit the wall behind him and bounced on the carpeted hallway floor. "Get out!" she shrieked.

He did. He ran to the kitchen, scooped his boots up without putting them on and burst into the hallway and down the stairs.

When he reached the ground floor, he passed a young guy walking in with a small fluffy dog on a leash. The guy grinned and winked at him as if they shared some secret, the secret of men running out of apartments with their shoes early in the morning. The secrets of weasels and snakes.

Jake slipped on his boots, climbed into this truck and gunned it for home.

A plain cardboard box sat on the stoop in front of Jake's house. He glanced at it as he unlocked the door. No label, no note taped to the outside. Reluctant to carry it into the house, he squatted down and used his key to cut the tape along the top of the box.

A time-worn Barbie doll lay inside. Its short blonde hair looked dirty. It wore a black-and-white striped swimsuit, but that too was smudged and stained. Otherwise the doll was intact, all of its legs and arms in place.

Something stirred at the sight of the doll, and he said the name it had once been given. "Greta," he murmured. "Greta?"

What made him think the doll would have a name at all? Why was it on his doorstep?

He considered calling Detective Bryant. Like the bloodied shirt in his office, this might be another clue to Petra's disappearance.

He left the doll outside and stepped into his house, picking up the cordless phone and punching in Norm's phone number.

Norm answered before it even rang. "Hello?"

"Norm, it's Jake."

"Oh, thank God. I'd hoped it was you. You got my message then?"

"No, what message?"

"I called last night and again this morning. I heard things next door, Jake. I heard someone moving around over there. I'd stepped on my back porch for a smoke. I quit five years ago, but all this with Petra... Anyway. I heard someone moving around in there."

"Did you call the police?"

"Sure did. Took them nearly forty-five minutes to get here and then they found nothing, but he was probably gone by then. You know?"

"Yeah," Jake sighed. "Norm, did Petra own Barbie dolls?"

"Barbie dolls?" Norm asked.

"Yeah, the toys."

"No. Not that I ever saw. Why?"

Jake stared toward his door where he knew the doll lay. Someone was trying to send him a message, but for the life of him, he didn't know what it was. "No reason. Never mind. I'll call you later, Norm. I'm just walking in the door and have to head to the office."

∼

"Hi, Jake." Adrian offered him a brilliant smile when he walked into the police station and his nerves about visiting the detective softened.

"Hey, Adrian. Is your dad here? I mean, Detective Bryant?"

She laughed. "He's not in the office, I'm afraid, but it's okay, the cat's out of the bag. People know he's my dad."

"Is that a problem for you at all? I mean, with the other cops."

"Nope. I grew up here. I've got fifty big brothers running around this place."

"I pity the man who crosses you."

She shrugged. "I've got a pretty good instinct about people. I steer clear of the dickheads of the world. It saves me the heartache and saves them the broken noses."

He laughed. "Well, any idea when your dad is coming back?"

"He's not in the habit of leaving a schedule, I'm afraid. Is there something I can help you with?"

Jake glanced down at the box and felt stupid. An armchair detective turning kids' pranks into evidence, or 'super-secret clues,' Faye had called them in years gone by when Lennon had set up some mystery in the house they'd spend a weekend unraveling.

"I've got a couple of things knocking around in my head that I can't seem to shake loose. For starters…" He set the box on the counter.

Adrian stood and peeled back the flaps peering into the cardboard box. Her expression became puzzled. "I never did understand the appeal of these things. Who wants to spend their days searching for itty-bitty high heels when there are trees to climb and BB guns to shoot?"

Jake laughed. "That's pretty much the way I saw it too. This was on my doorstep this morning."

Adrian crinkled her forehead. She reached beneath the counter and came out with a pair of latex gloves which she slid over her small hands. They looked like a child's hands. She poked around the doll, lifting it by one leg and looking beneath it. "No note?"

He shook his head.

"I'll have the crime scene investigators take a look."

"You don't think it's nonsense?"

Adrian leveled her bright blue eyes on him. They shone and he sensed her curiosity was piqued. "If it was, you wouldn't have brought it here. I'm guessing the kids in your neighborhood don't have a habit of leaving their toys on your doorstep?"

"No. I don't even know the kids in my neighborhood. I'm something of a workaholic. But I can't imagine how it could be connected to Petra."

"She showed up at your business the day she vanished; her bloody blouse appeared there days later. It's clear that something fishy is going on."

"Are you following the case?" he asked.

"Sure am. Don't tell Detective Bryant that." She winked at him. "He's possessive of his cases. 'Too many chefs spoil the broth,' is his favorite way of saying it when anyone is sniffing around his cases."

"Even his own daughter?"

She laughed. "Especially me. I don't follow etiquette. I have a bad habit of calling him in the middle of the night with my theories on his cases."

"Have any theories on this one?"

She rocked her head slowly from side to side. "Not quite. And duty forbids me from saying too much just yet. Not that you're a suspect, but..."

"It's okay," he said. "But just to throw in my two cents, I don't think Norm did anything to Petra."

"And why is that?"

Jake frowned. He didn't know Norm and his need to keep pushing Norm's innocence made zero sense, and yet there he was doing it again. "I just… I don't think he did it. I have good instincts about people too. Norm isn't a murderer."

"You'd be surprised how many people are capable of murder."

"Still…"

"You said you had a couple reasons for coming in. What else?" Adrian set the box containing the Barbie doll on a table behind her.

Jake thought of Norm's story about the asylum and his own discoveries at the hypnotist. Had a stranger told him the tale, he would have written them off as a person with a few screws loose.

"The day Petra showed up at my office…" he started and then stopped. He hadn't told Bryant about the asylum.

"Go on," Adrian prodded him.

"I… I didn't mention it to your dad. It didn't seem relevant at the time and, shit…" He brushed a hand through his hair. "And I thought it would make him suspicious of me. Petra said we'd known each other as children."

"I read that in my dad's report," Adrian said.

"Yeah, but she said we knew each other at an insane asylum where we both lived."

Adrian widened her eyes. "Okay, now that's interesting. Did you live in an insane asylum with Petra?"

Jake sighed and showed her his palms. "I guess. I didn't remember it at the time. I still don't exactly, but…there's something there. I think I probably did and I blocked it out or…" He chuckled. "I'm way out of my league here. The extent of my knowledge about amnesia is the soap operas one of my ex-girlfriends liked to watch and I wasn't exactly hanging on their every word. Anyway, Petra's neighbor, Norm, mentioned she'd been doing some digging into what happened during that time and she'd found a doctor. Norm wondered if the doctor might have been involved."

"Okay." Adrian had written his words down on a yellow legal pad. "And do you have any idea what doctor that might be?"

"Well, no, that's the problem. I can't even really remember being at the asylum. A couple things have come back. I sort of blocked out a big chunk of my childhood, which is a long story and a story that I can't even tell because…"

"… you blocked it out."

"Yeah. Sorry. Am I starting to sound like a crackpot?"

"They brought a guy in this morning who said he robbed a gas station because the man working at the counter had stolen the soul of his parrot and was auctioning it off through an underground club of soul-snatchers. Your story is pretty tame by comparison."

Jake chuckled. "I'm not sure if that makes me feel better or not."

"You can't remember the name of the doctors. What if I could get you a list of names? Doctors working at this asylum during the approximate timeframe you were there?" Adrian asked.

"Yes!" Jake exclaimed as he slapped his hand on the counter.

A man peeked around the wall behind Adrian, glaring at Jake. "You okay out here, Adrian?"

She nodded and waved back at him. "All good, Carl. Just getting some info on a case."

The cop stared at Jake for another moment before disappearing back behind the wall.

"Is it okay? For you to do that, I mean. Get the names?"

Adrian laughed. "I'm not pulling their bank accounts, Jake. It's public record. It's just easier for cops to grab that information than you. You'd probably spend a week at the library trying to find it. What was the name of the asylum?"

"The Northern Michigan Asylum in Traverse City."

Adrian frowned and tapped her pen against her teeth. "I've

heard of that place. You know what? I think they had a murder or something up there a few years ago."

"Really?"

"Yeah. Something anyway. Okay, I'll get those names and call you later today or tomorrow."

"Thanks, Adrian. I've been banging my head against the wall over this stuff."

17

Charlie had worked overnight shifts that dragged. Nights where the quiet hung heavy and thick and she waded through the minutes, looking at the clock too many times.

This night was not one of them. Two patients had coded, prompting hours of frantic rushing and CPR. One of the patients had had to be intubated.

By the time Charlie stood in the nurses' station at shift change, her muscles ached and the knots in her shoulders felt like two concrete slabs pinching each time she lifted her hands.

Worst of all was the young woman who'd died. She'd been in a head-on collision and survived, despite severe trauma to her brain. Emergency room doctors had managed to save her life, and when she was transferred to the ICU, she'd still been critical, but showing signs of improvement. Until just after midnight when suddenly her blood pressure plummeted. The nurses had scrambled, the doctor shouting orders that woke up half the floor, but it had been no use.

"A mother of three," Jane had told her sadly. "The husband's been a basket case. I don't envy that doctor's job."

Charlie and Jane had watched Doctor Pence stop at a drinking fountain and run water over his face, pausing for a long time to let the stream rush down his cheeks before gathering himself and heading for the waiting room where the woman's husband had been on constant vigil since the accident.

The woman had been badly swollen, much of her face black and blue or covered in bandages, but a family photo sat next to the bed, a photo her husband had brought and insisted they put beside her so if she woke up she saw the faces of her husband and children right away. She'd never woken up, but Charlie had studied the image. A picture-perfect family, the husband dark-haired with olive skin and his wife pretty and soft with wide-set blue eyes and wavy blonde hair that fell over her shoulders. Her children were a mix of their parents, two dark-haired boys and a little blonde girl. They'd been fidgeting during the picture, climbing on Dad's shoulders and into Mom's lap, and in the background a beagle puppy was sniffing a flower bush. He wore a bow tie and was likely meant to be in the picture but ran off before they could get the shot.

Tears welled into Charlie's eyes and she clenched her teeth together and willed them away. If she started to cry, it might get out of hand. Since the unraveling of her marriage, her emotions lived ever close to the surface. A pinprick of sadness could cause a geyser of emotion to erupt. She'd begin crying about the woman, but then she'd cry about the death of her unborn children, the end of her marriage, the years her mother had struggled alone as a working single mom. If she let it out, she might lose an entire day to the despair, and she refused go down that hole.

Charlie stopped at a gas station and ran in for a cup of coffee. She filled a Styrofoam cup, though the thought of drinking it made her cringe. The coffee was dark and sooty and she'd had too much during the night before. When she swallowed the first burning sip, her stomach lurched but she forced it down. She'd scheduled a massage the week before, a fate-filled move it seemed now, as she drove away from the hospital with a body as stiff as a tree trunk.

As she turned onto her road, she held her breath, releasing the pent-up air when she saw her lawn empty of dead things.

"The bird seed must have been bad," she murmured and made a mental note to take it into the store and tell them what had happened. There might be more in the batch. Who knew how many birds and other small creatures had died after eating it?

She parked and bent in half, letting her upper body dangle over her legs, attempting to release some of the tension wedged in her lower back. It didn't much help other than to remind her when she stood back up just how sore she was.

Inside, Bones meowed relentlessly and pawed at her legs as she walked. She hit play on the answering machine and sank to the floor next to him, smoothing down his tufts of unruly fur. He climbed high in her lap and nuzzled his damp nose against her face. She leaned into him, letting him pet himself against her jaw and chin. "Oh, Bones, I had one helluva night."

"You have three new messages," the machine told her in its dry electronic voice. "Message one."

Bev's voice came on the line. "Helloooo! This is your very best friend in the whole wide world calling to ask why you didn't call me back with details last night. Unless of course the sexy nurse stayed the night? Oh, I hope so, I do, I do. I've cleared Saturday with Rodney. The ferryboat tour is the next weekend. Okay, your machine is going to cut me off any minute. Call me. I want to hear about—"

The message abruptly ended and the second one began.

"Charlie, it's Mom. I just got home from the farmer's market and they had the cutest little jars of jalapeño jam. I've got a whole box of goodies headed your way. I hope you've taken some photos of the house. I'm waiting on pins and needles.

Arnie and I thought we might visit for the Fourth of July? He's looking at a camper, you know, one of these big rigs you drive. I told him I can't drive that big old thing, but—"

The machine cut her mother off.

Charlie laughed. "We've got some long-winded friends, haven't we, Bones?"

The third message clicked on. "Hi, my name's Nina. I'm calling about the room for rent. You can reach me at 513-9043."

The girl's voice stopped, but the message didn't disconnect. Silence followed and then a low soft sound like a little girl whispering.

"Shhh," the voice said. "She'll hear you."

Another sound followed as if the phone on the other hand had been dropped on the floor.

"End of messages," the machine announced.

"Well, that was weird," Charlie told Bones. "Maybe Nina has a little sister or a kid?" She frowned. If the woman wanted to rent a room with her kid, would Charlie say no? She had only intended to rent the room to a single person, preferably a woman, but what if she needed a home for her and her child? Could Charlie in good conscience say no when she had the huge house all to herself?

"We'll cross that bridge when we come to it," she told Bones, smiling because now when she talked it could be directed at another living being instead of to herself.

∼

AFTER SHE SHOWERED and put on clean clothes, some of the night's grime washed away, she felt better. Not great, but better. She scrambled three eggs and downed a glass of orange juice before feeding Bones half a can of tuna fish and locking up the house.

The massage studio was located in downtown Frankenmuth.

It had a little purple awning over the door. The sign painted on the window said Velvet Touch.

When Charlie walked in, a girl looked up from the reception desk. "Hi, are you Charlie?" She smiled and revealed shiny silver braces.

"Sure am. I have a ten o'clock appointment with—"

"Amy," the girl said. "She's my mom. She owns this place."

"Oh, wow. Well, that's pretty cool she lets you work here."

The girl grinned. "Technically I don't, but I'm on spring break and her receptionist called in sick. I don't mind. Lots of time to read." She held up her book.

'Sweet Valley High' curved across the top in red high school lettering. Beneath it two pretty blondes gazed out above the words 'Double Love.'

"Looks like a good one," Charlie said.

The girl nodded and her bouncy, shoulder-length brown curls bobbed with her. "It is. These are my favorite books ever," she gushed. "Do you read?"

Charlie nodded. "Spooky stuff usually. I just finished *Red Dragon* and I'm getting started on *The Silence of the Lambs* soon, though I think I'll wait until I'm more settled into my new house for that one."

"Where's your new house? Do you live here in Frankenmuth?"

"Not right in town. About three miles away on Elmwood Drive."

The girl wrinkled her brow. "Which house?" she asked, setting her book down.

"Wilder's Grove."

The girl shuddered, but before she could speak a door deeper into the office opened and a woman walked out. Her hands and forearms were oiled from just finishing a massage. "Hi, you must be Charlie? Let me give these a quick wash and then I'll get you settled in your room."

"What were you going to say?" Charlie asked the girl.

The door opened a second time, and a second woman emerged, a serene smile on her lips. "My goodness, I love a massage. I had the worst morning and now everything is right in the world. Mandy, your mother is a godsend." The woman stopped at the desk and dug through her purse, extracting a pink flowery wallet.

"That will be fifty dollars, Mrs. Clover."

"Here's sixty, honey. Little tip for your mom on there."

"Charlie?" Amy called, waving her down the hall.

Charlie glanced back at Mandy, but Mrs. Clover had her full attention.

Amy beckoned to a room at the end of the hall. "Go ahead and get undressed and lie under the sheet, face down. I'll come back in a few minutes."

"Thanks," Charlie told her, everything softening as she walked into the room lit only by a jar filled with pale twinkle lights sitting high on a shelf. A CD player released the sound of trickling water.

Charlie shrugged off her clothes and folded them on a chair in the corner. The sheets on the massage table were warm as if Amy had just pulled them from a dryer.

After her massage, Charlie drifted back to the waiting room on a satiny cloud of lavender oil and Enya. The girl who'd been at the desk, Mandy, was gone.

Charlie handed Amy cash for her massage. "Amy, I just bought a house in Frankenmuth called Wilder's Grove. Have you heard of it?"

The woman smoothed out the bills and put the money in the register, wrinkling her forehead. "I don't think so, but I love the name. Sounds like a bed-and-breakfast."

"Yeah. It'd be perfect for one, but your daughter Mandy seemed like she'd heard of it."

"Oh, yeah?" Amy turned away and picked up a spray bottle

of cleaner and a rag. "Well, she's a teenager. They know everything in small towns. I'm a single mom and a business owner. I'm afraid it doesn't leave much time for town gossip."

"Yeah." Charlie sighed. "You've got a point. Thanks again."

∼

AT HOME, she tossed a Caesar salad and ate it with pre-cooked chicken strips before settling onto her couch to watch *Total Recall*.

Two hours later, Bones dozed on the blanket beside her, emitting little broken meows and twitching his tail as he chased dream mice or bugs. Charlie brushed her fingers down his spine, but he didn't wake.

The credits rolled down the dark screen and Charlie flipped off the movie, dropping the remote control on the table and picking up Bones as she headed for the stairs. Halfway up the stairs, a sound jolted her. Bones woke up, digging his claws into her arm.

"Ouch," she yelped. "Bones, quit that." She set the cat on the stairs and returned to the living room, where the glow of the television spilled into the hall. The TV had turned back on.

On the screen, a scene from the movie *Misery* played. Kathy Bates stood over the bed where James Caan lay, a sledgehammer in her hands.

Charlie grimaced. "No, thank you," she muttered, picking up the remote and turning it off.

The blue glow slowly dimmed from the TV and Charlie looked at the remote to see if there was a stuck button. There wasn't. She returned it to the coffee table and went back to the stairs. Bones had disappeared, likely to the food bowl, his second favorite place after her lap.

Considering a shower, Charlie stripped down. Her skin still

had the sheen from the massage oil and the lavender smell to accompany it. She inhaled her forearm.

"Better just keep this on. Lavender helps with sleep after all." At least that was what her mother had told her a year earlier when she'd sent her a gift box stuffed with lavender everything—candles, lotion, eye pillow, and little satchels to hang from her rearview mirror and inhale when she felt stressed.

She slipped on her extra-soft Bourbon Street, NOLA shirt, one of the few items she'd kept from the New Orleans trip she and Jared had taken six months before the end. It had all been part of the last-ditch effort to save their marriage, though she hadn't known it at the time.

In a passionate fury, she'd thrown most of the stuff from the trip—including a necklace he'd bought her, mementos from a voodoo store and a book on the history of New Orleans—into the fire pit behind their house. She'd poured kerosene on the heap and lit it on fire before drinking half a bottle of wine and passing out on their couch. That had been one of the first of many nights when Jared hadn't bothered coming home.

She'd kept the t-shirt, rarely wearing it in the first months, but now it held only a dusting of those memories and it was so comfortable. Pulling the comforter to her chin, she watched the spots dance behind her eyelids. She was exhausted, beyond exhausted, but her brain did its usual hamster wheel activity as soon as she lay down.

The to-do list scrolled through her mind, including returning the bad bird seed, calling back Nina, the potential roommate, and getting into the attic to look at what other treasures, or more likely trash, had been left by the previous owners.

∽

SHE WOKE and stared at the dark ceiling. She'd been deep in a dream and the wisps of it played in her mind.

Charlie had been back in Dansville at the old apartment. Someone had been in the apartment with her, someone bad, and Charlie had crawled under the bed all the way to the wall, where she lay perfectly still, inhaling dust and watching the door on the opposite side of the room, knowing it would creak open and the bad person would step inside.

Relieved that she'd woken up before the worst part of the dream could unfold, she rolled over and looked at the clock. Three twenty-two a.m.

She closed her eyes, but a sound drifted from somewhere in the house, a murmuring like voices, and then...

"The TV," she whispered, frowning.

She sat up and squinted into the room, searching for her discarded slippers. She spotted them by the door and hurried over, sliding her feet into the plush fabric. The wood floors felt cold. The entire room felt cold, but she knew it was merely the contrast between lying in a cocoon of blankets and standing in the open air. She grabbed her robe and pulled it on, walking down the stairs. The television grew louder.

A song came on. "'People are strange when you're stranger...'"

Charlie stopped at the doorway, gazing at the television where the beginning scene of the vampire flick *The Lost Boys* showed the brothers, their mother behind the wheel, driving through Santa Carla, California. It flashed to a board thick with missing persons' flyers.

Charlie smiled. She'd seen the movie in theatres during undergraduate school. Gary, the guy who'd asked her out, had kissed her when she squealed as the vampires descended on the couple necking in the parked car.

She started into the room and then stopped cold. Someone sat on the couch in front of the TV. She could see their silhouette in the darkness lit by the blue glow of the television. A dark outline, the shape of a woman judging by the smooth line of hair from scalp toward shoulders.

Charlie froze—in every sense of the word, going cold all over, legs like two wooden stilts nailed to the floor, breath an icy balloon suspended in her chest.

18

On the screen, a carnival pirate ship swung into the air, a crowd of riders screaming in delight and fear.

Charlie's feet and hands went sweaty despite the icy cold in her blood.

And then she noticed Bones.

He stood on the chair, his fur a rise of spikes down his back and his tail stick-straight and frizzed like a feather duster. His two eyes, glowing yellow, were fixed on the woman.

Charlie managed to will her feet backwards, into the hall. She stood, back pressed against the smooth plaster, her breath squeaking out between clenched teeth.

The Doors song continued to play in the room. "'When you're strange, faces come out of the rain…'"

She eyed the door, struggling to form a solid plan. Run into the night? Pound on a neighbor's door and demand they call the police? She thought of racing to her car several nights before, her shame in the morning at her overreaction.

It was a woman in there. Maybe… maybe she'd walked in accidentally, confused this house with another.

Charlie slid a heavy silver candlestick off the entryway table, clutching it behind her back. She reached around the wall into the living room, searching for the light switch. She'd take the woman by surprise and if she seemed dangerous, Charlie would hurl the candlestick at her and run out the door.

She flipped the switch and light flooded the room as she stepped back into the doorway.

"Who are you?" Charlie shouted, but the words died on her lips.

The couch sat empty.

On the screen, the song moved toward the close as an old Jeep drove a dusty road into dense bush.

Bones hissed and jumped from the chair, darting out of the room past Charlie.

Charlie stared at the back of the couch, irrationally sure the woman had lain sideways and concealed herself, but when Charlie walked closer, she found the couch empty and the floor too. Shaking, candlestick slick in her sweating hand, she crept around the room peeking behind the furniture. There was only one entrance into the room from the hall. The woman could not have escaped without Charlie seeing her and yet...

"Hello?" Charlie called out.

No answer—only the voice on the television answered. Charlie grabbed the remote and stabbed her thumb on the off button. The picture disappeared and the silence took over.

Charlie lay awake the rest of the night, sitting up at every sound. When pre-dawn light turned her curtains from dark to a pale pink, the tension gradually drained from her body and she slept.

∼

THE FOLLOWING MORNING, Charlie drove the seventy-mile trip to Pontiac, arriving at her former therapist's door just after nine a.m.

"Charlie?" The woman looked up, surprised.

Charlie hurried over to help her with one of the two giant potted plants she was wrangling into her office. "Here, let me." Charlie took one and got a face full of palm leaves.

"Honey, what are you doing here? Did we have an appointment?"

Charlie maneuvered her face around the leaves and shook her head. "No, I'm sorry, Katherine. I just needed to talk and drove over here on a whim."

Katherine gazed at her thoughtfully, a glitter of concern in her eyes, but then she turned to the door and pulled it open, propping one foot on the bottom, so Charlie could hurry in first.

"Then I'll consider it my lucky day," Katherine told her. "Just stick the plant over there." Katherine nodded at the corner of the reception area where several dark brown leather chairs stood next to a small glossy table, stacked with self-help books.

On the top of one stack, Charlie noticed a book she'd flipped through every time she visited Katherine's for an appointment. *Breaking Up with a Narcissist,* the cover said above a shadowy man towering over a crying woman.

A pang of hurt coursed through her at the sight of it, the memory of all those days reading about gaslighting and shifting blame. Those had been hard days, some of the hardest of her life, and for a time, she'd wondered if she'd ever feel different. Would the fear, the downright despair, ever release her?

"How's the new house?" Katherine asked, sitting on her leather swivel chair.

Charlie settled into the gray-blue couch. At one end sat a throw pillow and a stuffed duck. Charlie picked up the duck, smiling at his worn beak, rubbed to sagging by so many of Katherine's patients, and not just the children. "It's beautiful and far too big for me."

Katherine smiled and balanced her notebook on her lap.

"That's a good problem to have. And the new hospital? How's that?"

"Good. I mean, the staff are nice. There's one guy who..." Charlie shook her head. "We had a weird encounter, but other than that, I like it."

"The guy? Is he a nurse?"

Charlie nodded.

"And is that what's brought you here today, Charlie?"

Charlie stroked Quack the Duck's beady black eyes, smooth and round beneath her thumb. "No. I mean, I should never have gotten involved with him. And I didn't, not really. He just came over one night and made me dinner. It didn't end well, which makes shifts together a little tense. Actually, I'm here about my house."

Katherine smiled. "Okay. Tell me about that."

Charlie uncrossed her legs, slipping her feet out of her shoes and pulling them up beside her. "Things have been strange. I've had a few unnerving moments and, well... I'm starting to think I've got some psychological issue that's manifesting as creepy experiences."

"Tell me about the creepy experiences," Katherine urged. "And not to derail the conversation, but the problem isn't always internal."

Charlie sighed and gazed at the duck. "Okay, well, the first happened a couple nights after I moved in. I woke up in the middle of the night and I felt scared, like maybe I'd heard something. I walked downstairs and found a silverware placement sitting on the table. I hadn't put it there."

Katherine nodded, jotted something in her notebook. "Okay, and how do you think it got there?"

"Well, at the time I thought someone was in the house. I spazzed and ran to my car and sat there until morning. That's crazy, isn't it?"

Katherine chuckled. "Not in the least. This has been a big

year for you, Charlie. A new house in a new town. That's just the tip of the iceberg. I remember when I lived alone for the first time after my divorce. I barely slept a wink for the first month. Every car horn that honked or toilet that flushed in the apartment building and I was out of the bed and smoking cigarettes in my bathroom."

"You smoked cigarettes?"

Katherine nodded. "Twenty years ago, I did. One of my many bad habits, but it helped at the time. I couldn't imagine giving up a toxic partner *and* my cigarettes, which I realize now were just another toxic partner. But the point is, I was scared and nervous. It didn't matter if there was a real threat somewhere nearby, my brain and body perceived one. As much as we want to rationalize ourselves out of those fears, we can't. Not in the moment. That change comes with time and practice and better coping skills."

"It must have been me, right? Who put the silverware there?"

Katherine cocked her head. "That's the logical explanation. Yes. We do things on autopilot all the time and have no conscious memory of doing them. Tell me about the other incidents."

Charlie considered the other things—related or not, she just didn't know. "I've been spooked a couple times. The other morning, I thought I saw a woman in the mirror standing behind me."

"And was there a woman?"

"Well, no. When I turned around it was a coat rack."

"An understandable mistake," Katherine murmured.

"And then last night..." Charlie turned the duck around and around in her hands. "I woke up because the television was on. Which was weird because I turned it off twice before bed."

"Twice?"

Charlie nodded. "Yeah. I turned it off and then started up to bed and heard it turn back on so I went back into the living room and turned it off a second time."

"Hmmm, that's a bit odd. Any idea why it turned back on?"

Charlie shook her head. "I woke up after three and I heard it again, really muffled because I was upstairs. I walked down and started to walk into the living room. *The Lost Boys* was on."

"Is that a Peter Pan movie?"

"No, it's about vampires."

"Yikes."

"Yeah, but it wasn't just the TV. There was a woman sitting on the couch. I could see her. She was just sitting there really still as if she were watching the movie, and Bones—my new cat—he could see her too. He was all fluffed up the way cats get when they're scared. And he was staring right at her."

"Wow. And then what happened?"

"I turned on the light and she was gone."

Katherine frowned and made another note on her pad.

"Did you just write 'Charlie's lost her shit?'"

Katherine smiled. "Not at all." She turned the notebook around so Charlie could see the word, Katherine had written 'ghost' with a question mark behind it.

"You think it's a ghost?" Charlie asked, surprised.

"Well, here's the thing. There are ghosts, like the spirits of the dead, and then there are the ghosts that live within us. Is one more real than another? I don't know. But I think it's plain to see you are haunted by something. Is that something outside of you or inside? That's the thread to follow now."

"And how do I follow it?"

"Well, if I were you, I'd think about process of elimination. The internal work is harder, it takes getting past our own patterns and belief systems and it's a job for life. So you might start by ruling out the external ghost. What do you know about the house you bought?"

"Are you serious, Katherine? I mean, do you think my house could be haunted by an actual ghost?"

Katherine wheeled across the room to her bookshelf. She plucked two books from the lowest shelf before returning to Charlie and handing them to her. "I'm open-minded, and remember, I've worked with a lot of people. I've heard a lot of stories. After a while, you start to believe there's more in this world than we're aware of."

Charlie looked at the books: *Poltergeist* by Colin Wilson and *Gothic Ghosts* by Hans Holzer. "Sounds like reading material that will give me nightmares."

"Or maybe they will put the nightmares to rest. Flip through them in the next few days. See if anything jumps out. And I think you should get some history on your house."

19

Jake heard a knock on the outer office door. He peeked his head out to see Adrian standing outside. She waved at him.

He unlocked the door. "Hey! What's up?" he asked.

It was a pleasant interruption, but he'd gotten behind on bids and planning projects. He'd finally started getting caught up, but now that his concentration was broken, he'd likely not find it again that day.

"I did some digging on those doctors and found some weird stuff. Have time to talk?"

He nodded and yawned, stretching his arms overhead. His lower back suddenly ached and his eyes felt gritty. He rubbed them and shook his head, peering glumly back toward his office. "How does a burger sound? I haven't eaten since breakfast." As if in agreement his stomach let out a whining growl.

Adrian laughed. "Yeah, a burger would be good."

Adrian followed him in her car to the Burger Hut. The place was dead. The only people inside were the owners who did the cooking and the serving.

"Jake, how are you, handsome stranger? I've been feeling

neglected that you haven't been in for a while," Lina pouted in her French accent.

Lina and her husband François—the cook—had come to the States from Quebec nearly thirty years before. They'd opened their very first Burger Hut in Detroit, a popular restaurant now run by their eldest son, Amos, and then set about building five more, one for each of their children. They took the idea of a family business very seriously.

Lina and François had taken the least profitable store for themselves in their retirement. The restaurant was only open for lunch and early dinner Monday through Saturday and closed on Sundays.

"Sorry, Lina. You know how it is when spring hits. Twelve-hour days and no time to eat."

Lina tisked and squeezed the skin on his arm. "You're getting skinny, Jake. Girls don't trust a skinny man, you know? They're scared he can't put food on the table." She shifted her attention to Adrian, pursing her lips and then smiling. "Now you are a very pretty young girl. And this man is much too old for you. Shame on you, Jake," Lina teased, taking his arm and steering him towards his usual table. "This girl should go out with my Samuel. Nearly thirty and still no wife." She hung her head.

Jake laughed and pulled out a chair for Adrian. "Lina, this is Adrian. We're working together, and it's strictly platonic. I'm guessing she doesn't need a matchmaker though." He winked at Adrian.

"I'm sure Samuel's great, Lina"—Adrian laughed—"but I'm pretty smitten as it is. And he's a cop, so I try not to ruffle his feathers."

"Oh, goodness me," Lina breathed, putting a hand to her soft bosom. "A man of the law. Did you hear that, François? This girl knows a police officer. We need to talk with a police officer, young lady, because someone has been dropping their trash in our dumpster out back. Twice now—"

"Crisse, Lina," François shouted in French. "Leave the girl alone and take their order."

"Don't you cuss at me, you old goat," Lina shouted back, though her smile stretched from ear to ear.

"Burger with all the fixings and fries," Jake told her. "And an iced tea."

"Same," Adrian told Lina. "Oh, but no pickles. Ick." She made a face.

"No pickles?" Jake demanded. "I'll take her pickle."

"Oh, yes, I know." Lina winked at Jake and headed for the kitchen, yelling out their order to François, who grumbled in response.

"They are hilarious," Adrian laughed. "I can't believe I've never been here."

Jake nodded. "They're great, and François makes the best burger in town. On Saturday afternoon there's a line out the door. Lina also makes French desserts once a week on Monday, they're sold out by six pm. Butter tarts and sugar pies. Damn, I'm getting hungry. Let's change the subject." He tapped on Adrian's folder.

She flipped it open. "So, I was able to get a list of names of doctors who worked at the asylum in the 1960s. From there, I tracked down each of the men. They were almost entirely men, might I add," Adrian told him, rolling her eyes.

"I can't thank you enough for this. Did you tell your dad?"

She grinned. "He's got enough to worry about. Plus, he'd have a hairy canary if he thought I was interfering in an ongoing investigation."

"But I'm not involved in Petra's disappearance," Jake reminded her.

"Almost all of these doctors are dead," Adrian went on.

"Really?" Jake leaned forward, trying to read her handwriting, but it looked like a five-year-old had been squiggling lines.

"I found records that said 'deceased' and where they'd been

buried, but I was curious about how they died. It seemed like so many of them were dead, too many really, because a lot of them weren't old even. I started putting them into our police system here and their names were popping up left and right. Now our records only go back so far, but still, the incidence of violence..."

She pointed to the first name, Doctor Pendleton. "Kenneth Pendleton, murdered during a home invasion in 1975. Harold Lundt, found shot in his car in 1968. Edward Coleman, strangled and left on the side of the road in 1967. Phil Stanton, missing, never found. Guy Lance, Fred Benevict and Joe Elmer all turned up dead on the asylum grounds in 1983. Coroner attributed the deaths to a violent animal attack."

"Holy shit," Jake muttered. "That's... I mean how is it even possible? What are the odds?"

"The odds are practically inconceivable, but it's true. Nearly every single one of these doctors met a violent end. And I found some other stuff in my digging. That hospital, the Northern Michigan Asylum, has been involved in a lot of shady shit over the years including the excavation of six bodies in 1993."

Jake's mouth dropped open. "No frickin' way."

"Yeah. Three years ago a woman in East Lansing went missing." Adrian pulled out an article. The headline read 'Co-Ed Missing for Seven Days. Foul Play Suspected.' A beautiful redhead gazed out from the picture.

"What does this have to do with the asylum?" Jake asked.

"Well, they ended up finding this girl alive. She'd been held hostage in an old caretaker's house on the asylum grounds. The woman who abducted her was the daughter of the caretaker who'd died in the asylum sometime in the 80s. The woman tortured the co-ed and basically tried to bury her alive. The perp—Greta Claude was her name—confessed to other murders. She also admitted that her father had been murdering people at the asylum for years. Six bodies were taken out of the ground."

Jake's head swam. Greta had been the name that had popped into his head at the sight of the Barbie doll. As Adrian spoke of the caretaker's daughter, an odd vision slipped into his mind. A two-story white, wood house. Heavy boots slamming across the porch. A little girl's face in an upstairs window.

He blinked at the article and then shifted his attention back to her list of names.

"How about this one?" Jake asked, jabbing his finger at a name that seemed to jump off the page. "Dr. Augustus Church."

"No records on that one. Wait." She looked at the little notation next to his name. "Cited for speeding in 1994."

"He's still alive then?"

"In all likelihood. Who is he?"

Jake frowned and studied the name. "Gus," he murmured, though he couldn't actually remember the man. Still his name brought that funny feeling, the sensation that somewhere in that ball of gray he called a brain, a memory of this man lived.

"Iced teas," Lina announced, stopping by their table and putting a tall glass in front of each of them as well as a little plate with lemon.

"Thanks," Jake murmured, not looking up.

Lina might have stayed to talk, but she likely sensed their conversation was serious and her interruption unwanted. She headed back to the counter and started spraying and wiping it with a rag.

"What's up, Jake? You just went three shades paler," Adrian said.

He frowned and searched for the thread of the man in his mind, but it had already begun to fade, like a dream slipping back into the chasm from where it came.

He shook his head. "I don't know. Something, but... What else did you find?"

"A lot," Adrian admitted. "And I'm not sure I scratched the surface here. In 1975 there was a scandal involving a doctor whose nephew was a serial killer up there. He murdered like five girls in a two-year span. When they caught him, it turned out his uncle, a psychiatrist at the asylum, and the kid's mother had been experimenting on the kid at the asylum. Not only that, they'd poisoned the kid's dad. Killed him. One of his victims somehow ended up imprisoned in the asylum, but that's not clear here.

"Another doctor, Stephen Kaiser"—Adrian leaned closer to her notes—"was accused of murdering his mother and another girl from his hometown of Gaylord. He ended up having a nervous breakdown and being committed to the asylum in 1965. They found him dead in 1966. Assumed to be suicide. There's a reporter, Abe Levett, who's written ninety percent of the articles I found."

"Damn." Jake scratched his head. "What a mind-fuck."

"Yeah, to say the least. I cancelled dinner plans with my boyfriend last night because I was waist-deep in this stuff, and I'm telling you, Jake, this is probably just the tip of the iceberg. Another weird thing, all of these deaths happened after 1966. Every one of them. I couldn't find any deaths by doctors at the asylum before that date. Not unusual deaths at any rate."

"1966," Jake repeated the date. It rolled out heavily. The year Lennon and Faye had found him; the year they'd found each other.

"Order's up, Lina," François announced.

Lina brought their burgers and fries, the smells igniting another rumble in Jake's belly.

He picked his burger up and took a huge bite, thanking Lina through his mouthful of food, and giving her an apologetic look for his bad manners.

She patted his head. "You just eat up, Jake. Can't have you wasting away on my time."

Adrian took a bite and nodded enthusiastically. After she'd swallowed, she announced, "This might be the best burger I've ever had."

"And that's the God's truth," he agreed.

The food served as a momentary distraction, but before he'd finished his food, his mind drifted to the tragedy and violence associated with the asylum. The first pinpricks of a migraine poked at the backs of his eyes.

"Shit, not again," he muttered, pressing his fingers into the hollows above his eyes.

"What's wrong?" Adrian asked.

"Migraine. I only get them a few times a year, but this is the second one this week."

"Ouch," she said. "Have any meds? My mom swears by essential oils, but she's a little out there."

He laughed, remembering the diffuser always running in Faye's room. Oils and herbs and monthly visits to an acupuncturist. They might have helped, but the headaches still came for her.

"I've tried oils a few times, but…" He shook his head. "Once it comes on, it's like a runaway train. A dark room is about the only remedy and that doesn't kill the headache, just makes it bearable until it goes away."

∼

TEN MINUTES LATER, he sat in his truck, engine idling, and closed his eyes. The pain had come on fast, too fast. He put both hands over his eyes to further block out the light.

Suddenly a weight leaned across his body. His engine turned off. He squinted through his hands at Adrian standing outside his door.

"Come on, get in my car. I'll drive you home."

By the time Adrian had pulled into his driveway, his brain

pulsed in waves. Nausea swirled in his head and the burger in his stomach threatened to come up. He heard the door open and the light of the day, despite his hands covering his eyes, seared through his head like a beam of hot steel.

"Ugh," he moaned as Adrian's hands pulled his arms.

He made it out, stumbled to the grass and dropped to his knees, vomiting up his lunch. His eyes were clenched shut, but he felt Adrian's hand on his back.

"Damn, okay. Umm... what can I do, Jake? A cold washcloth?"

"Yeah," he grunted, another wave of nausea rolling through him. He vomited again. In the street behind him, he heard a car door slam.

"What is this?" a voice demanded. A voice he knew. Allison's voice.

"Fuck," he groaned, but he didn't look at her. He angled away from the smell of his puke and dropped his face into the grass, digging his forehead down into the cool earth.

"Oh, hi," Adrian said, but she was unable to finish the introduction.

"Who the hell are you?" Allison's voice was angry, but tremulous as if she were on the verge of tears. "What, are you drunk, Jake? And dating a fifteen-year-old."

Now she was crying, big loud sobs as she ranted words that Jake could no longer hear. Adrian's voice was in there too, but hers was also lost in the waves of red and white light, like balls of fire bouncing in his head.

He pulled a handful of grass and dirt up and pressed it into his eyes, blotting out the light, the sounds, the world.

20

He woke to darkness and quiet.

Staring toward the dim ceiling, he put a hand gingerly to his head. The pain had subsided, though there was a small pulsing pressure still lingering behind his left eye.

He sat up, thinking he was in bed and then realizing no, he lay on the floor, the carpet prickly beneath his palms.

Someone else stirred in the room. "Jake?" Adrian asked.

"Yeah, I'm here," he whispered.

"Thank God. You scared the shit out of me. I almost called an ambulance out there in your driveway."

His mouth tasted sour and sticky. "What time is it?" he asked, climbing to his feet and bracing his hand against an arm of the couch.

"It's after three in the morning."

"Ugh," he muttered, blundering into the kitchen and turning on the faucet. He stuck his mouth beneath the cool water, letting it rush in. He spit the first mouthful into the sink and then drank in loud gulps, finally letting some of the water flow over his face. It streamed over his cheeks and ran back into his hair, a stream slipping into the collar of his shirt. After several seconds he stood and shut the tap off.

"Should I turn on a light?" Adrian asked from the doorway behind him.

"Yeah, it's okay. The headache's gone." And mostly it was, except for that tiny dull pulsing.

Adrian turned on the hall light rather than the overhead lights in the kitchen. He sat gratefully in a wood-backed chair and stared dully at the linoleum for several seconds.

"I've heard migraines are rough, but that was—"

"A goddamned earthquake," he mumbled. He pinched the bridge of his nose and blinked, willing away the little white halo that drifted in his left eye.

Adrian walked full into the kitchen. A golden hue emanated from her face and shoulders. Jake rubbed his eyes and looked again. The colored light remained.

"What can I get ya?" she asked, opening cupboards until she found the glasses. She filled a cup of water and set it on the table. "Food? You puked up your dinner."

She opened the refrigerator, and he grimaced and swiveled his head away from the light. It didn't hurt, not exactly, but like a vampire who slinks to the shadows when dawn creeps in, he wanted to stay in darkness a little longer.

"Oh." She scrunched her face and closed the door. "Sorry. Was that too bright?"

"No. It's fine." He rubbed his eyes again, trying to clear that white ring of light, but it merely blotted out and returned. "That was a doozy. I don't know if I've ever had one that bad."

"I suggest you get in to see your doctor, Jake. If I hadn't been there…" She didn't complete the sentence.

If she hadn't been there, he'd have likely puked all over in his truck at the Burger Hut before crawling down to the floorboard and curling into the fetal position. Lina and François would have called an ambulance.

"There's some crackers there in the cupboard. Saltines." He gestured guiltily at the pantry door. As a man he'd always been careful to be the caretaker, not the caretaken, but his knees felt wobbly even in the chair and he didn't fully trust his legs.

She grabbed the box, ripped open a package with her teeth and set them on the table, sitting in the chair opposite him and grabbing a handful of crackers for herself. She held one up and smiled. "I've lived on these things after every flu or stomach bug I've ever had."

Jake smiled and nibbled the end of a dry cracker. "I'm not sure why they haven't added them to the food pyramid," he agreed.

Adrian grinned. "A joke. Praise be to God, maybe you are going to live."

He finished the saltine and followed it with a gulp of water. The golden light around Adrian had begun to diminish. Soon it would disappear. The light ring also appeared softer, wiggly, as if it were losing its form.

He ate another cracker. "I'm sorry, Adrian," he said after he'd swallowed the dry bits coating the back of his tongue. "Here you showed up to help me and—"

"And I helped you," she finished. "End of statement. Listen, Jake, I can see you're one of these do-it-all-himself guys, but there's a reason human beings are pack animals. Our survival is dependent on our relationships. And in case you forgot, I'll soon be a cop. I'm doing that because I like to help people. If police hadn't run in the family, I might have chosen a more lady-like field for helping people—a nurse or counselor or God forbid a teacher—but when you're born into a family of cops, you tend to veer in that direction."

He smiled. "I think you'll be a great cop," he told her.

"A strange one, anyway. What with my barely being able to see into the driver's side window on the big trucks."

Jake frowned, a splinter of fear quivering in his stomach for

Adrian. "How do you handle that, Adrian? I mean, you're going to face some pretty nasty guys and—"

"And I'm so little?" She laughed. "You sound like my brothers. The gun is the great equalizer. I don't care if you're seven foot tall, a bullet will stop you in your tracks."

Jake shuddered. He owned a gun, two actually, but they sat in a locked box high in his bedroom closet. They'd both belonged to Lennon, who took him once a month to the local shooting range. The sound of the shot had always startled Jake. Whether it was the first round or the seventieth that day, he jumped every time.

"Do you like to shoot guns?" he asked.

Adrian bit into a cracker and chewed thoughtfully before nodding. "Yeah. I'm good at it. I started shooting when I was six. I started competitive shooting when I was nine. My dad wanted all of us kids to know the power and the danger of guns. My mom hated it, of course, but she never said no. She agreed with him on a fundamental level. It just scared her to see her little tow-headed princess firing off bullets at a sack of straw in the backyard."

Jake leaned back in his chair, surveying the petite but powerful woman before him. She was beautiful, and he felt an odd mixture of protectiveness and desire when he looked at her. He crushed the feelings away. Adrian wouldn't appreciate either of them.

She stood and bent her arm behind her, elbow overhead, and then did the other. "I'm going to need a back massage after sitting in that damn chair for five hours," she complained.

"Really, Adrian. I'm sorr—"

"Shush!" She silenced him before he could finish. "Don't say it again. Don't be sorry. Thank you for letting me help you. Nothing makes me happier." She grabbed her purse off his counter. "I'm gonna jet though. I'm working tomorrow and I'd like a few hours of shut-eye before I drag my sleep-deprived ass into the station."

She plucked a sticky note from a pad on his table and scrawled something on it. She slid the barely legible note in front of him.

"That's my home phone number. I live with my boyfriend, Stu, so if you call and a gruff-sounding dude answers, don't worry, he's supposed to be there."

"Stu," Jake repeated. "Is he going to be pissed that you were here?"

Adrian laughed. "Of course not. I called him, for starters. He and I drove back to the Burger Hut and picked up your truck. It's parked outside. Keys are on the chest in the foyer. Plus, he's a cop too, Jake. And he's not a power-hungry meathead. He's a guy who believes in helping the good guys. He's the one who got you off the front lawn," she added dismissively, walking backwards toward the doorway. "I'm going to call and check on you tomorrow, okay?"

"Yeah, thanks." He listened to her walk down the hallway and out the front door, trying not to imagine the sight his neighbors witnessed when Adrian's boyfriend had carried him into the house.

He remembered he'd heard Allison's voice at one point too. Had she shown up? Or had he merely dreamed her? It didn't matter now. He finished his water and plodded upstairs. Stripping, he climbed in the shower and let the water scald him for several minutes. His face had felt sticky when he woke and he'd been able to smell the putrid remains of his dinner.

After showering, he fell into bed, his mind trying to run but his body too tired to keep up.

21

Charlie refilled the large mixing bowl with popcorn and returned to the living room.

"He thought you poured gas into a charcoal grill? What a dumbass. I'm happy you ran him out," Bev said, taking a handful of popcorn and shoving it into her mouth.

"Seeing him at work has super sucked," Charlie said. "I don't know what I was thinking letting him come over to begin with."

Bev finished chewing and followed up her popcorn with a drink of margarita. "Sounds to me like he invited himself. Typical douchebag behavior."

Charlie laughed and stuck a piece of popcorn in her mouth. "Pretty much. I guess that's one good thing about the ghost. I've been so busy worrying my house is haunted, I haven't had time to feel completely mortified about what happened with Warren."

"I'd like to know where the damn ghost was when Warren was acting like an asshat. You hear me, ghost? If you're going to live here rent-free, the least you can do is cause the wanker's hair to turn white when he walks in the door."

"I'm pretty sure he dyes his hair, so it'd be a moot point," Charlie said.

"You know what sounds good all of a sudden? Peanuts! Have any peanuts?"

Charlie laughed and called out to Bev as she disappeared into the kitchen. "In the cupboard above the stove."

Bev stepped into the doorway a moment later, holding up a gray cashmere sweater. "Have you started keeping clothes in the kitchen cupboards?"

Charlie frowned and stood. "No way. I've been searching everywhere for that sweater."

Bev handed it to her.

Charlie stared at it and tried to remember unpacking it, but she'd been so busy the first few days in the house, it was impossible to remember when she'd unpacked the sweater. She laid the sweater over a chair.

∼

AT THREE AM, Charlie woke desperate for a drink of water.

She padded down the hall, eyes sandy with sleep. Moonlight filtered through the bits of window not concealed by drapes. At the top of the stairs, a woman stood, and Charlie froze.

The woman started down the stairs.

"Bev?" Charlie whispered. She'd forgotten her friend was sleeping over. Apparently, they'd woken thirsty at the same time.

Her friend hadn't heard her, continuing down the stairs and out of sight.

"Bev?" she called a bit louder, but saw no sign of her friend.

The downstairs hall was empty, and Charlie expected to find Bev in the kitchen, refrigerator open as she searched for juice. But the kitchen was dark.

Charlie poured a glass of water and walked to the living room and then the bathroom.

Empty.

She walked back upstairs and eased open the guest bedroom door. It was too dark in the room to make out Bev's sleeping form, but she heard faint snores from the bed.

She returned to her room and closed the door. As she stepped to the bed, something slipped over her head and cinched around her throat. Charlie's eyes bulged and her fingers scrambled to yank away the item strangling her, but she found only the bare flesh of her neck. The pressure released and she cried out, whirling around expecting someone, a man with a stocking or a rope, to be standing there.

Her room was empty.

⁓

"DID YOU HEAR ANYTHING LAST NIGHT?" Charlie asked Bev the following morning.

Bev sat at the farm table, drinking coffee and eating apple slices. "Nope. I slept like a log. Did it storm or something?"

Charlie shook her head and filled her own mug with coffee. She sat on the bench across the table from Bev. "I woke up to get a glass of water and I saw someone. I thought it was you walking down the stairs, but then I looked and no one was there and you were asleep in your bed."

Bev made a face. "The ghost," she said, nodding.

"When I got back to my room, I felt like... someone put a noose around my neck and tried to strangle me."

Bev paused with an apple slice halfway to her mouth. "Are you serious?"

"That was the sensation. It only lasted for a couple of seconds, but... it was real. I wasn't sleeping."

"That's completely terrifying. The ghost tried to kill you?"

"I don't know. There was no one in the room. What do I do, Bev?"

"I think you need to do what the therapist said and start tracking down the history of this place. Maybe… shit, I don't know. Maybe someone got murdered here and they need you to avenge them."

Charlie giggled and then Bev joined in, laughter rumbling the table between them.

When the laughter subsided, Charlie shook her head. "Whatever happened to the Ghostbusters?"

∼

AFTER BEV WENT HOME, Charlie dug through her purse and found her real estate agent's business card.

"Kate, hey, it's Charlie Pepin," she said when the woman answered the phone.

"Charlie. Great to hear from you. How's your new house? Loving it?"

"Yeah," Charlie lied. "Umm… I did have a few questions about it though. There are some neighborhood kids doing a school project on the histories of houses in the area. I wondered if anything significant ever happened at Wilder's Grove?"

The woman didn't answer right away, and Charlie could hear typing in the background. "Sorry, just finishing sending an email. Let's see, anything significant. Well, I don't know there'd be anything noteworthy for the kids. I wish I could tell you more about it, but the listing sort of fell into my lap and then you came along and poof, it was sold, so I didn't spend a lot of time getting to know the house. As I mentioned, the previous owners left quite abruptly. I never even met them. I handled the sale with their attorney."

"Do you have their names?"

"Somewhere, but it's on your bill of sale, honey. I would look it up for you, but I've got six showings today. There's a burgeoning market in Grand Rapids, and I have been slammed for two solid weeks. Maybe this weekend I could get around to it."

"No, that's okay. I'll find it. Thanks, Kate." Charlie hung up the phone.

She hadn't unpacked the paperwork from the sale of the house. It sat in a plastic folder on the top of a box she'd shoved into the study the day she'd moved in.

She grabbed the folder and opened it, flipping until she found the sales information. The prior owners had been Sarah and Michael Earhart, with a forwarding address in Livonia, Michigan.

Charlie dialed the phone number listed next to their address. A woman answered. "Earhart Residence."

"Hi, is this Mrs. Earhart?"

"Yes, speaking."

"I'm sorry to bother you, but my name's Charlie Pepin and I purchased Wilder's Grove."

The woman said nothing.

"Um… and anyway, some of the kids in the neighborhood are doing a history project on the old houses. I wondered if…"

"I find that hard to believe, Miss Pepin," the woman said crisply.

"I'm sorry. What?"

"The children in that neighborhood know better than to have anything to do with Wilder's Grove."

Charlie stared absently at the window in the study. It faced the side yard, where she spotted a woodpecker thumping his beak against the shed. "I don't understand," Charlie said.

"I think you do and I think that's why you're calling me. But the sale was final. I'm afraid if you have additional questions, you'll need to contact our attorney. Your real estate agent has his information."

The line went dead and after several seconds of incredulous silence, it started the whining beep of a disconnected call. Charlie turned off the phone.

∽

CHARLIE DROVE into Frankenmuth to the township building and parked.

A long blue carpeted hall, quiet in that stuffy way so many government buildings were, stretched beneath Plexiglas windows, each labeled with a sign. 'County Treasurer,' 'Permits,' 'Property Taxes.'

Charlie paused in front of the 'Property Tax' window. The thin, frizzy-haired man behind the glass stood hunched over a desk in the back of the room. She waited for him to notice her, but after several minutes passed, she tapped the little silver bell on the counter.

He looked up sharply and released a barely hidden sigh as he scurried toward her. "Yes?" he asked.

"I'd like the property tax records for 319 Elmwood Drive in Frankenmuth."

"For what year?"

She frowned. "Umm... I don't know. How about the past thirty years?"

He gave her an annoyed look. "Copies are five cents apiece."

"Sure, that's fine."

Several minutes later, the man returned and handed Charlie a stack of papers.

"Wait. I think you've given me extra. I just wanted title transfers for the last thirty years."

The man nodded. "That house has had seven owners since 1966."

Charlie's mouth fell open. She thumbed through the pages

seeing different names on each page. "Okay, then. Huh. That's... that's surprising. Thank you."

The man nodded and returned to his desk.

Charlie sat in her car and read the names.

Sarah and Michael Earhart had bought the house in July of 1994 and sold in April '96.

Jim and Linda Gilmore had bought the house in April of '93 and sold in July of '94.

Polly Tompkins had purchased the house in September of '91 and sold in '93.

Mary and Steven Dodd had bought in '89 and sold in '91.

Carl Wilhelm had bought in '88 and sold in '89.

Hal and Courtney Crosby had bought in '86 and sold in '88.

Faye and Lennon Edwards had bought the house in '55. The taxes had been transferred to another Edwards, Jake, in '84.

Every owner had sold within two years except the first couple, who'd owned the house for more than three decades.

She searched through the phone book, jotting down numbers for the names listed, some of which had multiple possibilities and others which had no listed number at all. For an hour, she dialed numbers and left messages, hitting a lot of dead ends.

Charlie sighed and dialed the last number. White pucker marks stood along her wrist where she'd wrapped the phone cord around her arm while talking.

After three rings, a message machine picked up. "This is Jake, leave me a message. If you're trying to order pizza from Reno's the number is 8723 not 7823. You're welcome."

Charlie smiled and waited for the beep. "Hi, Jake. My name's Charlie Pepin. I recently bought Wilder's Grove and had a few questions about the house. If you'd call me back, I'd really appreciate it." She left her number and hung up the phone.

The day before she'd had high hopes for her day off. Go for a run, sift through some of the boxes left behind in the formal dining room, which Charlie doubted she'd ever use for eating, and maybe plant some flowers. Instead, she'd sat indoors while the sun shone, tracking some elusive bit of history that might not even exist.

"It's probably not the house at all," she mumbled. "The ghost probably followed me home from the hospital when she saw a desolate soul who'd be easy to torment for the next twenty years."

Charlie punched in another number, and a woman's nasally voice answered.

"Frankenmuth Historical Society, Bernadette speaking."

"Hi, Bernadette. My name is Charlie Pepin and I recently purchased a house in Frankenmuth called Wilder's Grove. I wondered if you might know where I could find the house's historical records. Assuming there are any."

"You have called the right place, Miss Pepin! Wilder's Grove was built in 1907 by Dwight and Agatha Wilder. The Wilders were heavily involved in local business including beer-brewing, soap-making and even some ties to a local bank. They had three children, Emma, Theo and Seymour. The Wilders owned the house until the mid-1950s."

"Oh, wow, that's great. So, you're familiar with the house then?"

"Yes. We have a book on all the homes built in Frankenmuth before the turn of the century. I've found tourists like to hear about them so I pepper my tours with facts about the older houses."

"Bernadette, did anyone die in the house?"

Without skipping a beat, the woman continued, "Seymour Wilder passed in infancy in the house in 1924 and Dwight Wilder perished in the home in 1941 from natural causes."

"Have there ever been stories about the house? Ghost stories?"

"Any house built before 1950 tends to have a story or two

attached, but here at the Historical Society, we don't concern ourselves with campfire tales."

"Is there anyone who does bother themselves with such things? A paranormal group or anything?"

Bernadette let out an ear-shattering cackle, and Charlie cringed away from the phone. "Honey, this is Frankenmuth, Michigan. You'd be more likely to find a Bigfoot than ghost-hunters in this town."

"Okay," Charlie sighed. "Thanks for your time Bernadette."

"Pleasure's all mine, Miss Pepin. And if you'd ever like to open your house to tours, you just give me a ring."

Charlie hung up the phone. She'd written down the names of the Wilder family. Two people had died in the house, both male and one an infant. Neither fit the dark presence that had been plaguing the house. Whatever it was, it had once been a woman.

22

Charlie gave up on her search and organized ingredients on her table for her mother's famous blueberry muffins. She preheated the oven and poured blueberries in a strainer, rinsing them in the deep sink.

Baking had always been a reprieve for Charlie, a tactic she'd learned from her mother, who'd fill their little apartment with the smells of blueberry muffins or butterscotch cookies when struck by the blues.

The phone rang just as the timer sounded that the muffins were finished. She recoiled from the blast of hot air that surged from the oven, but inhaled the scent of fresh-baked muffins.

"Hello?" she said, sliding off her other oven mitt and poking a fork into a muffin to double-check they were cooked.

"Charlie, this is Jake Edwards returning your call."

"Oh, hi. Great. Thank you for calling me back. You're the only one who has. Is there any chance you'd be willing to come to Wilder's Grove? I mean, if it's not a huge inconvenience. I'm sure that sounds absurd but—"

"Sure. I can do that. I used to drive by every few months and now it's been a year probably."

"This evening? There's a fresh blueberry muffin in it for you."

He chuckled. "Sure. I'll come by in an hour."

∿

Jake stood in the driveway and regarded the home where he'd spent the best years of his life. He hadn't known it then. As Lennon liked to point out, Jake had already been rushing into the future. If he could go back, he would slow it down and savor every morning he woke in Wilder's Grove while Faye and Lennon still lived.

"Jake?"

A woman stepped onto the porch and waved. She was lanky, with tousled auburn hair, and flour peppered down her cut-off jeans.

"Hi, yes, I'm Jake," he told her after staring a bit too long. He strode across the yard and up the stairs, extending his hand.

She took it, beaming a smile that crinkled the corners of her deep-set blue-green eyes.

"I'm Charlie."

∿

The light drained from the sky and the citronella candles grew pungent, their scent drifting in woozy rivers between them.

Jake talked and laughed as he hadn't done in ages, not since the good years with Lennon and Faye. Maybe it was the house or the odd sense of stepping out of the strange reality that had recently plagued him. Maybe it was Charlie.

It didn't really matter, only the breathless stories and the laughter and the sense that slumbering hours had stolen in and cast them in a stupor, a magic place between waking and dreaming where anything was possible.

For now, all the dark mysteries had been cast aside and the light mysteries allowed to run gleefully as if through a spring meadow, as if there were not a care in the world.

"The realtor didn't tell you about the secret rooms and passages in Wilder's Grove? Terrible. You should demand part of your fee back."

Charlie laughed, finished her wine and reached for the bottle. He beat her to it, refilling both of their glasses.

"I wonder if she didn't know," Charlie mused, tilting her head and gazing at the house. "You should have heard her going on about the pocket doors. I'm sure if there were secret passages, she would have lit them with cinnamon-scented candles."

Jake grinned, remembering playing hide and seek with Faye and Lennon in the hidden halls. "Fire hazard," Jake mused. "We used headlamps."

"Headlamps?" She smiled.

He nodded, remembering the nylon bands with the little round lights in their center. "We looked like miners in there. After we played our games, all three of us would have these big red marks on our foreheads. Lennon's friend Willis stopped by once after an hour-long hide and seek session. We couldn't understand why he kept staring at our heads funny. Finally, he asked if we'd all been abducted by aliens." Jake chuckled.

Charlie laughed. "A totally logical question given the circumstances."

Jake hadn't told the stories in years. He and Willis had reminisced some in the early years after Faye and Lennon were gone, but then they'd become... a secret in a way—a cherished treasure that Jake never seemed able to share.

He'd tried once with a girl he dated for a few months. Corina. She'd been the first girlfriend after Lennon had passed.

Whenever he talked about Faye and Lennon, she'd get weepy-eyed and insist on rubbing his back and smoothing his hair. It drove him to the point of never mentioning their names in her presence.

Now he revealed those stories to a complete stranger, and yet nothing about her felt strange. He wet his lips and tried not to study the lock of cinnamon hair curling towards her left eye. The eye itself was the green-blue of a light-struck ocean, with long black lashes thick on her hooded eyelids. Faye would have called them sleepy eyes.

"Is your mom still living?" he asked Charlie.

Charlie nodded and sipped her wine. "In Arizona with my stepdad."

"And you didn't want to move back to Arizona after your divorce?"

Charlie shook her head. "I didn't grow up in Arizona. I grew up here in Michigan further downstate in a tiny town called Dansville. Truth be told, I bolted from that place the minute I graduated from high school. I left my mom behind. I have a lot of guilt about that now. She and my dad had divorced years earlier, and he'd bailed on us. She was a single mom. I graduated and moved to Kalamazoo to go to school at Western Michigan University. Any town was bigger than Dansville, I reasoned."

"I've been to Kalamazoo a few times. One of my buddies from high school attended Western."

"It wasn't exactly a leap into big city life, but when you come from a place like Dansville, it's definitely a culture shift. I called home but I was a typically self-absorbed teen and I made every conversation about me," Charlie admitted. "Ugh, what is it that turns teen girls into such brats?"

Jake laughed. "Believe me, it's not restricted to the girls. I celebrated my graduation from high school by getting drunk and running over the mailbox at Wilder's Grove. Mind you, it was brick and had been there for fifty years. Lennon made me rebuild it by hand."

"It must be raging hormones. Anyway, about two years after I left for school, my mom met Arnold at a cat show in Lansing. Ever been to one of those?"

He raised an eyebrow. "If I hazard a guess, I'd imagine it's a show that displays cats?"

"Oh, yeah." Charlie opened her arms. "Some of them are giant. Big fluffy Maine Coons and Ragdolls and Himalayans."

"Sounds purr-fectly wild."

Charlie grinned. "You have no idea. Some of those cat breeders are ruthless. My mom took me a few times. She loved cats, but we rented an apartment and were never allowed to have one. Arnold bred Maine Coon kittens. He lived in a big house in West Bloomfield, the Detroit area, and he'd been widowed a couple years before. He and my mom hit it off right away. They dated for a year and then he convinced her to quit her nursing job and move in with him."

"And that was a good thing?" Jake asked.

"Oh, yeah. He wasn't one of these guys trying to seize control of her life. He's a caretaker—not literally, but that's his personality. Every time I visit them, he spends hours cooking for us, planning fun mother-daughter adventures we can go on. He's pretty great."

Jake smiled and rubbed a thumb over his knuckles, remembering his own parents. "Faye and Lennon were great. Lennon taught me to change the oil in my truck, how to shave with a straight razor, how to re-roof a house, and probably most important of all, the business of excavating. Faye instilled in me kindness and compassion. My love of dirt came from her, oddly enough, though it was enhanced by Lennon and all the equipment. Faye spent hours outside in the garden, moving the dirt, planting flowers, finding special rocks we'd line up on the windowsills."

"Where are they now?"

"Both gone," he admitted. "I was twenty-five when Faye got the diagnosis, stage four colon cancer, and it moved quickly. She died eight months later. Lennon was heartbroken, but tried to put on a brave face. He suffered a heart attack three years to the day after Faye died. He passed in his sleep.

"We had a tradition in those days. Every Sunday I brought coffee and donuts to Wilder's Grove. He'd help me if I had any frustrating excavation projects that I needed a second opinion on. I was anxious that day—it was August third, the day Faye had died, and it was always a hard date for Lennon. I walked into Wilder's Grove and found him dead. He looked peaceful. It hurt but it also felt right. Lennon wasn't the same after Faye died. He wanted to be with her more than anything this world could offer. I think my only regret is they never got to have grandchildren. They would have loved grandkids, but…"

"You never wanted children?" she asked. Something passed over her face, but she smiled to hide it.

"I don't know. Maybe I was too young," he murmured. "I would have liked to have one for them, but that's not the right reason." He laughed. "I don't know much, but I know that."

"I think you know much," she said and they burst into laughter. She touched her face, flushed and pink. "I haven't laughed like this since…" She waved her hand. "Since who knows when?"

"Me neither. It feels good."

Charlie swept an unruly bit of hair off her face. Jake gazed at the delicate ear she'd tucked it behind. The lobe revealed three little freckles bunched together and he imagined the hidden freckles on her body, the ones in the center of her back that even she'd never seen.

She caught his eye and smiled. "What?" she asked and her tone held the soft note of an invitation.

He swallowed and broke the stare, gesturing at the house. "Ready for the Mysterious Wilder's Grove Tour?"

"Ready as I can be," she murmured. She stood and stretched her arms overhead and then swayed from side to side, releasing whatever kinks had lodged during their hours of chatting.

They stepped through the glass doors on the deck and Jake paused, breathing in the familiar scent of the house. "The best memories of my life happened in this house," he said.

Charlie glanced at him, running her fingers along the farm table as they passed it. "It's easy to see why."

He stopped in the doorway to the living room, eyes wide. "Are you an antique collector? This looks like the furniture that would have belonged to the original owners of the house."

Charlie shook her head. "They left it. The owners before me left all the furniture."

"Wow. Well, follow me, Miss Charlie, and enter if you dare..." He used a spooky voice, but rather than delighted, Charlie looked uneasy as he led her down the front hall.

Jake stopped at the hall closet and opened the door.

"Really?" Charlie asked as he pushed the coats open to reveal a blank plywood wall.

He squatted down, his large form filling the space, and pressed on the lower corner of the wall. It popped and the wall swung in to reveal a dark passage. "Have a flashlight?" he asked.

Charlie grabbed one from the shelf above the coats and flipped it on.

Jake shuffled to the side so she could squeeze into the closet beside him, their shoulders crushing against each other. She smelled of the muffins she'd baked earlier that day. He inhaled and smiled.

Charlie shined the light into the passage.

"I'd have to duck to go through there now, but when I was a kid, I'd run through this full speed. It opens into the closet in the washroom."

The beam of the flashlight caught on a gossamer spider web. A fat black spider fled from the light when she shifted the beam. "Yikes," she said.

"Creeped out by spiders?" he asked.

"Not usually, but it's a little big for my liking."

Jake shuffled forward and swiped the web down with one large hand. He emerged with his hand cupped. "I'll put it outside," he said.

"Did you crush it?"

He shook his head. "Trying not to." He shuffled out and went to the front door.

He returned to find Charlie hunched and shuffling into the closet. After only a few feet, she turned abruptly and rushed out, smacking into Jake. He steadied her with his hands on her shoulders.

"You okay?"

She laughed and blushed. "Yeah. Creepy passages have a way of flaring my claustrophobia."

"Let me show you the others," he told her.

She followed him to the second floor. Another passage fed into the closets in all four of the bedrooms.

"One more," he said, leading her back downstairs and into the study. He took hold of a grandfather clock.

"It's on wheels," he explained at her mystified expression. Behind the clock, he ran his fingers along the wall seam. "Here," he said, taking her hand and placing it on the ridge in the wall. "Press that."

She pressed and, like the passages, the wall opened, this time swinging out instead of in.

This space was tall, as high as the ceilings. Just a room, the size of a large closet.

"Why are all these hideouts here?"

"Well, the house was built during the early 1900s. The Underground Railroad ended when? Late 1800s. Maybe the family had done something like that previously and built the house with those ideas in mind."

"Oh," Charlie breathed. "That's kind of amazing."

"Or the original owner was just a nutter who liked to hide in his own house, spook his family, and pile up his money where his wife couldn't find it."

Charlie laughed. "I like the first story better."

"Me too," he agreed.

∼

"So, why didn't you keep this place, Jake?" Charlie asked after they'd returned to the patio. "With all those memories? I can't imagine you wanting to sell it."

Jake leaned back in his chair and tilted his head to look up at an oak tree, bushy with dark leaves. "I didn't sell it for a couple of years after Lennon died. I started my business and commuted to Saginaw, but… it's huge. I mean you've obviously noticed that. The space started to get to me after a while. I was working so much, I finally rented a little apartment in Saginaw. Then I met a girl and…" He shrugged. "I realized life was taking me somewhere else. I put it on the market, kind of an experiment really. Properties could sit for years after all. And I didn't lower the price, I asked for what it was worth and probably more than that, because to me the sentimental value made this house almost priceless. I had an offer two weeks later. I was swamped in those days with Dig Deep. I felt like I needed to unload some of the burdens. I accepted the offer and that was that."

"Did you ever regret it?"

"I've never given myself time to regret it. Lennon used to say I'm a future man. I never live in the past and I only spend enough time in the present to open a door and walk through it."

"I think I'm a past person," she confessed. "I've had a lot of sleepless nights mulling over how I might have done things differently. I'm trying to change that now though."

Jake smiled. "Maybe we can trade a little. You take some of my future and I'll take some of your past."

"I'd like that," she murmured. "But actually, I'd like to hear about some more of your past right now. This has been so nice, I'd all but forgotten the reason I asked you to come here."

"It wasn't merely to ply me with wine and muffins, so I'd reveal the secrets of this house?"

Her smile faded at his words, but then she forced it back on, though he'd seen the expression behind it. Fear.

"Ha," she laughed dryly. "Funny you should put it that way."

He cocked an eyebrow, curious to see where this was headed.

"Um... I don't know how to ask this question without sounding mental, but did you ever think the house was haunted?"

He gazed at her. Nothing in her face implied a joke. But in the midst of everything else he'd been discovering her words felt... significant.

"No." He shook his head. "Never. I never had an experience like that here."

"But you've had experiences like that? You don't think it's insane for me to ask?"

He thought of the asylum, the stories, the dreams that had started to turn his nights into murky pools of existence that seemed suspended between dreaming and remembering. "No. I don't think you're insane for asking. I am curious though why you're asking."

She blew out a long breath and then tucked both her lips in, creating a strange corpselike effect. "I've been hearing and even seeing things. At first, I thought it was me. The last year has been... hard, leaving my husband and getting divorced. I bought this place on a whim just over a month ago. I didn't come in with reservations though. I was excited. I still am, but the weirdness is getting hard to ignore."

"What kind of weirdness?"

Charlie squeezed her hands in her lap. "I've seen a woman in the house a couple of times. She's there and then she's gone. Stuff has been moved; the television has turned on by itself. Jake, did Faye die here in Wilder's Grove?"

Jake blinked at the house and then returned his gaze to Charlie. He nodded. "Yes. She had a hospital bed in the living room and a nurse who helped in the final days. They wanted to move her to hospice, but Lennon refused."

"Is it completely nuts to wonder if she'd be haunting the house?"

Jake frowned. "Honestly, I don't see Faye as someone who'd stay behind."

"Stay behind?"

"Yeah. Hauntings aren't just a result of death. Spirits have a purpose, a reason for staying in the living world."

"How do you know that?"

He dropped his head back and looked at the sky, suddenly reluctant to go on, wondering if his next words might kill the connection growing between them.

"When I was a little kid," he admitted, "I saw things—spirits. One in particular talked to me a lot. He told me why ghosts appear. Sometimes they're just passing through, saying goodbye, but hauntings, well, they're here for something. I don't believe Faye died unfulfilled in any way."

"What did Faye look like?"

Jake smiled. "She was little." He held a hand up to his chest. "I towered over her by the time I was fifteen. She had short hair, blonde but turning white when she died. Big blue eyes."

"That's not the woman I've been seeing," Charlie said. "This woman has long dark hair, dark eyes. Honestly, she scares me. It's not just the dead aspect, which frankly is scary enough. I think she's angry. Do you know that Wilder's Grove has been sold every two years since you left, Jake? No one has stayed here longer than that. I called all the previous owners, but other than you, I've only reached one of them—the people who sold it to me. The woman didn't come right out and say it was haunted, but she made it very clear the sale was final and I could contact her attorney if I had a problem with that."

Jake looked at her, surprised. "Every two years? That's crazy. Even if it is haunted, why sell? Are a few bumps in the night that big of a deal?"

"She strangled me," Charlie cut in. "I think. Assuming she's real, and I'm not completely losing my mind, the ghost in Wilder's Grove tried to strangle me."

"Holy hell." Jake ran a hand through his hair and gazed at the house.

It looked the same as it had when he'd first laid eyes on it as a boy. A fairytale house with blue shutters and gingerbread lattices. No dark faces leered from the windows. Even as he struggled to be more open, to feel more of the house, he sensed nothing dangerous within it.

"She wasn't there when we lived here," Jake said. "Have you asked her to leave?"

Charlie widened her eyes. "How exactly do I do that?"

Jake chuckled. "I don't know, but it seems like the easiest place to start."

~

THEY TALKED a while longer about the history of the house. When the fireflies started to fill the backyard, Jake stood and yawned. "I could sit here all night and talk to you, Charlie, but I've got a busy day tomorrow."

She stood with him. "Me too. Two twelve-hour shifts coming up."

They walked together to his truck.

"This was unexpectedly great," he admitted and he meant it. For more than three hours he hadn't thought about Petra or the Northern Michigan Asylum.

"For me too. Thanks for coming by, Jake."

"Anytime." He slid behind the wheel and looked at her, their eyes holding a few beats longer than necessary. He started to ask her out. The words filled his mouth, but he ground his teeth together. Allison's face swam up and the faces of the women before her. Distractions. He used women to escape. He had no business bringing anyone into his current mess.

"Thanks, Charlie. It was a pleasure." He started the truck and backed out of the driveway.

23

*J*ake usually worked on Saturday, often Sunday too, but not today. Today, he wanted to look at the forgotten places up close. He wanted to see what came back when he stood in the shadow of his childhood.

~

THE LITTLE TOWN of Alpena looked familiar, though not welcoming, as he drove into town. Instead of nostalgia overtaking Jake as he parked his car in the parking lot behind Burton's Department Store, he felt dread.

The store sold candy and toys, fabric and trinkets. He'd visited the store many times as a boy. His mother and grandmother had gone once a month to buy fabric they'd sew into blankets for church fundraisers. He remembered eyeing the candy, watching as other kids he went to school with walked in and their parents lovingly handed them giant spiral lollipops or bought them little paper bags of chocolate-covered peanuts. Not his mother, though. More than once, she'd dug her sharp fingernails into the back of his neck for getting too close to the candy displays.

Jake walked inside. The candy counter still stood, each bin filled with chocolates or brightly colored gummy worms and gumballs. The girl behind the counter looked barely fifteen, with a freckled face and reddish hair pulled into a high ponytail. She wore an apron covered in buttons.

"Hi!" She beamed. "Welcome to Burton's. Can I get you a sweet treat?"

He almost said no, but then he paused, the memory of wanting overpowering him, making his mouth water. "Yeah." He stared at all the choices. "I'll take a small bag of peanut clusters."

"Those are wicked good. The coconut clusters too," she told him, scooping a metal spoon into the peanut clusters.

"Add a bag of the coconut clusters too," he said.

She grinned. "Right on."

She handed him the bags of candy and he paid, a tremor of anxious delight coursing through him.

He laughed and walked away, wandering down an aisle filled with elaborately painted coffee mugs. The first chocolate-covered peanut cluster stopped him in his tracks. He closed his eyes and let the chocolate melt on his tongue. There was something painful about eating the candy, a mingling of guilt and also anger that his mother had never once let him try it.

He left the store, dumping the rest of the chocolate into a garbage bin outside.

Without consulting a map, he drove by memory to his childhood home. The little blue house sat on five acres of land a few yards back from the road. It looked the way he remembered it, though the porch he'd painted white with his grandfather now appeared spotted and brown. A large white Buick sat in the gravel driveway.

Jake stopped his truck on the road, shifting to park and staring at the curtained windows of the house.

Was his mother inside? She'd be in her sixties, not old by any means, but she'd seemed old even when Jake was a boy. She wore her hair pulled severely back from her face and pinned in tight buns at the base of her neck. Her dresses were hand-sewn, shapeless smocks decorated in dull blue or brown flowers. He'd never once seen her put on lipstick or a dusting of blush.

"How did she get pregnant?" he asked.

He'd never thought about it, never asked, but now it seemed impossible. Impossible that his mother with her tight-lipped scowls and her trembling stiff hands had gotten pregnant out of wedlock. That she'd had sex at all seemed to defy everything he remembered about the woman.

When he'd started the journey from his house that morning, he'd intended to knock on the door, to at least find out if the mother he hadn't seen in over thirty years still lived.

Something moved near the side of the house. He squinted through the windshield where a young woman, with curly blonde hair poking from a red ball cap, stepped from the garage with a pair of garden shears.

Jake shifted into drive and hit the gas, his truck lurching forward. His breath stuck in his throat and he rolled the window down, gulping the air as it rushed in.

He didn't look in the rearview mirror as he sped away.

∼

MEMORIES of his loveless childhood followed him on the two-and-a-half-hour drive to Traverse City. Each time he searched for warmth in the cramped little house in Alpena, he found only more instances of loneliness.

He stopped at a Shell station, refueled, and asked for directions to the former asylum. The man behind the counter looked at him funny, but didn't say much.

When Jake turned onto the tree-lined road that wound back toward the asylum, icy fingers tickled his spine. It wasn't a memory exactly that seemed to surface, more like déjà vu.

Through the trees, he spotted a massive white structure. He stepped from his truck and gazed at the buildings. The eye couldn't take it all in. He had to tilt his head back to see the top and shift his head from side to side. But he'd known that, hadn't he? He'd known it was huge. Its size remained, though the grandeur had dwindled. He saw smashed windows and graffitied walls.

The grass poked long and unruly. Patches of weeds and wild bushes jumbled around the base of the main building and the smaller buildings behind it.

Cottages. That was what those other buildings had been called. He stared at the TB house, which had once held people with tuberculosis.

The memories loomed like huge networks of tree roots growing beneath the ground, so close he could almost feel them poking through. But even in the face of it, in the shadow of the immense buildings, nothing rushed back.

~

JAKE STEPPED into the Traverse City Library feeling out of place and unsure where to start. The space was big, an entry that opened into a high-ceilinged room with a wide staircase at one end backed by two-story picture windows. Rooms stood to either side of the main entrance, each filled with shelves of books.

He stood, Styrofoam cup of coffee in hand, the silence before him like an invisible wall he needed a code to gain entrance to.

"Can I help you?" a voice asked.

He shifted his eyes toward the circular desk where a woman ten or so years his junior sat, hands primly clasped on the desk. She looked like a librarian—tan blouse, limp hair framing her face and spectacles that magnified her green eyes.

"I hope so," he said, stepping closer to her. "I need newspapers. Um… specifically stuff about the old asylum." He waved his hand as he spoke and a dribble of hot coffee splashed from his cup and scalded his hand. He grimaced.

The woman pointed at a sign. "No food or drinks in the building. You'll have to throw that away." She pointed at a trash bin.

He frowned. He'd just bought the coffee on his way to the library. He sighed and dropped it in the trash.

"Go to the second floor." The woman gestured at the staircase. "There's a computer lab. The man working there can log you into the periodicals."

"Sure. Thanks."

The guy in the computer lab was young, late teens, with a mop of unkempt black curls that stuck out at funny angles or flopped over his eyes. As he deftly clicked keys and swiped the mouse, Jake wondered how he managed to see with so much hair falling into his face.

"You're all set, dude," he said after several minutes. "Use the mouse." He tapped the black mouse to scroll. "This little box"—he pointed at the screen—"lets you search keywords, dates. I'm right there if you need something."

The kid returned to a desk by the door and resumed his paperback. Jake couldn't read the title but saw the author was Sidney Sheldon. Jake had never been a reader, but Faye read everything in sight and Jake remembered the author's name well. Half a row on Faye's extensive bookshelf had been filled with Sheldon.

Jake read a few articles about the removal of bodies, but most seemed lacking in details and implied a crazy caretaker and his family had committed the murders for no apparent reason. Most of the earlier articles about the asylum had been written by Abe Levett.

Jake wrote down the name of the newspaper Levett worked for and left the library, stopping at a payphone.

"Up North News," a man said.

"Hi. I'm trying to reach a reporter named Abe Levett."

"I'm sorry, Abe's no longer with us."

"He died?" Jake felt his momentum rushing out.

"Oh, no," the man quickly corrected. "Retired. He lives out on Treetops Road. Oh, I probably shouldn't have mentioned that."

"Do you have his phone number?"

"Sorry. I can't give out that information. Best of luck to you." The man hung up the phone.

Jake climbed in his truck and searched for Treetops Road on his map. It was a winding stretch of road in Grand Traverse County.

∾

TWENTY MINUTES LATER, Jake scanned the dense woods on either side of Treetops Road. He hadn't passed a mailbox in five miles. Up ahead he spotted a dirt drive and let his foot off the gas.

A ten-foot-tall, black metal gate blocked the dirt entrance, which had no mailbox and did not reveal what lay beyond it. A house? Oil refineries? A junkyard?

Jake parked and walked to the gate, tugging on the metal bars, only to find they didn't budge. A chain-link fence, as high as the gate, and topped in barbed wire, ran the length of the property. There was no way to get inside.

On a tree beside the fence someone had posted a metal sign that read 'I'm Watching You.'

24

A voice bellowed from overhead. "What do you want?" a man demanded.

Jake jumped and spun around. It took him several seconds to find the dark speaker perched in a tree. He searched among the canopy of trees for a camera, but found nothing.

"Uh, yeah, hi." He waved at the speaker for lack of another option. "My name's Jake Edwards. I'm looking for Abe Levett. A guy at Up North News told me he lived out here on Treetops Road. Maybe you know where I can find him?"

"What's your business with him?" the voice boomed.

"The Northern Michigan Asylum."

"Are you friend or foe?" the man asked.

"I'm sorry, what?"

"What do you want with the asylum? What's your connection?"

"Well." He sighed and searched for his reasons. "I lived there when I was a kid, and now I'm trying to make sense of some things."

"Abe, just let him in." A woman's voice drifted from the speaker.

"Shh... I've got the speaker button depressed. He can hear—"

The buzz of the speaker cut off, and Jake imagined a man and woman arguing on the opposite end about whether to let him in.

A moment later, a grinding started, and the gate slid open. Jake climbed in his truck and drove down the dirt driveway.

Nearly a quarter mile in, he spotted the house. The quaint white and blue cottage surprised him. He'd expected something industrial or fortress-like. Instead, he found a home that wouldn't have been out of place on Martha's Vineyard.

Abe Levett had a full dark beard, streaked in silver, and a head of hair to match. Two dogs crowded the space on either side of him when he opened the front door. Jake recognized Rottweiler characteristics, though the dog's long snout and tail showed a mixed breed rather than a purebred. The second dog looked like a hunter, long and lean with short brown and silver speckled fur.

Jake took an automatic step back, expecting a snarl from the larger dog, but they both merely scrambled around Abe, attempting to get a closer look at the stranger outside.

"Twain, Dickens, get out of here." Abe wiggled from side to side and pushed the dogs back into the house. "Orla, the hounds of Hell are trying to escape the underworld again," he shouted.

Jake laughed, but Abe swiveled his head back to him, eyeing him suspiciously. "Don't be fooled. They're trained to kill on command."

"I bet." Jake tried to keep a straight face.

"What's your full name?"

"Jake Fritz Edwards."

"Occupation?"

"I own an excavating company called Dig Deep."

"What machine would I use to dig a well?"

"A well driller," Jake said.

Abe frowned.

A woman's laugh trilled from the house. "Abe. You're going to scare the man away. Open the door. And asking him questions you don't know the answers to is unlikely to be very helpful."

Abe hardened his jaw and locked his eyes on Jake for another moment before coming to some conclusion and opening the door. "Come on in, Jake," he said.

Jake stepped into the sunny interior. The wood floors were polished and framed photographs of a beautiful young woman with dark hair and bright green eyes hung from the walls.

The woman he'd heard stepped into the foyer and waved. "Hi, Jake. I'm Orla. Don't let Abe scare you. He's a tad cautious."

"Better to be safe than dead," Abe grumbled.

"Is someone after you?" Jake asked.

"The Grim Reaper's after us all," Abe quipped. "But I'm more worried about flesh-and-blood men, especially where the Northern Michigan Asylum is concerned." Abe waved for Jake to follow him.

They walked into a spacious kitchen and living room combined. A large green sectional sat on a charcoal area rug. Pillows in varying colors were strewn across the couch.

On the long marble kitchen island, jars stood in a row. Orla scooped globs of something purple into each one. "Blackberry jam," she told him when she saw him looking. "My friend Hazel brings me hoards of them. I've had these frozen since last summer. I'm finally getting around to making jam. Can I grab you a beer, Jake? Or coffee?"

"Coffee for me, honey," Abe said, settling into an overstuffed black chair. He propped one ankle on his knee and surveyed Jake.

"Yeah, coffee would be great. Thanks, Orla, and nice to meet you."

"Likewise." She smiled and tucked a strand of long black hair behind her ear. She'd tied her hair in a long braid, but some of it had pulled free.

More photos lined the shelves in the sitting room. The girl in the images bore a striking resemblance to Orla.

"Is that your daughter?" Jake asked.

"Sure is. The apple of her father's eye." Orla winked at Abe, whose face had darkened. "Her name's Dawn and she's a sophomore at the University of Michigan this year, studying special education."

"That's great," Jake said, noticing the worry lines that creased Abe's mouth as he gazed at the pictures.

"Dangerous is what it is. More than a few predators have roamed those streets," Abe muttered.

Orla carried in two mugs, handing the first, a lopsided ceramic thing painted in shades of purple, to Jake and the second, equally deformed, but rainbow-colored, to Abe.

Abe held his up and shook his head. "Orla and Dawn became potters a few years back. We bought a kiln and everything. I'm not sure their glassware business will take off anytime soon."

"Oh, quit it," Orla laughed. "The point is, Jake, there're no holes and they're pretty."

Abe looked cross-eyed at his mug. "If by pretty you mean the ugliest damn coffee mug anyone's ever laid eyes on, then yes, they are quite pretty."

Jake chuckled and sipped his coffee, hot and rich. He eased back into the couch.

"I hate to encourage you to get down to business, since we rarely receive pleasant news associated with the asylum, but I'm guessing you didn't drive out here to talk about pottery," Abe said, resting his mug on the arm of his chair.

Jake sighed. "I found your articles about the asylum at the library. I lived at the asylum when I was ten, but…" He made like his brains were flying out of his head. "I don't remember.

There's a shimmer of something. I've even seen a photograph of myself there, and it was definitely me."

"What then? Are you trying to trace your past?"

Orla came in and sat on the arm of Abe's chair, moving his mug to the table. He took her hand and ran his fingers back and forth across her knuckles. Jake noticed she wore nude gloves.

"I wish it were that simple," Jake admitted. "A girl I was at the asylum with, Petra, showed up at my office recently. I didn't know her. Like I said, I had no memory of ever being there. She came to see me and that afternoon she disappeared."

Orla visibly tensed.

"She didn't just disappear," Jake continued. "Something happened to her. There was blood all over her apartment."

Abe shut his eyes, and Orla took her hand from his.

"I think I'll take the dogs out," she said. She kissed Abe's head. "Twain, Dickens, come on, guys. Walkie time." The dogs jumped from their respective beds beneath a picture window and crowded around Orla as she herded them toward the door.

"I'm sorry. I didn't mean to upset her," Jake said.

Abe watched her leave and then shook his head. "She's okay. Since Dawn moved downstate, it's harder for her to hear this stuff."

"I read about Orla," Jake admitted. "I read that they had held her in the asylum against her will?"

Abe nodded. "I wrote that. The hospital tried to cover it up. They tried to claim she was just another of Spencer Crow's victims, and she managed to get away, but she wasn't. It was Crow's mother and uncle who tortured her."

"I can't imagine that what happened to her relates to Petra, but—"

"Oh, but it does," Abe said. "It's all connected. That place is a fucking spiderweb. In the twenty years since they abducted Orla, I've heard thirty stories of bad doctors in there, and they were not doing ordinary evil things—and by that, I mean lobotomies and straitjackets. That level of torture is tame compared to what these doctors have been up to."

"But it's closed now. Right? All the doctors are gone?"

Abe stood and disappeared down the hall. He returned with a cardboard box and dropped it at Jake's feet. "It's everything I've written, plus the stuff I'm convinced is connected to whatever dark pursuits have gone on at the asylum. The stuff on the top is the most recent.

"A woman named Crystal Childs was abducted from Lansing, Michigan and held captive in the old caretaker's house on the asylum property. I wrote her story down. I didn't publish it because I'm retired and the editor at Up North News changed a few years back and the new one wants nothing to do with asylum stories. The cover-up is still going on, and when you start sniffing around, some nasty elements come out of the woodwork to shut you up. I've stepped away from it a lot. A hard decision, but when Dawn was born, I had to protect my family. Simple as that." Abe tugged at his beard. "Messing with that place is like poking a hornet's nest. I used to throw fire on them, but now…" He waved toward the door Orla had left through.

"I get it," Jake admitted. "And I don't want to bring any grief into your house. I'd just like to know where to start with all this. There was another little girl in the asylum with us. Maribelle. Something about her is important. But how I even begin—"

"Maribelle," Abe murmured, nodding. "You need to talk to Crystal Childs."

"The woman who was abducted?"

Abe nodded. "She can talk to you about the Claudes. A terrifying posse right there, but the little one, Maribelle, never made it out of that family alive. Maybe Crystal can help you put some pieces together. She's pure sunshine. She and Orla hit it off right away. Crystal's even gone to visit Dawn a few times in Ann Arbor. Takes her eggs from their farm and homemade gift baskets. Go see her. She can shed some light on what happened to Maribelle Claude."

"Would she be open to that? Talking about what happened to her?"

Abe nodded. "Crystal's a helper. It's not easy to talk about in much the same way it's hard for Orla, which is why neither of them is penning a book about the horrors they suffered, but if their stories will help someone, then that's different." Abe stood and grabbed a sheet of paper off a notepad stuck to the refrigerator door. "I'm writing her address down. I'd say to give her a call, but she lives in a community of sorts and they only have one phone. It's easier to just show up." Abe folded the paper in half and handed it to Jake.

~

"JAKE." Orla stopped in the open door of his pick-up after he climbed behind the wheel. "I don't know if Abe mentioned it. I'm sure he didn't. But… sometimes when I touch things…" She looked down at her gloved hands, winding her fingers together. "Sometimes I can see stuff. It might not help, but if you had something of Petra's…"

"I'm not sure I understand," he told her, studying the complex expression on her face.

She laughed. "I don't do it anymore, hardly ever, but if I were to touch something of hers, well, I might be able to give you some clue about what happened to her. Just think about it. Okay?" She didn't elaborate, but turned and walked back to the house, the dogs following behind her.

25

"Hi, Chloe. How are you today?" Charlie asked.

The sandy-haired eight-year-old who lived down the block stopped jumping rope and turned to look at Charlie, who'd paused from her run to say hello.

"Hi, Miss Charlie. My head feels all better. Mommy said your magic salve made the ouchy go away." Chloe touched her head where a shovel that had fallen off the wall in her garage several days before had struck her. The damage had been minor, a small split that needed two stitches, but she'd cried something fierce when her mother brought her into the hospital. Charlie hadn't been Chloe's nurse, but she'd encountered her in the hospital lobby and helped Chloe's mom pick out a salve in the pharmacy for her daughter's head.

"Are you exercising?" Chloe asked.

Charlie nodded. "I try to go for a run every day when it's nice out."

"I like to go outside when it's nice too."

"Well, listen, I made some blueberry muffins yesterday if you want to come over and have one. I also have a new kitty."

Chloe's eyes lit up, but then she looked past Charlie toward

Wilder's Grove. "I better not," she murmured. "The mean-eyed lady doesn't like kids."

Charlie frowned and glanced at her house, half expecting to see a woman sitting on the porch. "What mean-eyed lady?" Charlie asked. "The woman who used to live there?" She heard the tremor in her voice and hoped the little girl thought it was merely from the run.

"The lady who watches us out the windows," Chloe whispered as if the lady might hear.

Charlie remembered the tightening around her neck. She absently put a finger to her throat. "Has she always been there, Chloe? The mean-eyed lady?"

Chloe nodded. "My big brother and all his friends were scared of her too. Mrs. Larson, the lady across the street, tells all the kids to stay away. The mean-eyed lady killed her dog."

"What? Not Howie."

Chloe shook her head. "Howie's brother, Barney. He used to hide his bones in other people's yards. Mrs. Larson said Barney went to Wilder's Grove to hide a bone and she saw the lady's hands reach up from the ground and strangle him."

Charlie gaped at her. "My God. That's a terrible story to tell children."

"Chloe!" Chloe's mom appeared at the end of her driveway. She waved at her daughter. "Time for lunch, honey. Hi, Charlie."

Charlie waved and started to ask more about the lady, but Chloe took her jump rope in one hand and skipped off down the block. "Bye, Miss Charlie," she called over her shoulder.

"Bye, Chloe," Charlie replied. She jogged the last half a block to her house, pausing on the sidewalk to look in each of the windows. No one returned her gaze, and yet a prickle of gooseflesh rose across her chest.

Across the street, Mrs. Larson's windows were dark.

The phone rang when she opened the door, and she hurried

to the living room, grabbing the receiver and offering a breathless hello.

"Have I got Charlie Pepin on the line?" a woman's husky voice asked.

"Yes, this is she."

"This is Polly. You called me about Wilder's Grove."

"Yes, Polly, great." Charlie searched for the woman's details, but couldn't remember her last name or when she'd owned the house. "I recently bought Wilder's Grove and had a few questions, if you have a couple minutes to talk."

"Well, well... that house sure does make the rounds." The woman made a sound as if she were sucking something through a straw.

"That's kind of why I'm calling. I wondered if... I wondered why you sold it."

"Because that place is more haunted than a corpse."

"I'm sorry?" Though she'd heard her perfectly well.

"Haunted, my dear. Spooks, ghosts, demons for all I know. I saged that place every morning for a month. No good."

"What kinds of things happened to you here?" The question hung strangely in the air. All around Charlie, sun cast the carpets and furniture in a warm glow. The house itself beckoned you in as if it were an old friend inviting you over for a cup of tea, and yet here she stood talking about something malevolent that lived beneath this very roof.

"It'd be faster to list the things that didn't happen," Polly said gruffly. "My stuff got moved all over. I heard voices, slamming doors, someone running down the stairs. I'd wake up some mornings to find every window in the house wide open in the middle of January. Snow ankle-deep, drifting into the living room. I had a few witchy friends come over and they tried to rid the house of the spirits. I even resorted to a Catholic priest. Nada. Whatever's livin' there is there to stay. I lasted for two years and then—"

"What happened?"

"I fell down the stairs and broke my leg. But—and I'll never prove it—I was pushed. That demon shoved me down the stairs after luring me out of bed in the dead of night. I lay there until my sister came over in the morning and found me. I put the house on the market a week later."

"Polly, did you ever try to find out the history of the house?"

"You bet I did, but I came up empty. I thought for sure somebody must have been murdered there, but if they did, it never made the news."

"Did you ever hear anything like that?" Charlie whispered, turning to look behind her.

A sudden feeling of eyes on her from every corner stole in and she wrapped one arm protectively across her chest.

"No. I looked into the families that once owned it as best I could, but none of them had committed crimes. There's an old biddy down at the Historical Society who'll chew your ear off all day long about the history of that place, but when it comes to the important stuff, she didn't have a clue."

"So, you have no idea who or what is haunting Wilder's Grove?"

"Not a clue. But my advice to you is this. Get out, Charlie. I only broke my leg, but it could have been my neck."

~

CHARLIE READ UNTIL MIDNIGHT, hoping to find some shred of a solution in the books her therapist had given her. There were none. Some people had had success with blessings by priests, others had rid themselves of haunted objects, a few held séances and politely asked their ghosts to leave.

In the morning, with eight uninterrupted hours of sleep pepping her step, Charlie took her coffee and newspaper and went to the porch, settling into her chair.

Despite her previous night's reading, she'd woken refreshed and again steeped in the overwhelming delight of her new home. Yes, she'd have to deal with the ghost sooner or later, but for the next hour, she could savor the pink and saffron light of early morning.

As she sipped her coffee, Charlie's eyes drifted to the yard. Three dark lumps lay beneath the feeder. Trembling, Charlie set her mug on the arm of the chair and stood.

She walked haltingly down the porch steps and across the dewy grass. Three dead birds lay beneath the feeder, their bodies stiff and their spindly legs sticking into the air.

26

Jake parked in the circular driveway, double checking the address Abe had given him for Crystal Child's. A hand-painted wooden sign read Earth Voices.

Surrounding the drive but set further back from the road stood five dome-shaped houses. They reminded Jake of gnome huts. Wildflowers grew unkempt between the houses. Behind the domes, he saw a cream-colored barn and a white fence with two horses grazing in a pasture.

Three small kids played on a wooden play set off to the side. A little girl, maybe five, with glossy red hair down to her butt hung from the monkey bars.

"Hey, does a woman named Crystal live here?" he asked the children.

The girl with the red hair released the bars and landed barefoot in the grass. "That's my mom," she said. "She's in the chicken coop. I'll take you." The girl skipped over and reached for his hand.

"Jo?" a man called from the doorway of one of the little

houses. He stepped out. He was tall and broad with dark wavy hair that brushed his shoulders.

Jo stopped and waved eagerly. "Daddy, this man is looking for Mommy!"

The man gestured at the other kids. "You play. I'll help the man," he told her.

Jo bobbed her head and ran back to play. A boy with white-blond hair, wearing corduroy overalls and no shirt, called out to her as he pushed down the slide. "Want to play hide and seek?" he asked.

"Yeah," Jo shouted.

The other child, likely a couple years older than the other two, sat on a swing reading a book. "I'm in," she announced, folding the book closed and tossing it on the wooden platform.

The man strode to Jake, eyeing him and his truck. "You're looking for Crystal?" he asked.

"Yeah. Hi. Jake Edwards." Jake stuck out his hand, and the man shook it.

"Ezra. Can I inquire what you want with her?" He asked politely, but Jake sensed that if his answer wasn't satisfactory, he wouldn't get anywhere near the woman.

Jake glanced toward the kids as they disappeared behind the house. "Well, it's a long, weird story, but I lived at the Northern Michigan Asylum when I was a kid."

The man frowned, clearly not liking where Jake had started.

"I'm hoping Crystal knows what happened to a girl there—"

"Crystal isn't in the habit of dredging all that up, friend," the man told him.

Jake started to say more, but stopped when a stunning woman with long red-gold hair came. He recognized her from newspaper clippings he'd seen about her abduction.

Her hair swayed as she walked. She wore a long paisley skirt and a man's flannel shirt, mismatched and yet perfectly falling on her curvy body. Green eyes gazed from her milky face, and a touch of pink lit her cheeks as if she'd spent the day in the sun.

"Ezra?" she started and then she noticed Jake. She paused, studying him. "You're here for me," she said, not asking, but seeming to know. "Ezra, honey, Merriweather is plucking Belle's feathers again. Do you think you can put Belle in the happy room?"

"You're okay?" Ezra asked her, shooting a wary glance at Jake. "He's here about asylum stuff."

Crystal smiled. "He has good reasons," she murmured. "I'm fine. We'll have some tea on the porch?" she asked Jake.

"Uh, yeah, sure. Tea would be great."

Ezra headed toward the barn, turning twice to cast backward glances at Jake.

"Come with me," Crystal said, beckoning to Jake as she walked up the stairs to the dome house Ezra had stepped out of several minutes before.

Despite its bizarre exterior, the interior of the house was relatively normal, though rustic, with unfinished wood furniture, eclectic and brightly colored mismatched couches and chairs, and stacks of books on every surface. A scattering of children's toys lay around the room.

"Don't mind the mess," Crystal laughed, stepping over a pile of little wooden cats painted in shades of pink and purple. "Housekeeping has never been my strong suit."

Jake chuckled. "Mine either. My saving grace is working a lot. It doesn't leave me much time to mess things up."

Crystal nodded. "That would work for me if I didn't have Ezra and Jo in here when I'm gone. Jo moves through the room like a whirling dervish and Ezra can't put an item in the same place twice. But don't think for a minute I'm any better. I start a new project every day and I'm likely to take a year to finish it." She pointed at an enormous drafting table along one wall scattered with words cut from books and magazines. "Poetry collage," she said.

She took a pitcher from her refrigerator and poured them each a glass. "It's hibiscus tea. But I can also make coffee if you'd prefer?"

"No, tea is great," he insisted, though he'd never had hibiscus tea and doubted he'd have ordered it if he saw it on a menu somewhere.

She led him to a back porch. Each of the houses had a little half-moon porch attached to the back.

Crystal waved at another woman two houses away. "I've collected the eggs, Marnie. I'll bring some by later," Crystal called.

The woman gave her a peace sign. "Thanks, Crys. I'm heading to a reiki share in the morning if you and Ezra want to join. Doug said he'll stay home with the kids."

"Maybe," Crystal told her.

She sat on one of two wooden benches, both covered by purple and turquoise cushions. On the porch rail an incense burner released a stream of woody-smelling smoke.

"You work with the earth," she said. "And hate"—she squinted as if trying to catch the tail end of a vision jumping out of her line of sight—"watermelon. And you get headaches." She tapped a finger to her temple.

He stared at her, not sure how to respond. "Umm... yes. That was weirdly accurate. Are you a mind-reader or something?"

She laughed. "Or something. So, what brings you here to Earth Voices?"

"I saw the name on the wooden sign. What does it mean?" Jake asked.

"It's a poem by Bliss Carman. We are a community of poets and nature lovers. One evening, before we started the community, Ezra was reading aloud from a book of poetry. He read 'Earth Voices,' and there was this hush.

I heard the spring wind whisper
Above the brushwood fire,
The world is made forever
Of transport and desire.
I am the breath of being,
The primal urge of things;
I am the whirl of star dust,
I am the lift of wings."

Crystal closed her eyes as she recited the poem and when she opened them, they sparkled as if she might cry.

"It's nice," he told her.

Jake had never been a reader of poetry and the few times he studied it in school, he'd complained incessantly to Faye and Lennon. However, he'd never heard a woman as beautiful as Crystal speaking the words as the sun played on her crimson hair. The place felt like a poem, an unreachable dream that frankly he found disconcerting.

"Tell me your story, Jake," she said, leaning back and drawing her legs up on the bench and stretching them long. Silver rings decorated her slender toes and she'd painted her toenails in alternating shades of green and purple.

"I lived at the asylum when I was a boy. Not for long, maybe six months. My memory is..." He shook his head. "Cloudy. In fact, I didn't remember it at all until a week ago. I started working with a hypnotist and he regressed me or whatever. The memories have started to come back. Not all of them, just like..." He pointed at the incense. "Like the sky is the complete story and I'm getting that tendril of smoke."

She looked at the drifting gray and nodded.

"I had friends there," he continued. "Two girls. Petra and—"

"Maribelle," Crystal whispered knowingly.

27

"Maribelle." He echoed the name back to her. "Something happened. I got out. I don't know how or why, but… she must have died."

"She did die," Crystal confirmed.

"It feels important, her death. I just…" He slapped both his hands against the side of his head. "I wish it would all just fucking come back. Do you hear me?" He knocked hard on the side of his head.

Crystal swung her legs down and planted her feet on the porch. "Let's go for a walk. Those feelings need room to move around."

"Sure, yeah." He stood and took a quick drink of his tea. It was cold and refreshing but a little floral for his liking. He followed her off the steps.

A large fenced-in garden stood next to the barn. When they passed the chicken coop, he noticed Ezra squatting in a separate enclosure talking with a chicken who looked half plucked. She clucked at him and nuzzled her beak against his hand.

"There, Belle, see," he reassured the chicken. "Your own little oasis free from that mean old Merriweather."

Crystal laughed, and Ezra looked up. He stood as they passed. "Going for a walk?" he asked, eyes shifting to Jake.

"Yep. See you in a bit." She waved and walked on, barefoot, into the trees. A dirt trail cut through the forest.

Crystal leaned down and brushed her fingers over a patch of fat green leaves coming up from the dirt. "Ramp season," she told him. "Ezra makes the most delicious soup."

"What are ramps?" Jake asked.

"Wild onions."

"Yum," he said. He liked onions, and Faye had made delicious soups, but years as a bachelor had him ensconced in the eggs or sandwiches camp. Easy, fewer dishes and no need to forage in the woods. He enjoyed the woods well enough, but rarely found the time to make nature walks a priority.

"How can I help you, Jake?" Crystal asked, turning and walking backward so she could face him. He started to tell her to watch out, but she deftly stepped over a root in the path.

"I don't know. I think I've reached desperation. Petra appeared at my office, and ever since it's like I've been living in a nightmare and I can't seem to wake up."

"Petra was the girl you knew at the asylum?"

"Yeah. But I didn't remember her. She showed up at my office and told me we'd lived at the asylum as kids and I thought she was yanking my chain. I told her as much. And then…" He paused, remembering Norm's stricken voice on the phone. "And then something terrible happened to her. No one knows what. There was blood all over her apartment and she disappeared."

Crystal's face fell. "That's horrible."

Jake nodded. "And maybe nothing would have come of her showing up at my office except I tried to call her back, and that's when her neighbor found the blood and he started screaming, so I called the police and I went to her house. Now I'm on this madman's rollercoaster and I can't seem to get off. I want my old life back. I just want to get up and go to work and dig dirt and go have a few beers and—" He threw his hands up. "I didn't ask for this and I don't want it, but it won't go away. I'm not sleeping right and someone is screwing with me. Petra's blouse ended up in my office, and someone left this creepy Barbie on my doorstep. I'm starting to think I'm having a nervous breakdown." The words rushed out like a dam breaking. Finally, he clamped his teeth shut.

Crystal continued walking backward, and he was grateful not to see judgment in her face. "We don't get to choose. Not really. When it's time, it's time. This is your time, Jake. Life isn't meant to be that thing, that get-up-and-work-and-drink-a-few-beers thing. Sometimes I think the cold water in the face happens when we're living with our eyes closed. That's what you've been doing, right? Living on autopilot. You've blocked out whole chunks of your existence. You're not integrated. Now it's time to do the hard work. It's time to live again."

"Fuck all," he muttered, tilting his head back.

Crystal grinned. "It's not easy. I know. I lived it once myself, and I had nowhere near the battle you're facing because I hadn't repressed things. And really, my role was to facilitate the awakening of others. It awakened me too. I lost the love of my life. I went through pregnancy and childbirth without the father of my child. I was starved and hated and nearly murdered." She smiled as she spoke, but her eyes looked haunted. "But I grew through that pain and I wasn't the only one. I see it differently now. As a crucible. Maybe we're all just playing our part in the awakening of the land itself, in whatever trauma it's trying to evolve out of."

Jake frowned. "I'm afraid you're losing me."

She nodded and turned forward, slowing so they walked side by side. "There's something in the land at the asylum. There's a life there. Just as we're on a journey, it is too. You're part of its journey. It's part of yours.

I am the master-builder

In whom the ages trust.
I lift the lost perfection
To blossom from the dust."

"Huh?"

"The poem, 'Earth Voices.' The earth has its own story, its own return to balance when things have been disrupted."

"I think you have a much loftier view of all this than I do," Jake admitted, tempted to kick a sapling beside the trail. The urge almost made him laugh. It was the behavior of a grumpy child.

"Life's bigger than us." Crystal gestured at a tree. "Look at that elm. You're a single leaf, Jake. Does the leaf know that? Not if it functions like a human being, it doesn't. In our minds, we're the center, we're the whole thing, but we're not. Theoretically we know that, but in our brains and bodies, we continue to feel individual. The story of your life isn't merely about you. If the leaf gets sick, where is the origin of the disease? In the leaf? Or is it in the tree, the trunk, the roots, the ground? How can we know without going further back, deeper into the story that came before yours?"

"Which I'm trying to do. I mean, I think I am. Right? I'm trying to find out what happened at the asylum—what happened to Maribelle."

"Maribelle Claude," Crystal confirmed.

"And Maribelle's sister was—"

"Greta. The woman who abducted me," Crystal said. "I'll tell you what I can, but like you, I only glimpsed a fraction of the story. Maribelle and Greta were the twin daughters of Joseph Claude, the asylum caretaker. According to Greta, their father killed people as sacrifices to the land. It all comes back to the land," she murmured, brushing her fingers over the soft purple flower on a tall thistle. Beneath the tuft of purple, sharp green prickers poked from the stalk of the plant. "For a long time, the girls believed there was a monster in the woods. Later, Greta believed the monster was the land itself. Which I don't think is quite right. Something dark exists there, but I don't believe it always has."

"But you just said it all comes back to the land," Jake countered.

"I did, but I think it's what happened on the land. I don't think the soil and grass and trees on the asylum property are evil. When have you ever met a malicious flower? Men, on the other hand..."

"You said their father murdered people. Is that what made the place...?" The word 'evil' stood on the tip of his tongue but he couldn't force it out.

Hypnotism, repressed memories, ghosts and now evil land. He wanted to shake his head and laugh and then hop in his truck and speed back to the ordinary world.

"It started before Claude," Crystal said. "Joseph Claude believed he was servicing some other force that already existed."

"But he ended up in the mental institution. Who's to say this entire nightmare wasn't born from his"—Jake twirled his finger by his head—"craziness?"

"You spoke to Abe Levett?" Crystal asked.

Jake nodded.

"Then you know it goes back further than Joseph Claude."

Jake sighed and threw his hands up in the air. "A bunch of whacko doctors and a crazy caretaker doesn't equal a supernatural mystery."

"Jake." Crystal stopped and put a hand on Jake's arm. The touch jolted him as if a current of truth he'd been denying coursed through him at her touch. She faced him and stared into his face. Her gaze was intense, and he wanted to look away. "Don't," she told him. "Open up. Allow yourself to know the things you already know."

He frowned, held her stare for another second, and then shifted his eyes to the high trees and chuckled uncomfortably.

Crystal released him and resumed walking.

"When Greta and Maribelle were young," Crystal said, "Maribelle kept a ring from one of her father's murder victims. She intended to take it to police and turn her father in. She wanted to escape the house. But Greta told Joseph, and he forced Maribelle into the institution. He and the doctors in the asylum were in it together. Maribelle died in the asylum. I don't know how or why. My sister did some looking after I went missing. She discovered that police covered for the hospital. Despite the condition of the little girl's body, which a nurse said showed clear signs of foul play, they ruled it an accidental death."

"I think she died the night we tried to run away," Jake murmured.

They said little as they wound their way back through the trees toward the barn.

As they stepped from beneath the shade of trees, Crystal stopped. "Listen," she said, stepping closer to him. "This may sound far out, but if you're open to it, we might be able to help you here. We have a space where we do healing rituals with sacred medicine. Mushrooms might help to open the doorway into your past."

He smirked. "Are you talking about magic mushrooms?"

"Psilocybin. Yes. One of our group is a professor. He's a psychiatrist who specializes in mycology. He works with people suffering from severe PTSD. My healing after the experience at the asylum was accelerated by Gerard's work. I'd be happy to facilitate something here for you."

Jake stuffed his hands in his pockets and gazed at the fields on the opposite side of the road. He'd never taken drugs. He'd smoked dope a few times in college, but whenever a friend had pulled out strips of LSD or a handful of pills, he'd adamantly refused to try them.

Mind-altering substances spooked him. He didn't like the thought of being out of control.

"This is a safe place," Crystal continued. "Let me explain it to you. We have a small cottage out back. Gerard would attend, and Marnie with the singing bowl. You'd take a prescribed amount of psilocybin and then Gerard would help walk you back in time if that's possible. I'd be there making sure you were fed and watered. It's really a beautiful experience. I understand your hesitation—truly, I do—but the modern world of medicine disregards so much of the human experience. We're meant to be whole, but living with trauma creates fractured people. You're fractured, Jake. Let's try to put you back together."

Jake hadn't spoken since she'd asked the question and his thoughts were flipping and flopping. His normal brain shrieked, *No, no, no.* But another voice, barely audible, whispered, *Yes...*

"Okay. Let's do it," he blurted.

Immediately he wanted to take the words back, but Crystal's eyes lit up and she beamed, grabbing his hand and pulling him back toward the houses.

28

The cottage included a single square room, the floor covered in orange and burgundy rugs. Throw pillows sat in a circle.

Crystal arranged candles on the wood floor as Ezra tugged heavy dark curtains over the windows.

"There's no electricity out here," Ezra explained. "We try to keep the space clear."

"Clear?" Jake asked.

"Free of manipulated energies," a man said, slipping through the door and bringing with him a surge of amber light as the sun set beyond the trees. "Electricity conducted through wires, for instance." He held out his hand. "I'm Gerard Gunter."

"The professor," Crystal told Jake with a wink.

Jake shook the man's hand, taken aback by the sight of him. He towered over Jake, who was tall at six feet. A masculine square head sat on his thick neck, his hair was buzzed close to his scalp and he wore an army fatigue jacket paired with rumpled blue jeans.

Gerard squinted at him in the firelight and then glanced

down at his outfit and laughed. "It's my day off. I promise, I didn't print my PhD off at Kinko's."

Jake smiled and shrugged, wiping the surprised look from his face. "I think I expected someone more..."

"Nerdy?" Gerard asked, stacking two pillows before plopping down on his butt.

"Small," Jake admitted.

Crystal laughed. "Yeah. He's extra useful when apple-picking season comes around."

Gerard nodded. "Not to mention when Ezra throws the frisbee on the roof, which happens at least once a day all summer long."

"I'd hardly say once a day," Ezra grumbled, though he suppressed a smile.

"I'd like you to meet the golden teacher," Gerard said, pulling a glass jar out of the leather satchel slung over his shoulder.

Jake gazed into the bottom of the jar where several shriveled mushrooms lay coiled together. "The 'golden teacher?'" he mused, struggling to reconcile the name with the gnarled glob before him.

Gerard grinned. "It's the name given to this strain of mushroom. And it's a worthy one. I promise you."

Ezra grabbed a pillow and sat down near Gerard.

A single hollow knock sounded on the door. Crystal opened it to reveal Marnie, the woman Jake had seen earlier. She walked into the cottage carrying a stack of blankets. Balanced on top sat a large copper-colored bowl.

"Crystal said you've done this before?" Jake asked, shifting from sitting on his butt to his knees. He wasn't used to sitting on the floor and it had his joints muttering in irritation.

Gerard beamed. "Two or three times a week for more than five years."

Jake glanced at Ezra, wondering if the man was kidding.

"It's true," Ezra assured him.

"Not often here in the cottage," Gerard went on. "I have an office where I work with clients. My teaching assistant at the university is my sitter."

"Your sitter?"

"She tends to the needs of the patient. Water, food, blankets—that kind of thing. I talk them through the experience."

"But aren't those illegal?" Jake nodded at the jar.

"Yes," Gerard admitted. "They're a schedule one controlled substance."

"So how—"

"Healing with psychedelics is my life's purpose," Gerard said, unscrewing the top on the jar. "I adhere to the laws of men but not at the expense of my humanity. We created Earth Voices because all of us here understand that our work in the world is bigger than collecting a paycheck and following the rules. Is it risky to perform these healing rituals? Sure, I'm breaking laws that could cost me my job and possibly my freedom. Is it worth it? Absolutely."

Crystal listened to Gerard, her eyes shimmering as he spoke.

"And we're careful," Ezra added. "Gerard has worked for years with a lot of his patients. He rarely does a mushroom healing with someone he just met." Although he tried to hide it, Jake sensed a note of disapproval in Ezra's tone.

Crystal looked at him sidelong, but it was Gerard who acknowledged the comment. "Not always, Ezra. And who better than Crystal to recognize a person who would benefit from such a journey? Mind you, we can all benefit from the journey, but certain people need it more than others."

"Oh, great, I'm that guy, huh?" Jake muttered.

Crystal and Gerard laughed, but Ezra remained impassive.

Marnie sat on a pillow in the room's corner, the copper bowl resting in her lap. She picked up a wooden mallet and gently tapped it against the side of the bowl. It released a low ring like a church bell, which ignited goosebumps along Jake's arms.

"Background music?" he asked.

She smiled and closed her eyes, tracing the mallet around the outside of the bowl where it released a steady hum. "This," she told him, "is a singing bowl. The sound is soothing, but it's the vibration we're after. Close your eyes, Jake, and feel it."

The others in the room closed their eyes and after a moment, feeling like the only person in the chapel who hadn't bowed his head to pray, he let his eyelids drift shut.

Jake listened to the ting as the wooden mallet struck the bowl's edge. The sound stretched and filled the room. After several seconds, the hum stopped.

When he opened his eyes, they all gazed at him.

He laughed uncomfortably. "Yeah. That was interesting."

"You ain't seen nothin' yet," Gerard told him.

Crystal handed him a jar of peanut butter and a spoon.

"Don't tell me peanut butter has some spiritual purpose here," Jake said. "All this time, I've had a jar sitting on my counter at home."

Crystal laughed. "The peanut butter helps cover the taste of the mushrooms. It makes swallowing them a little less unpleasant."

He eyed the dried mushrooms. "Are they gross?"

Gerard shrugged. "To each their own. They taste like earth to me."

"They're gross," Crystal countered. "But you're not eating them for flavor."

She unscrewed the lid, and Gerard stuck a spoon into the soft wave of peanut butter. Jake smelled it and thought of the peanut butter cookies Faye used to make for Lennon. He thought then of Charlie roaming the same halls he'd run through as a kid and smiled.

Gerard pulled out three withered mushroom caps and pushed them into the nut butter. He handed the spoon to Jake.

"Bottoms up," Jake said, sticking the spoon in his mouth and grimacing as he chewed.

The peanut butter hid whatever flavor the mushrooms released, but it did little to help with texture. When he finally choked it down, Crystal handed him a glass of water, which he swallowed in two large gulps.

"Now what?" he asked.

"Now we wait," Gerard told him.

∽

TWENTY MINUTES PASSED, and he took a sip of water.

"I don't feel anything."

"You will," Gerard said. "Just remember you're safe. Whatever arises for you in here, it's a temporary state of consciousness. Regardless of what your mind tells you, the usual constructs of reality will return."

It started with color. Jake looked at Crystal, and then shifted his eyes toward the candle flickering near the door. As his eyes moved, the green of Gerard's jacket streaked with him, leaving a trail of moss green across the space between them. The candle flame danced and grew tall and then short. It reached up and up and he held a breath, expecting it to catch the ceiling on fire, but then it shrank and he saw that it was merely the tiny flickering orange of a candle.

"I think it's starting," he blurted, eyes darting to Gerard. Relaxed a moment before, he suddenly felt the muscles in his legs and arms tense. He wanted to backtrack an hour and turn down the offer.

"Good. Let's get ready then, shall we?" Gerard nodded his head at Marnie, who traced the singing bowl, its haunting cry pouring out.

Jake tilted his head forward, chin resting on his chest, and listened to the sorrowful call of the bell.

Another bell clanged in his mind, the church bell at Sacred Heart. He felt his mother's rough dry grip on his hand as she pulled him toward the cement steps that led up to the narrow white church. The priest watched him with unreadable eyes, but Jake knew he disapproved of the boy born out of wedlock who claimed to see visions of the dead. His feet grew leaden, and he tried to pull back.

When Jake opened his eyes, the floor of the cottage swam before him. He snapped his head up.

Gerard smiled at him. Ezra had left, but Crystal sat in the same place on the pillow. His eyes followed the blue of her shirt down to her milky hands resting in her lap, fingers woven together. He studied her pale pink cuticles and her fingernails trimmed to meet the tips of her fingers. Her hands were powder white against the bright skirt whose colors and patterns whorled and orbited. He blinked at the swirling design.

"Would you like to lie down, Jake, and put a lavender pillow over your eyes?" Gerard asked, patting the bed they'd made for him on the floor.

"Uh-huh," he murmured, lying on his side. His hand brushed the blanket beneath him and he swiped his palm back and forth across the fabric, soft and velvety and deep. He felt if he pushed, his hand would pass through the blanket and into another dimension, a world where everything was plush and enveloping.

The room throbbed around him. The images expanded out and drew back in as if it breathed, the wood beams above him, the soft purple-hued pillow as Gerard lowered it towards his eyes.

The scent and weight of the pillow swaddled his forehead. It did not merely press upon his eyes but seemed to wrap fully around his skull, cool and silken, and the scent...

"She smells like a garden," he whispered and giggled as he had as a boy when Maribelle had spoken the words about

Nurse Minnie—the nurse in the children's ward whom they'd all loved, who snuck in treats for the kids and told stories when you had to take the icky medicine to distract you from the taste.

Minnie. He didn't know if he'd said her name out loud, but slowly a vision of her emerged—tall and slender with delicate features and long brown hair she kept tight in a bun, except once in a while when she played ring-around-the-rosie, and her hair pulled loose and flowed over her white smock. She'd seemed old to him then, but now Jake knew she hadn't been a day over forty. Unless her hair fell down and then, she seemed like a girl dressed in a nurse's uniform.

"It's in the ground," he shouted and sat up.

The pillow flew to the wood floor.

The room had gone dark except for the candlelight. The bowl sang on. Molten eyes peered out from the faces of Gerard and Crystal.

Jake jumped to his feet and ran from the cabin.

"Jake!" Gerard called behind him, but Jake leapt from the top step to the ground.

The night burst with dark colors and sensations. He felt as if he'd plunged into an ocean on a black night. He gasped and stumbled forward.

Gerard touched his shoulder. "Jake. What do you need?"

"It's okay, Jake," Crystal told him. "Remember, you took mushrooms, and this is just a temporary condition. It's already receding the moment it begins."

"Exactly," Jake exclaimed as he turned to look at them. His eyes felt enormous, the size of bowling balls. "I have to find the knife before it's gone, before I forget."

He ran across the yard, studying the trees and the ground. It all moved—waves of shadow and light. Nothing was separate. It flowed together in a symphony, a dance. He might have been looking at a river rather than a forest.

"I can't find it," he muttered, looking and looking, but the earth didn't match his memories of that place.

"Jake," Gerard told him, "you're here with us at Earth Voices. It's not here. Let's go back into the room and you can speak what you remember and I will record it all. Tomorrow, when the effects have cleared, you will know where to look."

Jake shook his head and dropped to his knees. He crawled across the ground, seeking the pulsing. That was how he'd found it before. It breathed below the earth.

The grass was cool and fragrant beneath his hands. He leaned down and pressed his face into the stalks of green, smelled the dirt and smiled at the ground.

"I've always loved it," he murmured. "This."

He dug both hands into the soil and came back up with two handfuls of dirt. He held it out to Crystal and Gerard so they could admire it, the freshness. He wanted to be neck deep in it. He rubbed the dirt and grass over his face and head. He grabbed two more handfuls and inhaled it before pressing it against his cheeks. He held it there, and then he remembered the knife and resumed his digging, throwing handfuls of dirt behind him.

He heard Crystal asking Gerard what to do and Gerard insisting they let him be, but their voices, their presence, barely registered.

As he stared into the black hole, two hands stretched out to grab his face.

He screamed and reeled backwards, scrambling away from the hole. When he looked back, the hands had vanished. The hole looked bigger, as if a whole person could fit inside, as if he'd dug a grave.

Jake jumped up and looked wildly at Gerard.

"Jake," Gerard told him slowly. "Let's go back to the cottage and lie down. Things are coming up, and you wanted to talk about them. Remember? You wanted to tell us, so we could write it down and help you remember."

"Did you see her hands?" Jake shrieked, though some part of him knew they hadn't seen the woman's hands. Only he could see them and that thought tumbled into another. "Only I could see them," he told Gerard and Crystal. "The ghosts. Only me. No one else could see them."

"Good. That's good." Gerard steered him back toward the cottage. "That's a memory you didn't have and now we will go inside where it's safe and we're going to write it all down."

Jake walked heavily back toward the cabin. A woman stood near the stairs. He slouched forward, trying to make her out. All the world seemed oozy and soft. Her dark hair gave way to dark streaks on her face and on her pale skin.

Petra Collins stood beside the cottage. Her arms hung slack at her sides. A gash had opened her throat and released a plume of red down her white shirt. She didn't look at him, but behind him, eyes wide and round as if the man who'd slashed her throat crouched behind Jake.

Jake whipped around, startling both Gerard and Crystal. Crystal started and let out a little yelp.

A sea of darkness stretched beyond them and no shadowy man emerged. Above them the stars glittered like a billion seedlings in the blackest soil he'd ever seen.

Gerard put a hand on his back and guided him back toward the cottage.

Petra was gone.

29

Charlie set her coffee mug on the counter and started back to the porch. Before she'd walked through the doorway, the shattering of ceramic made her jump. She turned around to see her mug broken on the wood floor.

Unnerved, but refusing to think about what had made it fall —she knew full well she'd put the cup a good three or four inches away from the edge—she walked to the hall closet for the little broom and dustpan. When she opened the door, cold air flooded out.

Behind the coats she could see a crack in the wall. She must not have fully closed it when Jake had visited days before and shown her the secret passages.

Bones meowed at her from the doorway to the living room.

"Come here, Bones. Want to go exploring with me?"

He started over and then stopped, his tail pricking and the fur on his back slowly rising as if someone had just rubbed a helium-filled balloon down his back. He stood perfectly still, gazing at the open closet.

"Bones," she said, taking a step toward him.

He spun around and raced down the hall and disappeared up the stairs.

Charlie bit her lip as a sudden surge of tears welled behind her eyes. "What do you want?" she shouted into the empty house.

She hadn't expected an answer, and truth be told, she didn't want an answer. She wanted the ghost to go away, leave her to start her new life without dishes breaking and invisible hands snaking around her throat.

Grabbing the broom and dustpan, she returned to the kitchen and swept up the cups, dumping the ceramic pieces into the trash bin. When she returned to the closet, she studied the crack in the wall for a long time.

"I will not be afraid of my own house," Charlie stated loudly.

She grabbed the flashlight off the shelf above the coats and flipped it on. When she pulled the panel of the wall back, another gust of cold air surrounded her.

The chill hadn't been there days earlier when Jake revealed the secret hall. Although that evening, she'd been floating on a wine buzz and the fuzzy feelings of attraction to Jake Edwards.

Charlie edged into the narrow space, ducking slightly. Her breath grew shallow and rapid, as if the cold were so cold it had constricted her diaphragm. Except it wasn't cold that choked her breath, but fear. Eyes wide, flashlight extended and ready to club anything that moved in the dim space, she walked forward.

A kind of peaceful quiet generally permeated Wilder's Grove, but in the murky passage, the silence descended like a callused hand clamped over her mouth and nose.

Five feet in, the tunnel made a hard right, moving between the walls that separated the study from the downstairs bathroom. As Charlie crept, her foot struck something soft. She gasped and spun back towards the opening.

Remembering her flashlight, Charlie forced her feet to stop. She swung back to face whatever lay in the tunnel. As she focused the beam down, she peered at a lumpy blue mass on the floor. Dark nylon handles stuck from the top of the fabric and after a moment, she made sense of the object.

"It's a backpack," she murmured.

Charlie grabbed the bag by one strap and turned back toward the opening, carrying the bag out of the closet and onto the front porch. She needed the comforts of bright light, the warmth of the day and, most importantly, sounds. Birds chirped in the trees, and down the street an old man in khaki shorts and knee-high socks tackled bushes in front of his house with a weed-whacker.

Charlie sat on the top step and savored the noise, shaking off the oppressive quiet from the tunnel.

The backpack was old and ragged, its front pocket ripped and hanging. She unzipped the inner pocket and reached in, pulling out a yellowed envelope. Tucked inside, she found three faded photographs and a list written in a child's sloppy writing.

She looked at the photos. In the background of each stood a massive brick building.

In one photo, a boy with light-colored hair stood next to a diminutive woman wearing a plain gray dress. Her hair was pulled tightly back from her face and she looked beyond the picture-taker as if in a hurry for the ordeal to be over, so she could walk away. Her lips were pressed in an unsmiling line. The boy also did not smile. His confused eyes were tilted up towards the woman and his mouth drooped as if on the verge of tears.

The second two photos also captured the boy, but now he did smile. In one, with the same towering buildings in the background, he was bundled in winter gear, a scarf dangling from his neck and a checkered winter hat covering his blond head. A girl buried in an oversized coat stood next to him, her face as pale as the snow and her hair dark and long.

The third photo revealed the same boy and girl a second

time, but now a third girl had joined the pair. She had dirty blonde hair and shy downcast eyes. The dark-haired girl held a Barbie doll in a striped bathing suit. The boy made a face at the camera while the dark-haired girl smiled big and cheerfully. Only this photo had writing on the back in pretty cursive. *Jacob, Maribelle and Petra. The Northern Michigan Asylum, May 1966.*

Charlie leaned in closer to the picture, recognizing the shape of the boy's nose and mouth. The little boy was Jake Edwards.

She smoothed out the crumpled list that she'd found with the picture and read the clumsy writing of a child.

Getaway Plan
Pants, shirts, underwear
Sneak two pudding cups, two apples and two rolls
Dagger
Nurse Minnie keeps twelve dollars in a tin box in her cubby. Leave IOU.
Two bus tickets to Christmas town. Leave Petra a note.

She smiled at the kids' sloppy handwriting, their cute plan. She looked a second time at the pictures, puzzling at the large buildings. A boarding school? Except the note referenced a nurse. The children didn't look sick. Then again, maybe the note had nothing to do with the photos.

Bones shimmied along her back and walked across her lap.

"Hi, Mr. Bones?" She rubbed beneath his chin. "Think we should call Jake about this?"

Bones purred and wandered away, jumping onto the porch railing and eyeing a blue jay perched in a magnolia tree in the front yard. The tree had begun to flower and pink blossoms clung to its spindly branches.

Before she could talk herself out of it, she stood and hurried into the house, grabbing the cordless phone in the living room. Jake's phone number was written on a notepad in her desk. She punched his numbers in and waited, nervously tapping her fingers on the walls as she walked back to the porch.

His message machine greeted her.

"Jake, this is Charlie Pepin. I found something of yours in one of the secret passages. I thought you might want it. Give me a call, it's Charlie. Oh, I already said that." She laughed and hung up, resting the phone against her head.

"What are you, twelve?" she murmured, but she felt suddenly giddy.

30

"Jacob... Jacob..." The woman's voice whispered across the room.

Icy cold, he pulled his thin blanket tighter to his chin and rolled over. "No," he murmured, half awake, shivering.

"Jacob... follow me..."

The voice registered, the words sliding cold and slick into his head and pooling in his skull. He felt the fingers of a migraine kneading the soft tissue of his brain.

He stuffed the pillow over his head and drove his face into the mattress. Everything felt cold. He wanted another blanket, another layer of clothing.

"Socks," he muttered, still in the indistinct murk of half-dreaming.

"Jacob. It's up to you. Set me free, Jacob..."

He sat up in bed and saw her. Dark hair and eyes as black as a raven's. She put a finger to her dead lips and beckoned with the other hand.

Dazed, he stood and followed her. The hall lay dark except for the light at the far end, the nurses' station. Several doors away he heard the orderly, Ralph, performing nightly checks.

His feet were cold, and his skin prickled and wrapped tighter against his muscles and bones.

The woman did not walk. She floated in an icy vapor. Her white dress billowed out and wrapped him in a frigid cloud. He gasped and stopped, and she drifted far enough away that he could breathe again.

"Come," she whispered, and he went.

He followed her down the corridor and to the door that was always locked but somehow, on this night, was not.

Down the cement stairs, through another door. The station where the night people watched stood empty. Out into the night, stars bright and glittering in the huge sky. He tilted his head up and tried to see it, but it went on forever.

"Jacob," she urged, and her voice slithered like poison dripped into his ear.

He followed her into the black woods where anything might hide, but nothing crept among the leaves, no yellow eyes peered at him from the darkness. *These are her woods*, he thought, and nothing dared disturb him when he walked with her.

Down the hill he trod where the willow had died and now the trees grew horizontal across the ground. He ducked beneath a crooked trunk, branches splayed, and there she knelt, a hand resting on a patch of earth that seemed to glow red.

The soil pulsed beneath his feet.

"Dig," she whispered, and he did.

~

JAKE WOKE with his hip aching and a blanket tangled through his legs. He thrashed until he managed to pull the blanket off and fling it aside, where it hit a candle that rolled across the wood floor.

The dream, or had it been a memory, tumbled through his mind.

Dull morning light, mostly blocked by curtains, leaked into the room. No hangover plagued him, but he did feel… odd. As if the night before he'd journeyed into another dimension and the residue of the place still clung to his skin.

A glass of water sat near the door along with a folded note. He opened and it read, 'Come have breakfast with us.'

When he creaked open the cabin door, the light hit him full force, and he shielded his eyes and leaned against the door frame until his legs agreed to successfully navigate the wooden steps down from the cottage. He couldn't remember the last time he'd slept on a floor, but it hadn't been a regular occurrence since his twenties and his hips, lower back and ankles all seemed to be queuing up to give him their opinions on the matter.

"It's official," he muttered, walking gingerly down the steps. "I'm old."

"Nah." A voice startled him, and he turned to see Marnie guiding a horse through the open fence of the small pasture. "I like to call a man your age ripe."

"Ripe? I don't think I've been ripe since I was nineteen."

Marnie laughed and closed the gate, pointing to the back deck of Crystal's house. "Ezra made pancakes," she told him.

Jake saw Crystal and her daughter Jo on the wooden benches. Crystal looked up and waved. He limped over, the movement slowly oiling his rusted joints.

"That wood floor did a number on ya?" Crystal asked, nodding at his legs.

"Yeah." Jake stretched his arms overhead and then did a few squats, his knees and ankles popping with each movement.

"Snap, crackle, pop," Jo giggled. "You sound like Rice Krispies."

"I feel like Rice Krispies," he laughed, holding the rail as he walked onto the porch.

"Coffee?" Ezra called through the open glass door.

"Please," Jake responded. "I may need a half gallon to get this engine started."

"Marnie's husband roasts our coffee," Crystal explained. "He sources it from a farm in Ecuador. It's really lovely."

"So long as it's caffeinated, I'm in," Jake told her, easing onto a bench and rolling each foot.

"Would you like to do some tai chi after breakfast?" Crystal asked. "It might ease that soreness."

Jake chuckled and shook his head. "I appreciate it, Crystal. All of this, truly. But I've got a lot to digest after last night. A strong cup of coffee and I'll be on my way."

Crystal offered him a sad smile and nodded. "I understand." She stood and disappeared into the house, emerging a moment later with a sheaf of papers. "These are Gerard's notes. He wrote everything you said verbatim and, in the margins, he explained what you were doing at the time."

"Cream or sugar?" Ezra asked, sticking his head through the open door.

"Black for me," Jake told him, taking the notes from Crystal.

His eyes grazed the words. The night before was grainy and the sensations had already begun to fade. Still, he remembered the revelations that had come swimming up and taken hold of him like a shark in night waters. He shuddered at the memory of the woman's hands reaching for his face.

"It's intense," Crystal agreed, watching him.

Ezra stepped onto the porch and handed him a brown mug. Jake sipped the rich coffee and continued skimming: *Buried dagger, asylum escape, steam tunnel, the woman in the woods, Horace...*

He'd thought the memories might flee when the mushrooms wore off, but they remained, nebulous but intact.

"I wrote mine and Gerard's phone numbers on the last page," Crystal told him. "You might need clarification or to talk about some of your memories. Don't hesitate to call, Jake. Even if you don't need help remembering, we'd like to know what happens."

"Pancakes?" Ezra asked, squatting to let Jo climb onto his back from the bench. Jo clung to the man, her arms wrapped around his neck.

"Can I ride with Marnie and Olive now? Please, please. I ate all my pancakes." Jo pointed toward a yellow plate on the bench, empty except for a glistening residue of syrup.

"Sure, Jo-Jo," Ezra told her. "If Mommy says it's okay."

"Give me a kiss first," Crystal told her. "And make sure Marnie sees you before you walk up to Olive."

Jo struggled down from Ezra's back and gave her mom a sticky kiss on the mouth before bouncing off the porch and running across the field where Marnie walked the dark horse toward the trail in the woods.

"We've got half a dozen flapjacks left," Ezra said, mopping his neck with a rag where Jo had left her syrupy fingerprints.

"No, this is perfect. Thanks." Jake finished his coffee and folded the notes, sliding them into the back pocket of his jeans. "I need to get on my way. But thank you both. This was unexpected, but maybe just what I needed.'

Crystal followed him to his truck and handed him a glass jar of water. "Drink the whole thing," she said. "You'll feel better once you're hydrated. And call me, okay?"

"I will. I promise," he assured her.

She took his hand and squeezed and then stepped back so he could close the door of his truck. He watched her return to the little dome house where Ezra stood, waiting.

Jake swallowed the entire jar of water and rested the empty container on his passenger seat. He started his truck and pulled out of the circular drive.

A strong hand suddenly rested on Jake's shoulder. His eyes darted to the rearview mirror as he let off the gas and for an instant, a man's smiling face flickered in the rearview mirror.

Jake slammed the brake, but the face was already gone.

Jake twisted around and looked in the backseat of his truck. Empty except for his toolbox and a rolled print.

"Horace," he whispered.

～

JAKE DIDN'T DRIVE HOME. The thought of sitting in his little house and mulling over the details of the previous night bugged him for reasons he didn't understand. When a sign for Wanda's Waffle House appeared, he hit the brakes and drove into the parking lot.

He sat in a booth with red pleather seats and ordered chicken and waffles. His appetite had risen unexpectedly when he'd walked through the door to the smell of sizzling bacon and the sweet aroma of waffles.

His waitress, Luann, a fifty-something woman with powdered skin and burnt-blonde hair, delivered his coffee and water before bustling down the restaurant to greet a group of older men who'd shuffled in, all clutching newspapers and talking over one another.

Jake pulled the notes from his pocket and spread them on the table. Petra was mentioned nowhere in the neat lines of notes, but he'd discovered something about her the night before as well. She was dead. The mushrooms hadn't conjured the nightmare of Petra's ghost. Instead, they'd opened him to something he'd always known.

"A sixth sense," he said, but that wasn't what his mother and grandparents had called it. *Visions from the devil*, they'd whispered.

But now he knew he'd been able to see the dead as a boy. Like everything else he'd repressed it, but it had returned.

He read Gerard's words: *Dig, dagger, the woman with black eyes...*

"The dagger," Jake murmured. He remembered digging the night before. The belief that the weapon lay in the ground had overwhelmed him, the need to find it. But why?

The memories of his time in the asylum were there now. Not vivid, but they existed. He could see them. Blurred, a little out of focus, but yes, he'd been there.

We were supposed to go back for Petra, he read and knew it was true.

He and Maribelle had plotted their escape. They would go back for Petra, but then...

"Then what?" he whispered, shuffling through the notes.

Something had happened and they'd had to leave right then. Maribelle had run to get the backpack hidden in the cleaning closet.

Outside the diner, the morning sun had been replaced by thick gray clouds. A light drizzle began to fall washing down the windows. Luann returned and filled his coffee. He thanked her and slid the mug toward him.

A crack of thunder split the air and Jake jumped, slopping the scalding coffee onto his hand. A flash of lightning followed and several patrons in the restaurant let out little gasps of surprise. Jake plucked an ice cube from his water and pressed it against the red skin near his thumb.

"Lightning," he murmured.

It had been raining that night. Not drizzling as it was now, but a deluge of rain. It had pounded against the tall asylum windows. Some of the kids on the ward had been agitated. Storms scared them in much the same way dogs got spooked. They whimpered when the thunder cracked. The nurses and orderlies had been busy soothing them.

"We have to go tonight," Jake had insisted, because—

"Chicken and waffles," Luann announced, sliding a plate heaped with fluffy, bronzed waffles and wings of fried chicken in front of him. "Syrup and butter. Can I get you anything else?"

"No. Thanks. This looks great," he told her, but he wasn't looking at the breakfast, he was looking back through time to the dark hallway they'd shuffled into. Horace had told Jake tonight. That was why. The doctors had been planning something, something bad. Maybe Jake wouldn't survive it. They had to go that night.

Maribelle had looked frightened for only a second as she looked at the dark stormy night and then she'd pulled herself up taller and put on her serious face. "At midnight, we leave."

And at midnight, they had left. They'd met in the hallway and slipped down the stairs. The steam tunnel was their way out.

It was there that something had happened. The tunnels were pitch black. They had one flashlight as they ran through the brick pathway, but he couldn't get to that last shred of memory.

∼

JAKE STOOD in the rain and thought of Ricardo's advice that he buy a cell phone. He'd started to see them more and more, but the thought of the constant interruption of a ringing phone on the job made him grind his teeth.

"Dig Deep Excavating," Barbie's chipper voice announced.

"Barbie, it's Jake. I'm not going to make it in today."

"Jake? My goodness, I've called your house five times already. I was starting to worry. I thought I might lock up and drive over there."

"I'm fine. Not at home though. I'm up north and can't get back until tomorrow."

"Oh, my. Well, okay, but Dave Wilson called about getting started on the foundation at his daughter's house. And the neighbors at Stowers' house are threatening to call the DOA unless they see a permit posted about the work near the stream."

"I'll take care of it all tomorrow, Barbie. I've got to go."

She started to say more, but he hung up the phone and walked in the rain to his truck, his boots sloshing through puddles and soaking the hem of his jeans.

31

The rain had stopped by the time Jake reached Traverse City. He parked in an old lot at the asylum where the concrete had cracked and weeds grew through.

The door to the network of steam tunnels beneath the buildings stood in a boxy brick structure no large than a portajohn. A rusted metal sign read 'Private Property.'

Jake smashed the crowbar against the lock. Blue sparks flared, but the lock didn't break. He hit it again and then a third time. It broke off and dropped to the ground with a clatter.

A thick dark yawned below him when he opened the door. He stepped into the black stairway and closed the door firmly before pulling out his flashlight.

Seconds passed as he fumbled to turn it on. He gripped the barrel so hard his hand ached, but if he loosened it, he might drop the light and never find it again.

Click. The light illuminated the dark stairs. A narrow passage took him down, and the dense concrete swallowed the sounds of his footfalls as he descended. At the bottom of the stairs, he met another long narrow concrete hall. He walked slowly, searching for a familiar feeling, a memory tucked in the forgotten place.

The door at the opposite end loomed tall and thick. If it was locked, he'd never get it open. Worse, if someone had followed him in and locked the other door... It was a thought he couldn't avoid, like the terrible what-ifs that plagued children at night when they imagined the black crevices beneath their beds and the hand that might reach out to grab their foot and drag them down.

Jake clutched the door and pulled. It didn't budge, and he grunted and jerked it harder, fighting the rising panic. It flung open, and he stumbled back, his flashlight hitting the wall and blinking out.

"Oh, shit, no," he muttered, twisting the flashlight head back and forth. It turned back on. He moaned, relief flooding through him and dissolving the cement block in his gut.

He stepped into a round room with low ceilings. Old furnaces stood bunched together. Forward, through another door, he moved, and this one opened easily. When he shone his flashlight beyond it, he saw a round brick tunnel.

This was it. The steam tunnel where he'd lost Maribelle.

He blinked and tried to wet his lips, but his mouth had suddenly gone dry. He stepped forward into the brick corridor and the door behind him swung closed. His palm grew slick around the flashlight. He switched it to the other hand and wiped his palm on his jeans, wondering why he'd left his crowbar outside. A plastic flashlight would make a flimsy weapon and if he broke it... well, he'd be lucky to ever find his way back out of the tunnels beneath the asylum.

Jake hesitated, the white circle of his light wobbling over the curve of brick. The keening voices of the Munchkins from *The Wizard of Oz* skated through his mind. 'Follow, follow, follow, follow, follow the yellow brick road.'

The grimy brick slowly melted away. It was lighter, the color of yellowed cream beneath the lantern Maribelle had clutched in her outstretched arm. They'd been halfway through the tunnel when they heard the footsteps behind them.

"Run," she'd screamed and Jake had run.

He'd gotten the door open and rushed through the other corridors, up the stairs and into the night. He'd been almost to the woods when he realized Maribelle hadn't followed him out of the tunnel. He'd turned and started back…

The door had been closed and when Jake had edged it open, the tunnel was black and silent. She had screamed. The sound had pierced the dense hush, and it had faded as if someone carried her away.

Jake had started down the stairs, but Maribelle had had the lantern. The blackness had crowded around him. Afraid, he'd turned and fled back to the rain-drenched forest. He'd waited for hours, but she never appeared.

In the gloom of early morning, he'd walked to the bus station and bought a ticket to Frankenmuth like they'd planned. He'd left her. He'd left her behind.

∼

JAKE DROVE TO TRENT'S, found the door locked. He called Trent from a payphone. "Trent, I need to talk. I've remembered stuff. Can you meet me at your office?"

"Of course. Give me twenty minutes, Jake."

∼

JAKE DIDN'T SIT. He paced around the room, babbling faster than Trent could write.

"I remember! Petra, Maribelle, the asylum. Everything. I

mean, almost everything. Something was happening to me. You know what I think?" He stopped and stared at Trent, but didn't really see him. Instead he looked through him, looked back in time. "I think they were doing experiments on me, like... like in *Jacob's Ladder*. Have you seen that?"

Trent pursed his lips. "The movie where the man believes he was given a drug that turned him into a homicidal maniac?"

"Yes!"

"But then it was all a dying hallucination," Trent countered. "Remember, at the end, we see the principal character was dying in Vietnam. None of the other things happened, the experiment included."

Jake shook his head and walked away. "I don't think his story is literally what happened to me. Just something like that. The doctors at the asylum were experimenting on me. Maybe on all of us little kids... I don't know. Maybe that's why we decided to run away."

"That's very interesting," Trent said, crossing one ankle on top of his opposite leg. "Can you remember any of these experiments?"

"No."

"How about any of the doctors or nurses who might have experimented on you?"

Jake bit his lip hard between his teeth. "Kind of. I remember a room filled with faces. They were all men and a doctor we all liked, us kids, but... I think he was there the night Maribelle died."

"Do you remember his name?"

"I think we called him Gus."

"Gus..." Trent murmured. He crossed and uncrossed his legs. "I must admit, it seems strange that a psychiatric doctor would permit patients to call him Gus, especially children."

Jake nodded. "Maybe so, but... that's what I remember."

"And the night you escaped. What do you remember? You must have had some money? Did you take personal items with you? Toys, clothes?"

"Maribelle had seen Minnie, one of the nurses, take cash out of a tin box in her cubby. Sometimes she'd give it to us kids for the canteen. We stole it, stuck it in our backpack. We had a plan that night and we tried to run away. I waited for Maribelle in the woods, but… she died. I think… someone hurt her. They killed her."

Trent clicked his pen shut and set it on the paper. "Those are serious allegations. Can you prove them?"

"Of course not," Jake huffed. "I ran. I left her. Petra too. We were supposed to come back for Petra. I got on a bus and I never looked back."

"What happened to the stuff you took with you? You said you had a backpack."

Jake thought of the dagger, how he'd buried it in the yard. He started to describe it and then stopped, suddenly chilled. He glanced toward the air conditioner, but it was off. He rubbed his hands over his bare arms. "Did you feel that?" he asked Trent.

"What?"

"A blast of frigid air. It just…" He waved his hand. "I guess the bag is still at Wilder's Grove. There couldn't have been anything important in it. Maybe a change of clothes. For all I know, Faye threw it away."

"Wilder's Grove was your home in Frankenmuth?"

Jake nodded. "Yeah."

"What will you do, Jake? Do you intend to tell the detectives working on Petra's case about the things you've learned?"

"I don't know. Should I? I'm afraid he'll think I'm a lunatic."

Trent chuckled. "Interesting choice of words, considering. And I hate to agree, but I do. Law enforcement officials can be very close-minded. Any evidence that you're unstable and—"

Jake paused by Trent's desk, trying to imagine the look on

Bryant's face if he revealed his latest theory. "They'll think I did something to Petra, but I didn't. And I have an alibi. I worked that day. The thing that worries me is what if I keep my mouth shut and somehow this is related to her disappearance?"

Trent stood and walked to his desk. He tensely shuffled papers and notebooks together. Jake caught a glimpse of a funny looking black journal decorated in red kisses.

"Oh," Jake said, remembering Trent probably had confidential notes from other patients' sessions on his desk. "Sorry, I wasn't reading anything."

Trent waved the comment away. "I've been thinking a lot about the possibility that the mental hospital was connected to Petra's disappearance, and here's my issue with that line of thought. You and Petra were in that asylum thirty years ago. A doctor working there would have been, what? In his thirties or forties? That would make him high sixties, seventies, even eighties today. Petra wasn't a sizeable woman, but... could a seventy-year-old man have incapacitated her? Furthermore, why would one of these doctors have felt the need to silence her?"

Jake collapsed onto the couch, banging his head against the back. "I don't know."

"It's good, the work you're doing to figure out your past, but I'm beginning to think Petra's disappearance is unrelated. Realistically, it's much more likely that a previously abusive boyfriend, even an abusive family member, did something to Petra."

"But"—Jake sat up abruptly, swinging his legs over the side—"someone put her blouse in my office."

Trent nodded. "I've thought about that too. What if a previous boyfriend followed her that morning? Thinking Petra was seeing you, he attacked her in a jealous rage and then put the blouse in your office to send you a message."

Jake bit the side of his hand and nodded. "Wow, yeah. That

makes more sense than I care to admit."

"It makes a lot more sense than an asylum doctor coming after Petra three decades after she was institutionalized."

32

The knock sounded a second time.

Charlie wiped her floury hands on the dishtowel Bev had made her. She'd stitched the words 'The only man I chase is the ice cream man' above a heart-shaped ice cream cone. Charlie smirked and hurried toward the door.

As she walked down the hall, she could see the inky silhouette of the person standing behind it, a man based on his build. She reached for the knob.

"Don't open it!" A woman's voice boomed behind her.

Charlie spun around, more surprised than fearful in those initial seconds. Emptiness down the hall. No woman stood there, but the sound had come from there and it had been a woman's voice.

The man knocked a second time.

Charlie stepped back from the door. The deadbolt was engaged. She suddenly thought she shouldn't open the door, shouldn't slide the deadbolt open and allow the man standing outside into her house.

The glass was opaque. He couldn't see her, but still she

ducked behind the coat rack and peeked out from the black fabric.

He knocked again, louder. And then Charlie heard the rattle of the knob. The man was trying to open the door. She gasped and stumbled backwards, hitting the wall.

The door thumped in the frame as the man shook the knob harder, and then he abruptly stopped and disappeared from the glass.

Charlie scrambled from behind the stand and raced into the kitchen, where she yanked down shades and flipped the lock on the door that led to the porch. There was only one other door, leading from the washroom on the opposite side of the house, but she never unlocked that door.

Charlie ran back to the front hall and sprinted up the stairs. She moved from room to room, searching for the man in her yard and on the street. In a small bedroom at the back of the house where the previous owners had left boxes of antique books, she spotted him. The silver haired man stood tall, over six feet, Charlie thought and the grooves in his face appeared to deepen as he scanned the yard behind her house. His eyes, light initially, darkened when they locked on the window Charlie peered out of.

"Oh, shit." She ducked behind the curtain and stood frozen, her hands two balls of white tension clutching the maroon curtain.

Charlie hadn't recognized him, but his expression made her uneasy.

Crouching, she ducked down to a squat and then crawled on hands and knees to her bedroom, mentally running through every window in the house. Two were probably unlocked—the window above the kitchen sink that looked into the backyard and the window in the study downstairs.

In her room, she jumped up and locked the bedroom door, hurrying to her phone. She didn't care if she sounded nuts to the police. The man had wiggled the doorknob. He'd had every intention of walking in if it were unlocked. She snatched up the phone and punched 911.

Nothing, no dial tone.

She frowned and hit the end button. When she powered it back on, no green light glowed behind the power button. Had she left the cordless off the base? She didn't think so, but she must have.

There weren't any other phones on the second floor, but there were two on the first floor. Charlie grabbed a brass turtle she used as a door stop and crept down the stairs. No sounds. Surely, she'd hear if he was trying to get in.

Bones greeted her at the base of the stairs, meowing and rushing to his food dish, which stood empty.

"Not yet, Bones," she whispered. She slipped into the study and ran to the curtains, raking them over the window. Concealed behind the curtain, she reached one arm around and felt along the window pane for the lock, finding it secured.

Next, she went to the phone, pressing it to her ear, finger poised over the number nine.

No dial tone.

He'd cut the phone line to the house.

∼

FOR TWO HOURS, Charlie cowered in the locked bathroom. Bones slept on the rug in front of the sink.

Rather than quelling her fear, the passage of time had amplified it. Sweat dripped down her back and her legs shook beneath her when she edged the door open and peered into her bedroom.

She made a run for it. If he'd gotten into the house, it would only be a matter of time before he broke open the bathroom door.

Charlie ran through her room, down the hall to the stairs. She leapt down the stairs three at a time and jerked open her front door. She dove off her porch and sprinted to her car. Grasping on the handle, she jerked the door open.

A hand closed around her free arm, and she shrieked, raking her fingernails across the man's wrist.

"Ouch, Charlie. What the fuck?"

She jerked away and stumbled backwards across her lawn, registering the man's familiar voice.

In the dark, she squinted toward him. The interior light in her car had come on when she'd opened the door. The figure gradually came into focus, the blood roaring in her ears still too loud to hear the sounds of the night. His voice seemed far away.

"Charlie?" Jared asked.

Charlie burst into tears, and he ran to her, kneeling and gathering her close. She sobbed into his neck.

~

JARED LED her back into her own house, and she sat at the kitchen table trembling. He felt his way around her kitchen, turning on lights, opening cupboards until he found the new wine glasses she'd bought, grabbing an unopened bottle even though there was a perfectly good half bottle of merlot right next to it. He unscrewed the cork and poured them each a glass. She looked at his pale fingers on the delicate flute, the fine blond hairs on his knuckles.

They'd had beautiful wine glasses that Jared's aunt had given them for their wedding. They were piped in delicate black and gold spirals. Charlie had left them behind. Every item she had a happy memory of was abandoned in their house in Pontiac. But now here he was creating a memory with her new glasses, leaving the invisible traces of himself, fingerprints and the cells of his skin, on her glasses.

He sat on the long bench beside her, straddling it and smoothing a palm across the smooth wood surface. "This table is beautiful. This entire house. What a find, Charlie."

She stared dumbly at his hand on her table, and then up his arm, to his pretty face. That was how people described Jared. He had high cheekbones and a soft, heart-shaped mouth. He was thin, pale and angelic. She'd called him that when she first told her mother about him after they'd met at a party in college.

"He looks like an angel, Mom," she'd said.

"Honey, are you okay?" Jared asked. "I thought you might claw my eyes out a minute ago."

Charlie grimaced and picked up the wine, downing the contents in two shuddering gulps. When she looked back at him, his eyes were concerned, but she refused to make an excuse. "There was a man here. I think he cut my phone lines," she whispered.

She stood and filled a second glass, not returning to the bench where she could smell his Irish Springs soap and just a hint of his Cool Water cologne. She leaned against the counter.

"Really? Cut your phone lines?" He stood and walked to the phone hanging on her kitchen wall. He picked it up and listened. "Charlie, I passed a utility truck down the street on my way here. It looked like a tree fell on a phone line. I'm guessing that's what happened to your phone. What makes you think someone did it on purpose?"

"What?" she asked. "Where? Where was the utility truck?"

"Not even a block away. Here, look." He walked to the front window and peeled back the curtain.

When she pressed her face close to the glass and looked to the left, she could see the orange pulsing of lights down the street. She sagged forward, her forehead going cool against the window.

After a moment, Jared tugged her away. "Come on, Charlie girl, sit down."

Charlie girl. He hadn't called her that in years. It had been his nickname for her at the beginning, but as the years went by, it had become straight Charlie.

She returned to the bench, her stomach turbulent with contradictory emotions—relief at his appearance coupled with fear. "Why are you here, Jared?"

His face softened and he reached one delicate hand to hers. "I was worried about you, honey."

"Don't call me that," she snapped.

Charlie stood from the bench abruptly and her elbow struck her wine glass. It tipped, dark cabernet splashing onto the table. The glass rolled sideways, but Jared caught it before it could fall to the tile and smash.

"It's okay," he insisted. He grabbed the dishtowel by her oven and dropped it onto the wine.

"No," she shouted, snatching the towel that Bev had made for her.

She hurried to the sink and turned the tap on cold, bunching the towel beneath it and watching the red swirl into the sink. Something like agony lay coiled in her throat, reaching up, threatening an eruption of howls or sobs. She clenched her eyes shut, the icy water numbing her hands.

Jared grabbed a paper towel and finished wiping up the mess. Charlie turned off the faucet and draped the rag on the edge of the sink. Half of it was no longer white but a light pink hue she knew would never wash away.

"How did you find out where I lived?" she asked, back still to him, the mass of emotion hovering, waiting.

He came to stand beside her and reached for her back, but he let his hand fall. He tucked both hands into the pockets of his jeans. "Ginger from Pontiac General. I called her for your address because you'd gotten some mail at the house and I wasn't sure where to send it."

Charlie felt a flutter of rage at her former co-worker.

Charlie had had a group of wonderful friends at Pontiac General. Ginger was not one of them. Competitive, shallow and using every spare moment during their nursing shifts to paint her nails and brag about her boyfriend's yacht, Ginger had rubbed most of the nurses the wrong way. She'd been especially venomous to Charlie, and it didn't come as a surprise that she'd be all too willing to pass on her address, which Charlie had asked the staff to keep confidential from her ex-husband.

"Slag," Charlie muttered.

"What?" Jared asked.

Charlie didn't respond, but smiled thinking of James, a fellow nurse originally from Britain, who'd first called Ginger a 'slag' during a late-night shift when she was droning on about how sad it was that some women thought cubic zirconia was the real thing. From that night on, it had stuck.

It was mean, but Ginger was mean. She wasn't merely boastful. She constantly insulted patients, commenting on the saggy ass of Brenda in Room 6 or how Mr. Elmer stank as if he were rotting from the inside out. More than once, Charlie had wanted to cram her hands over her ears and scream to drown out the woman's voice.

"Jared, why are you really here? Where's Sheila? Hmm… thinking you're working late?" Charlie demanded.

"What was that outside, Charlie? You were crying. You seemed so happy to see me."

She clenched her teeth together. "I wasn't happy to see you. I was scared. You could have been the mailman and I would have reacted like that."

"I miss you, Charlie. I've missed you for months. I never wanted this."

Charlie's mouth dropped open. Fury, grief—both vying for the chance to talk, for the chance to choose what came next.

"No." She shook her head. "It's too late. It's too fucking late. Do you know how long I wanted to hear you say those words?

And actually mean them?" Charlie scoffed. It took every ounce of her self-control not to snatch the glass in his hand and throw the wine in his face.

He seemed to recognize the impulse and took a step away from her.

"Get out," she muttered. "Leave, Jared."

"You need me, Charlie. I saw you out there. My God, you were terrified. Let me help you."

33

Jake parked his truck nearly half a mile away and slipped on leather gloves. He stared at the dark duplex and wondered for the millionth time what in the hell he was doing. The police had searched Petra's apartment, and they'd found nothing of significance.

"But maybe they didn't know what to look for," Jake murmured, steeling himself against the voice urging him to go home and go to bed.

He climbed out of his truck and shut the door, walking quickly down the quiet street. Norm had mentioned the sliding glass doors into the duplex, which never felt quite secure. Norm lodged a stick in his door so that it couldn't be opened, but Petra, Norm said, did not.

At the sliding door, Jake grasped the handle and rocked the door up and down. He leaned close to the glass to see how it locked and wiggled the door until it pulled away from the latch. It was easy and very possibly how an intruder had gotten in to Petra's to begin with. Unless, of course, she'd let them in.

The apartment smelled of cleaner. Jake wondered who'd

washed it. He couldn't imagine the police allowing Norm to go in and clean up if they considered him a suspect.

Despite the cleaning, the streaks of dark remained on the cream-colored carpeting. He couldn't distinguish a color. In the darkness, they merely looked like misshapen stripes against the light backdrop.

He flicked on his flashlight and moved slowly, lighting up the pictures on the walls. Petra, in much the same way as she dressed, did not include much color in her home décor. Black and white paintings of silhouettes covered the walls. The furniture and side tables were in varying shades of black and dark brown. Even the dried blood in the beam of his flashlight seemed to match the dark furniture.

He walked into the small adjoining kitchen. A pile of mail lay neatly stacked on the countertop. The sink was empty. He could smell the bleach. The kitchen had been scrubbed clean.

He thumbed through the mail quickly. A gas bill, an advertisement for half-off pizza, a notice from the Census bureau and a copy of *Glamour* magazine offered little insight into Petra's life.

A noise startled him and he froze. Ice cubes spewed from the automated dispenser in the refrigerator and shot across the floor.

No one had touched the dispenser and the ice lay gleaming in the beam of his light. Frowning, he scooped it up and dropped it in the sink and started out of the kitchen.

Something cracked behind him. He spun back to see the refrigerator ajar, a sliver of light spilling onto the linoleum.

"Holy hell," he muttered, stepping toward it. He started to close the door and then, curious, he opened it wider. The top two shelves were packed with vanilla pudding cups. Rows of six or eight were stacked nearly to the refrigerator ceiling.

Disturbed by the finding, but making little sense of it, he closed the door firmly and walked back toward the living room.

The creak sounded again, followed by a crash.

Heart thumping, he stepped back into the kitchen. The refrigerator door stood all the way ajar and at least twenty pudding cups had fallen to the floor.

Dumbfounded, and uneasy, he started back toward the puddings when he heard a sound near the glass sliding door. He slipped back into the living room and a beam of light burst through the sliding doors, blinding him. Jake threw up a hand to shield his eyes and stumbled forward, hitting the coffee table and hurtling over it. It broke beneath his weight and he sprawled onto the carpet, yelping as pain shot into his elbow. He rolled sideways, panting, and held his hands in the air, getting slowly to his feet.

The light stayed trained on him. He waited for a cop's voice over a megaphone or for the door to burst open. It didn't. Unwavering, the beam held him in its sight.

When no one ordered him to freeze, Jake's unease turned to fear. Covering his eyes, he ran down the hall. He plunged into a bedroom and closed and locked the door behind him.

Seconds passed, a minute. He listened, frowning when a muffled noise came to his strained ears. It was the glass door sliding open.

There was no trickle of light beneath the door. The beam had been turned off. Footsteps moved slowly down the hallway, achingly slow and deliberate, following the path that Jake had taken seconds before.

Panic seized him and his throat locked on the howl he almost released. His legs pedaled him backward into the wall and his breath died in his chest, heavy, incapable of the burst it needed to escape back into the still room.

For an instant, he stared down a dark tunnel through the eyes of a young boy and he listened to the screams of his best friend fade into the black.

The handle on the door squeaked and the sound reached

into Jake's chest and squeezed the still balloons he called lungs and set the air rushing up through his trachea and out of his mouth in a whoosh.

Jake dove to the window and wrenched it open. Clumsily, he fell through it and into a prickly bush that clawed at his face and clutched his shirt as he lurched away from the house.

34

Against her better judgment, Charlie had agreed to letting Jared sleepover on her couch.

That night she dreamed of the Jared who'd loved her. They celebrated Christmas at his parents' house, laughing as they struggled to thread popcorn on a string. Jared shoved handfuls in his mouth when his mother wasn't looking. When she twisted around to make sure he didn't eat them, he and Charlie burst out laughing. They sat pressed close together on a dream couch that had never existed. Warm red and green lights filled the room, and everything hovered in a misty glow of goodness that only dreams can create.

"What the hell are you up to?"

The voice, angry, ripped Charlie from sleep.

The lamp beside her clicked on, and she squinted into the too-bright light. "Huh?" she grumbled, shielding her eyes with her hand. She registered Jared's face in the halo of light, lips pressed together and eyes narrowed to points. His naked chest rose and fell as if he'd just run a sprint.

"Don't fuck with me, Charlie. Okay, I get it. You're still pissed, but—"

Charlie scowled and struggled up in bed, pulling a pillow to her chest and hugging it. "What are you talking about, Jared? You just woke me from a dead sleep."

His eyes lit as if he couldn't believe her nerve. He scoffed and made one full turn, shaking his head angrily. "I saw you, Charlie. I saw you standing in the doorway with a fucking knife. Don't lie to me."

"Oh, wow, isn't that the pot calling the kettle black," she snapped, sitting up taller now, the pent-up rage at all the hurt foaming forth as it had so many times in their last year together. But all those other times, she'd swallowed it.

Rage and shame, rage and shame, those had been the two prevailing emotions, and he'd punished her every time either had reared its ugly face.

"You are a piece of work," he spat. "I knew it was a mistake coming here. You know what, Charlie, have a nice fucking life." He saluted her with one hand, fingers curling down to leave her with only the middle finger as a farewell.

Charlie grabbed a pillow and chucked it at his retreating form. She burst into tears when she heard the front door slam.

The sobs came hard and fast. Her diaphragm ratcheted against the soft tissues inside her body. She collapsed and curled herself around another pillow. Her breath slowed and the fury, the anguish, subsided.

When she finally sat up again, she felt woozy from the upheaval. She sat on the edge of her bed, feet dangling over the wood floor, and stared in stunned silence at her slippers. It wasn't the slippers that alarmed her, but the slowly registering words Jared had spoken.

He'd accused her of standing over him with a knife.

∽

Bev hadn't ignored Charlie's early-morning call or told her

she was overreacting. Instead, she'd gotten out of bed, gotten dressed and driven more than an hour to Charlie's home. She arrived as the sun crested the trees, orange embers lighting the western sky.

Charlie sat on her porch, wrapped in a blue fleece blanket, sipping her second cup of coffee. A cold had blown down from Canada and swept across the Midwest. The air held a chill that wiped the sleepiness from Charlie's limbs. A layer of cool fog hung above the ground, enchanting and strangely mesmerizing. Charlie stared into the white void, tempted to run barefoot through the mist and watch it scatter across the clammy grass.

A car door slammed, and Bev dispersed the fog as she walked to the porch. Bev hugged her and took the seat next to Charlie, opening a white paper sack and handing her a pastry.

"You went to Amelia's Bakery?" Charlie stared at the gooey pecan roll and tried not to cry.

"Sure did, and I got your favorite. Amelia said she misses your face. I told her she wasn't the only one."

Charlie smiled and took Bev's hand, kissing the back. "Thank you for coming, Bev, and for not calling me a mental case."

"The only thing mental about you, Charlie, is that you let that son of a bitch into your house." Bev grabbed a glazed donut and took a bite, chewing angrily.

Charlie thought of the dream she'd had before Jared woke her. It had been so sweet. Now that the anger had worn off, the strands of those old feelings filled her with loneliness. "You know, I think the hardest part of seeing him is there's the Jared who exists now, the person he became, and then there's the Jared I met and fell in love with, the Jared I married, the Jared who was jumping up and down with me the first time I got pregnant. There's so many more memories with that first Jared that it's almost impossible for me to extract the new Jared and see him for who he is."

"And maybe for who he always was?" Bev asked.

Charlie sighed. It was possible that Bev was right and Jared had been a terrible human being from the beginning, but Charlie didn't think so. In fact, she still didn't think he was a terrible human being. She thought he was just human—fallible, selfish and choosing instant gratification rather than working harder to repair what they had damaged, to breathe life back into the love that had once swept them both away.

Charlie would never convince Bev that for years Jared had been a good husband, a good partner and a good friend. In a way, Bev's stubborn refusal to see him in that light was part of what made her a good friend. She fought for Charlie; she refused to let her waffle in that space where Jared's high points overshadowed all the cruel things he'd done since.

"He's not sincere, Charlie. Okay? Just trust me."

Something in her tone caught Charlie's attention. "What? What do you know, Bev?" Charlie had moved more than sixty miles away. She no longer had access to the ring of gossip that drifted around Pontiac. That had been one of the deciding factors in her choice of a new location, but Bev still lived there. Her husband's best friend worked with Jared.

"Sheila's pregnant."

The muscles in Charlie's abdomen spasmed as if someone had sucker-punched her. She put a hand to her belly and closed her eyes. "How far along?" she whispered.

"I don't know. I didn't want to tell you. I can't believe he showed up here. What a creep."

Charlie tried not to care, but the months and the therapy and the new life didn't erase her suffering. It was better than it had once been, but it lived on.

"Screw him," Bev said. "Let's talk about last night. You said he accused you of standing over him with a knife?"

Charlie nodded. "And I didn't, Bev. It's been a rough year,

but I'm not a psychopath. I was sound asleep, and I woke up to him shouting at me."

Bev huffed and chomped another bite of her donut.

"I think... I'm seriously starting to believe I bought a haunted house."

Bev chewed thoughtfully, craning around in her chair to gaze into the window of the house. "I believe it."

"You do?"

"Sure. I've never had those experiences myself, but remember my roommate in college? Dana?"

"Yeah."

"She used to talk about ghosts all the time. It got old, to be honest. I figured she was vying for attention. All the other girls on our floor were long-legged and blonde. Dana's only way of standing out was the ghost thing."

Charlie giggled and took another bite of her roll. "Seems like there are easier ways to win popularity contests."

"Oh, she wasn't winning any popularity contests, believe you me. But... well, I ended up believing her. I came home from class one day and she was arranging this bouquet of flowers she'd picked around campus. I asked what they were for, and she said she planned to give them to Teresa. Teresa lived on our floor, one of the leggy blondes. And I thought she was nuts because Teresa had never said a kind word to her in her life."

"Why did she want to give her flowers then?" Charlie asked.

"Exactly. That's what I asked her and she said Teresa would need them. Not two hours later, there was all this ruckus in the hall. I walked out to find Teresa with her groupies huddled around her. She was crying hysterically. I mean, she could barely breathe she was crying so hard. I asked one of her friends what had happened and she said Teresa's little sister got hit by a car and killed that morning. She'd just gotten the call from her parents."

Charlie stopped chewing. "Wait. Does that mean your

roommate—?"

"Yeah. I'm pretty sure. I bugged her about it and she wouldn't say much, just that she'd had a visit that morning from the other side and knew Teresa would need cheering up. Not that the flowers did much. Maybe they did. Who knows? But... it shifted my opinion of Dana. I'll tell you that."

"I always thought people just made it up," Charlie said. "I remember in high school having sleepovers and we'd tell spooky stories. There was always a girl or two who claimed to have seen a ghost, but..." She shrugged. "I figured it was all talk, maybe sprinkled with paranoia. You know? The way you sometimes wake up and the dream was so real, you think it happened."

"Yeah. Though I've never been much of a dreamer."

"I had a vivid one about Jared last night. I think it made his... his leaving the way he did so much worse because I'd had this beautiful dream where we'd been together and we were happy."

Bev didn't probe. She never encouraged Charlie to wax poetic about the good times with Jared. "How do we figure out if this place is haunted?" Bev asked. "Let's talk about that. Okay? Forward, not backward. Remember?"

Charlie nodded and finished her roll.

"Want another one?" Bev asked. "I brought reinforcements."

Charlie shook her head. "I need another hit of coffee though. Want a warm-up?"

"Yeah, no better way to start the day than a caffeine and sugar high. I'll come with you." Bev followed Charlie into her kitchen.

"I don't think it's a question of if anymore," Charlie answered. "A woman who used to own this place called me back. She said the ghost pushed her down the stairs."

"But you said the guy who lived here for like decades said it wasn't haunted, right?"

"Yeah, Jake Edwards." Charlie warmed at the thought of him.

"Okay," Bev said, leaning against the counter and giving Charlie a mischievous smile. "I see that look on your face. Tell me about Jake Edwards."

Charlie smiled and filled their coffee cups. "He lived here until he was in his early twenties and then he moved back after his parents died, but sold it a couple years later."

"Is he devilishly handsome?"

Charlie let out a strangled laugh. "Let's avoid words like 'devilish,' shall we?"

Bev smirked. "Good point."

"Handsome though, yes, he is. Big sparkly blue-green eyes and full lips. And he's strong. He looks like a guy who has spent ten years hauling timber on his back."

Bev nodded approvingly. "Yes, out with those scrawny androgynous Jared types and in with a nice rough-hewn lumberjack."

"Nothing happened," Charlie said, walking back to the porch with Bev in tow.

"Not yet," Bev insisted.

"Maybe never. I had the feeling he wanted to ask me out, but he didn't. Maybe he's got a girlfriend or, worse, a wife." Charlie wrinkled her nose.

"Was he wearing a ring?"

Charlie thought about his hands and shook her head. "No, but not every married man wears a ring. Jared used to tell me he preferred not to wear it because he might lose it."

"What a crock of shit."

"Yeah. I wanted to believe him though. Even last night. I wanted so much to believe he'd had some… I don't know, some premonition I was in trouble, that I needed him."

Bev stood and leaned against the porch railing, sipping her coffee and gazing seriously at Charlie. "Jared's got his head stuck so far up his own ass, he wouldn't know if he was in trouble, let alone someone else."

Charlie laughed and felt tension from the previous night running out of her. Bev could do that. Her presence seemed to act as a beacon to Charlie's nervous system: *It's okay, everyone, the emergency is over.*

"While we're on the topic though, who was the creepy guy who spooked you yesterday? Just some deranged Jehovah's Witness trying to meet his pamphlet quota?"

Charlie remembered the woman's warning. *Don't open it.* "I couldn't see him through the glass, but Bev, the ghost told me not to open the door."

Bev's eyes went wide. "No way."

"Yeah. I have goosebumps just thinking about it." Charlie held out her arm.

Bev shuddered. "Me too. Damn, that's freaky."

"What terrified me is he tried to get in. When I didn't come to the door, he started turning the knob and trying to open it. Then I spotted him on the back deck and he was staring right at me."

"Did he try the other doors too?"

"Probably. I don't know. I was running through the house locking windows and wishing I'd taken your advice and bought a gun."

"That was a joke," Bev told her.

"Still, I wished I'd done it. I tried to call the police, but the line was dead."

"He cut the phone line? Holy crap."

Charlie shook her head. "No. A tree fell on a line apparently, but I didn't know that at the time. I thought he'd cut it too. When Jared showed up, I was making a run for it. I thought Jared was the guy, and he intended to drag me back in the house and chop me up into little pieces."

"Whew," Bev breathed. "That's terrifying, but what I'd like to know is why didn't the damn ghost tell you not to let Jared in either?"

35

Jake was hurrying out the door when his phone rang.

"Jake, something happened at Petra's last night," Norm blurted the instant Jake put the phone to his ear.

"I broke in," Jake said, mouth flopping open when he realized he'd just admitted to something he'd sworn to himself the night before to keep secret. He hadn't intended to tell anyone, ever, and sure as hell not Norm, but there it was.

"What? You? I called the police, Jake! Why did you break in? Did you find something?"

"Meet me at the Pink Drink tonight. I'll tell you everything."

Norm was an unlikely confidante and yet in the midst of all that had gone on, Norm believed in the bigger forces at work.

In Bryant's face Jake had seen suspicion, in Adrian's a reluctance to believe. He didn't dare tell Barbie or Willis because then he'd have to meet their concerned looks every day at the office. But Norm knew things the others didn't know. He knew about Maribelle's ghost and the hypnotist. He also had the most to gain from finding the real kidnapper. After all, it was Norm the police had set their sights on from day one.

Jake expected Barbie to give him a hard time, the guys for sure, but instead of irritated, she looked worried when he walked in. She and Willis stood by her desk, and he had the distinct sense they'd been talking about him before he stepped through the door.

"Jake," Barbie said, relieved. "I wasn't sure..." She waved weakly at the clock.

"It's not even seven o'clock," he reminded her.

"You called in yesterday. I just thought..." She cast a flustered glance at Willis.

"It's all good, Barbie. He's here now," Willis said. "We need your expertise on this one, Jake." He gestured at the desk calendar. "Allen and Jerry are scheduled at the Gillespie house today. They've got gravel getting delivered at ten. The problem is Brody Harris has called all pissed that the water washed out the grade in his driveway, which is damn well not true. I drove by yesterday and it looked fine, but he's kicking up a shit storm, so somebody has to go over there with the skid steer."

"I'll meet the gravel truck with Jerry," Jake told him. "Send Allen to Harris's. He likes Allen. He won't give him a hard time."

"And that's why you're the boss." Willis tipped his ball cap at him. "Ricardo and I will be at the Wilson property pulling stumps."

"And you've got ten, maybe fifteen, requests for bids," Barbie added. "A new insurance guy stopped by and he'd like to go over company health insurance plans, which I'm not saying a thing about, but you know my Edmond will need a knee replacement sooner rather than later and his insurance is the absolute pits."

"Okay, gotcha. I need to make a few phone calls." Jake ducked into his office. He'd barely closed the door when someone knocked on it.

"Yeah?" he asked, trying to make sense of the list of names and messages Barbie had dropped on his desk.

"Boss?" Ricardo peeked his head in.

"Yeah, what's up?"

Ricardo walked full in and shut the door. "I just wanted to let you know that the detective who was out here the other day called me. He called Jerry and Allen too."

"Detective Bryant? Why?"

"He was asking about where you were the day the lady disappeared."

Jake frowned and studied Ricardo. The younger man looked worried. "It's okay, Ricardo. I'm sure that's the standard thing they do."

Ricardo nodded, but his troubled expression didn't change. "Okay, just wanted to give you a heads up."

"Thanks, Ric. I appreciate it."

After Ricardo left, his look, more than his comments, niggled at Jake's mind. He dialed Bryant's phone number,

"Detective Bryant," the man said.

"You've been talking to my guys?"

"Who is this?" Bryant demanded.

"It's Jake Edwards," Jake said, rattled but trying not to show it.

"I would like to know, Jake, why are you so interested in Petra's case?"

"Seriously? Her goddamn bloody shirt was sitting on my desk. Wouldn't you be interested?"

"Ricardo Denaud told me that on the day Petra disappeared, you left the job site for an hour."

Jake frowned. "Why are you questioning my guys?"

"Merely corroborating your alibi. It's standard procedure."

"I told you that the night I came in. I left to call my girlfriend, Allison."

"And that took you more than an hour?"

Jake stared at the wall above the phone. "I ran into a gas station for coffee and I had stuff on my brain. I sat in my truck and thought for a bit. I highly doubt it was an hour."

"You were working at a property near Bay City. That property was only fourteen miles away from Petra's home."

"Okay," Jake said, irritated.

"An hour could have had you at Petra's and back to the job."

"Bullshit!" Jake snapped. "I didn't know where Petra lived. I didn't find out until I called her apartment after five o'clock. And what? I went to her house and murdered her and drove back to the job site to work another six hours? Where was her body then? Huh? Stashed in the backseat of my truck?"

"Are you willing to let us search your pickup truck?"

"Have at it," Jake shouted. "Keys are inside."

He slammed the phone down.

∽

JAKE DIDN'T BOTHER GOING HOME after work. He drove straight to the Pink Drink to meet Norm, who'd already picked a table at the back beneath a mirrored wall.

Jake drank a beer while telling Norm the story of his foray into Petra's the night before. "The refrigerator door opened and about twenty pudding cups fell out. To say it was a weird is a gross understatement."

"Maribelle's pudding," Norm said, nodding.

"Say that again?"

"Those are puddings for Maribelle. You couldn't have force-fed those to Petra. She started buying them for Maribelle. She'd peel open the top and put one out for her every night. Kind of like feeding a stray cat." Norm giggled. "Petra believed Maribelle liked them. She said sometimes half the cup was empty when she woke up in the morning."

Jake tried to wipe the incredulous look from his face, but the story was so ridiculous, he struggled not to laugh out loud. "Someone showed up, Norm. They must have followed me."

Norm's eyes went wide. "Did you see who it was? It has to be the guy who took her, right?"

"I don't know. I hid in a bedroom and climbed out the window. I didn't take a weapon with me." Jake didn't add that he'd been scared shitless, that for a moment he'd been sure the boogeyman stood on the opposite side of Petra's door waiting to gobble him up, boots and all.

Norm licked his lips and then chewed the lower one. "I've got to get out of there. Maybe I'll stay with my mom for a while. Ugh. The thought makes me gag. Not that I don't love her. I do, but she smokes like a burning house. Bleh." He grimaced. "I'll have to fumigate my clothes after."

"That's probably for the best. You said you called the police last night. Did they show?"

"Oh, sure. And they looked at me like I'd called because my cat was stuck in a tree. Gorillas," he huffed.

"Did they go into Petra's house?"

He shook his head. "'It's a crime scene,' they said. And I told them, 'No kidding. And somebody, probably the bad guy, was just in there. He might still be in there.' They walked around outside with their flashlights for about five minutes and then drove off."

Jake frowned and crossed his arms. If they'd gone into her apartment, they might have found the man who'd murdered her.

"Hey." Norm suddenly perked up. "Did you find her diary?"

"Petra kept a diary?"

Norm nodded and fished an ice cube from his glass, rolling it around in his mouth. "She wrote everything in it. If she'd met someone and hadn't told me about him, he'd be in that diary."

"Did you tell the police about it?"

"Yeah, definitely. I asked Detective Bryant the last time he called if they found it and he said no diary."

Jake frowned. "What did it look like?"

"It was pretty distinctive," Norm said. "A black leather cover spotted with red lips. I've never seen another one like it. Her boss gave it to her as a Christmas gift a few years ago."

"And the police searched for it?"

"The detective implied they did, but..." Norm crunched the ice cube between his teeth. "I don't know if I believe him. People hide their journals. She probably has it under a mattress or in a cereal box or something weird like that."

"Why though?" Jake countered. "She lived alone. Why should she hide it?"

Norm paused in his chewing. "That's true. I hadn't thought of that. She probably wouldn't hide it."

"Did you ever see it when you went into her apartment?"

"Yeah. In different places. On her coffee table. Sometimes it was sticking out of her purse like she took it with her."

"Then it seems like it would have been in an obvious location. The police should have found it easily. Unless..."

Norm's eyes widened. "Unless the guy who abducted her took the journal."

Jake nodded. "And why would a stranger take her diary? If an unknown man broke into her house to rob her or attack her, why take her diary unless he thought she mentioned him in it somewhere?"

Norm propped an elbow on the table and rested his chin in his hand, nodding. "You're good at this."

Jake chuckled. "Hardly. I've just watched a lot of *Law and Order*."

∽

As Jake drove home, he thought of Petra peeling back the little tinfoil tops on vanilla pudding cups and leaving them out for a ghost child.

Had it been Maribelle in the apartment the night before?

He remembered the taunts from his childhood, the fearful strangeness in his mother's eyes when she looked at him. But that had been thirty years ago. Thirty years without so much as a chilled room or a whisper in the night. If he'd been able to see spirits, if there'd really been spirits at all, where had they gone? Why had they vanished all those decades ago when he'd fled the asylum?

He thought about the apartment, trying to imagine a black journal covered in lips. He hadn't seen one, he was sure of it, and yet the image seemed familiar to him. Had he seen one like it somewhere else?

As his mind churned through forty years of data, Jake felt a twitch as the memory came to him. He let off the gas, drifting to the roadside when a Jeep blared its horn behind him.

He had seen the journal on the desk of the hypnotist, Trent Henderson.

36

Jake called Trent all afternoon, but the phone number, initially going to voicemail, soon emitted a message which stated the line had been disconnected. He drove to Trent's office and tried to peek in the window, but drawn shades blocked his view.

"Shit." He kicked a cement parking block.

As he considered his options, a black sedan pulled into the parking lot. Detective Bryant climbed out.

Jake narrowed his eyes at the detective. "Are you following me?"

"Does that bother you?"

Jake sighed, exasperated. "No. But I think the guy we need to be talking to is right here." He gestured at the dark office.

"It looks closed," Bryant said, staring at the door.

Jake frowned and pulled the handle, surprised when it swung open. He stepped in and his mouth fell open.

"What the..." Jake scanned the bare carpeting and the white walls. The reception area lay void of the furniture that had been there the day before. Trent's inner office was equally deserted.

The couch and desk, the diplomas, the bookshelf stacked with texts, the phrenology sculpture—all of it was gone.

Detective Bryant didn't even walk in. He'd placed his hand on his gun, but now he dropped it to the side. His eyes narrowed on Jake. "Is this a joke, Jake?"

"No, God, no. It was here. I've been here three times. There was a desk right here. I'm telling you." Jake got down on his hands and knees, but the carpeted floor didn't so much as reveal an indent.

Jake stood, blinking around the room. "He had Petra's journal. I saw it."

"But you'd only just met Petra the day she disappeared," Bryant said coolly. "For less than five minutes, if I remember correctly."

"Fuck!" Jake shouted. He kicked the wall and the hard toe of his work boot broke through the plaster.

Bryant returned a hand to his gun holster.

Jake put his hands up. "I'm sorry. I just... I'm telling you this guy was here. I've come here three times. He was here."

Bryant walked to his car and got on a radio.

Jake stood in the middle of the office, eyes bulging, a vein in his forehead pulsing with the threat of a migraine. He wanted to pound his fists on the walls.

Bryant returned several minutes later, his eyes hard. "I contacted the manager of the building. That office has been vacant for two years, Jake."

"That's not possible," Jake whispered. "It's not fucking possible!" He roared it now and ran into the interior office, dropping to his hands and knees, searching for indents in the carpet, a scrap of paper, some proof the man had been there.

"We'll be in touch, Jake," Bryant told him.

Jake stood slowly, a sick feeling swimming in his stomach. He walked outside and watched the detective drive from the parking lot. He walked to his own truck, his feet heavy and leaded, his hands shaking as he climbed behind the wheel.

"What the fuck?" he shouted, slamming both hands on the steering wheel.

He stared at the building, at the place where the hypnotist's office had been two days before. Empty, nothing.

"I'm not losing my mind," he said, but the quaver in his voice scared him, as did the look in his eyes when he glanced in the rearview mirror.

He turned the key and his engine sputtered and died.

"You've got to be kidding me," he muttered. His truck had never stalled, not once.

He tried it again. This time the engine didn't even offer a hopeful gasp.

Jake climbed out and kicked the tire. As he stomped toward the hood, a flash of movement at the back of the building caught his eye.

A large, industrial dumpster stood behind the building and beyond that, in a pocket of shadow, stood a man with a bristly red-brown beard. The man in the mirror.

"Horace," Jake whispered. He walked toward him, but the man faded until Jake stared at nothing but trees.

"Horace?" he asked, starting when a crow burst from the dumpster. It shuddered its large wings as it rose into the sky and flew away.

Jake walked to the dumpster and looked inside. A jumble of black trash bags lay amongst a pile of sagging boxes. He walked to a wooded area behind the dumpsters and searched the ground until he found a long stick. Returning to the trash container, he leaned over the side, opening the flaps on the boxes to see papers. One box contained a broken lamp. He shoved the black bags aside, noticing a jumble of miscellaneous junk strewn across the floor of the bin.

As he studied the stuff inside, a familiar pattern caught his eye. He leaned closer, his pulse thumping in his neck.

In the dumpster's bottom, a black journal lay bent in half. Pairs of red lips speckled the dark cover.

Jake threw the stick and braced both hands on the dumpster edge, hoisting himself up and in. His feet crunched over bags of garbage. Wiping away coffee grounds, he shoved the journal under his arm and continued poking.

He recognized other items from Trent's office, but nothing that included a name. Two books Jake had noticed on the man's bookshelf lay haphazard amongst the debris. He even found the yellow legal pad Trent had used when taking notes from Jake's own sessions. The notes were useless—a string of words that Jake recognized but wouldn't prove that he'd been meeting with a hypnotist.

In his truck, the engine failure all but forgotten, he pulled out the notebook and opened it.

Empty.

Only a dozen white-lined pages remained. Someone had ripped most of the pages free and their jagged edges poked from the inner bindings.

"No!" He flung the notebook against the dashboard, where it slid and got stuck.

He fished it out a moment later and opened it back up, squinting at the blank pages. The indentation of words she'd written still remained. The sentences were illegible. Words had overlapped as she'd pressed harder on some pages than others. Halfway down the page, he stopped. The name Gus was there. It had its own little blank spot. He could read nothing of what she had written around it.

Jake returned to the dumpster and climbed in. He got in deep, grabbing handfuls of paperwork and skimming them before tossing them aside. Ripping open trash bags, he wrinkled his nose at a putrid smell like curdled milk, which he quickly realized came from the contents of a paper coffee cup, which had cracked open and spilled down his pant leg.

At the bottom of the dumpster, in a back corner, he grabbed a brown paper sack, like a kid's lunchbag. He opened it and looked inside. He stared at a matted ball of paper.

"Please," he whispered, pulling the ball out and extracting the outer page.

December 26, 1995

Yesterday was Christmas, and I spent it alone. No, not entirely alone. Norm came over with a guy he's seeing—David. They brought a lemon raspberry soufflé, and we watched A Christmas Story, *though they mostly groped each other on my couch. I never feel more alone than I do at Christmas. Norm decorated his bushes out front with twinkle lights, but the decorations only remind me of the year I lived with the foster family in Flint and the father who dressed as Santa Claus was hard when I sat in his lap to tell him what I wanted for gifts. I hate Christmas. If I could take a pill and sleep through the month of December, I would. Next year for Christmas I vow to save enough money to go on vacation to some tropical place that doesn't celebrate Christmas.*

He'd found them, the pages of Petra's journal. They didn't list her name, nothing indicated who'd written the passage, but he knew.

Jake rifled through the entries, putting them in order. When he reached an entry dated May 7th, 1996, he stopped. The entry was from two days before she'd vanished.

May 7, 1996

I found Jacob Dunn. I still can't believe it. For thirty years I thought he died that night with Maribelle. I figured they just hid his body, but no. What does it mean? That he left? Why didn't he ever find me? Send me a letter?

But that's not the big news. The big news is that something happened in Henderson's office the other day. I walked in and his shirt sleeves were pushed up to his elbows. He had a funny scar on his arm.

It's shaped like a stalk of broccoli. It didn't come back to me right away, not until I got home and put out Maribelle's pudding. I suddenly remembered Gus, the doctor who was always so nice to us. Some of the little kids called him Dr. Broccoli because of his scar. Trent Henderson is Dr. Gus!

Stunned, Jake read the words a second time and then a third.

"Trent is Gus..." he muttered.

The explosion of anger spasmed like a seizure flinging Jake's legs and arms out simultaneously. His feet slammed against the floorboards as his fists hit the wheel.

He stared hard through his windshield and beat back his desire to jump from his truck, grab a brick, and hurl it through the window of the man's office.

Instead, teeth gritted, he climbed out and walked to the building where a phone number for leasing inquiries was posted on a door.

∼

JAKE DROVE HOME, gulped two glasses of water, and punched the building's number into his phone.

"Milo's Property Management deals with all of our rentals. You can reach him at 328-1965," the man on the phone explained.

"Great, thanks." Jake hung up and dialed the number.

A man with a wheezing voice answered. "Hello?"

"Hi. I'm trying to get in touch with the person who leases the spaces at 218 Industrial Street."

"That would be me. Milo Bates at your service." The man sounded like a chronic smoker or an asthmatic.

"Milo, I need to know about the guy who's renting Suite C—the hypnotist."

The man on the other end didn't respond for several

seconds. "I think you must be mistaken, sir. No one is renting Suite C. It's been vacant for two years."

"It hasn't been vacant for two years, because I was there last week meeting with Trent Henderson. Now either he broke in and has been using that space without your knowledge or you're covering for him. But let me tell you this, friend, he's wanted in a murder investigation, so if you don't want to end up behind bars, I'd suggest—"

The line went dead and the loud intermittent beep-beep sounded in Jake's ear. He slammed the phone down and grabbed his phone book, searching for the address of Milo's Property Management.

He drove to Bay City. Half a block down from 218 Industrial, Milo's Property Management occupied a utility trailer in a large cement parking lot littered with rusted equipment for sale and stacks of tires. A small, newer-model pickup truck sat outside the trailer. The truck was blue and had a decal on the side that read 'Milo's Property Management.'

Jake walked up the two metal steps outside the trailer and pounded on the door with the side of his fist.

A scrawny man in his thirties answered the door. His receding hairline left him with an unnaturally large forehead, which rose over squinty brown eyes, and a spattering of brown facial hair speckled his upper lip and chin.

"Can I help you?" the man asked.

Jake didn't answer. He shoved the door in hard, hitting the man's outstretched hands and sending him stumbling back into the trailer. The linoleum floor had a noticeable sag and the space stank of wet dog, though Jack didn't see an animal in sight.

"Hey," the man shouted, scurrying behind his desk and grabbing his phone.

Jake slammed a hand on top of the man's, pinning the phone to the table. "Milo, I take it. We spoke on the phone. I'm here to ask you again about Suite C. Either you're going to give me an answer or we're going to take a little drive."

The man's beady eyes widened. His face seemed to shrink deeper into his suddenly glistening forehead. Jake had never seen a man break into a sweat so quickly. It rolled toward the ridge above the man's eyes.

"Do you have children, Milo? A wife? Anybody who'd notice if you never came home?" Jake crunched the man's hand harder beneath his own as he questioned him. "I don't think so. I think you're one of those guys who could be missing for weeks, maybe months, and no one would be the wiser."

"You're... you're breaking the law," Milo stammered.

"Am I?" Jake asked. "I'm just here to have a friendly chat. I haven't broken any laws... yet. Have you, Milo? That's a fine little truck outside. How'd you get the money to afford that? Somebody slipping you some extra cash? Hmmm... maybe to let them use a space without leasing it. Maybe the money never made it to the building owners at all, huh? I bet they wouldn't like to hear that."

Milo's eyes darted toward a drawer in his desk.

Jake suspected he'd hit the nail on the head. Either the drawer contained money or the man kept a pistol in there. Jake had no intention of letting him get anywhere near it.

In one swift move, Jake jerked his hand off Milo's and shoved the smaller man in the chest. Milo stumbled backward, his legs hitting his chair.

"Sit down," Jake barked. "And put your hands in your lap."

The man did, fingers trembling as he laced them together.

Jake walked around the desk, keeping his eye on Milo. He jerked open the drawer, empty except for a single envelope. He recognized the neat square handwriting of Trent Henderson.

Jake plucked the envelope out and thumbed it open. A stack of hundred-dollar bills lay inside. "So fucking predictable," he muttered.

"What are you gonna do?" Milo yelped, eyes watering.

"Nothing." Jake flung the envelope back into the drawer. "But you're going to call Detective Bryant and tell him all about Trent Henderson."

"Who's Trent Henderson?"

Jake stomped toward him, but the little man threw up his hands and cowered lower in his chair.

"Gus," he sputtered. "He called himself Dr. Gus."

37

"Hey," Adrian said, glancing up from her car. Her eyes darted to the police station, and Jake knew her dad had gotten to her. *Stay away from Jake Edwards. The guy is nuts.* "Jake, you probably shouldn't be here. Fly under the radar for a while. Okay?"

"Your dad told you about Henderson?" he asked.

Again, she glanced at the police station. Jake wondered if Bryant watched them.

"Jake." She brushed a hand through her flowing hair. Her head barely reached the roof of her car. "When my dad found out I'd been digging around for you, he was irate. I start basic training next week and I just… I just can't. Okay?"

Jake nodded. "I get it. Sure. I just… Trent is Gus. They're the same guy." He fumbled in the folder he'd brought, pulling out the wrinkled pages. "This is Petra's journal. I dug it out of the dumpster behind the office on Industrial where I've been meeting with Trent. Petra found out it was him. That's got to be it."

"Jake, no one can find the hypnotist."

"But Milo called your dad. He told him that a guy named Gus has been using that office on Industrial on the sly."

"But there's no way to verify that Milo is telling the truth," she murmured. "This thing—it's getting out of hand and I think you just need to let the detectives do their jobs. Okay?"

"How can I do that?" he demanded. "When this guy is clearly trying to frame me?"

"Why? Why would he frame you?"

Jake continued holding out the papers. "I don't know yet. Maybe Petra threatened to tell police about the stuff the doctors did to us as kids."

"What did they do?"

"I can't remember that part, but something. They did something."

Adrian reluctantly took the papers and dropped the folder on her driver's seat. "You should have given those to my dad."

"He doesn't believe a word I say. I feel like I'm losing my mind here, Adrian. There's no proof, but… it's not your problem. I really appreciate all your help. I do." He turned and walked back to his truck.

Adrian watched him. She lifted her hand in a half wave and then dropped it back to her side when the door to the station opened and Detective Bryant marched across the lot toward his daughter.

Jake glimpsed the man's glare in his rearview mirror as he drove from the lot.

∼

JAKE SPENT the rest of the day on a muddy piece of property that needed seeding. He returned home, tired, but grateful the work had emptied his mind for a little while. He played his phone message.

The first was from Charlie, left a few days earlier. She'd found something in one of Wilder's Grove's passages. He listened to the others after hers, one from Barbie and another from Willis, but they barely registered.

He dialed Charlie. "Want to watch airplanes?" he asked the moment she picked up the phone. "And drink a few beers?"

She laughed on the other end. "And here I thought you were Freddie's Insurance calling for the third time today to ask me to switch my policy to their company."

Jake chuckled. "I'm afraid I can't make such an appealing offer."

"Airplanes and beer sound great."

∼

He parked in the lot across the street from the airport. Grabbing the six-pack from his back seat, he climbed out and opened the tailgate. He sat on the back edge.

As he watched the black sky, headlights illuminated the lot. The lights stung his eyes, but he didn't bother to shield them. He imagined her behind the wheel, seeing him suddenly lit in the darkness, muddy jeans, bare feet. What if she just turned around and drove away? He wouldn't blame her.

"I see you got started without me," she said, stepping from her car.

Like him, she hadn't dressed up for their outing. She wore light blue surgical scrubs. Her honey-brown hair was pulled into a messy bun at the base of her neck. No makeup. She smelled of strong soap when she shimmied onto the back of the truck.

She opened a paper bag. "Serendipity or a fluke?" she asked, pulling out a matching six-pack of Miller Genuine Draft.

"That's impressive," he laughed.

She removed one from the plastic ring and popped the top. "This was on sale. But fate sounds more fun."

He took a sip and set his beer aside, lying all the way back. He'd propped up bags of mulch to cushion their heads. "Fate has a sick sense of humor if it meddles with beer."

She surveyed the mulch. "I like your style, Jake Edwards."

"I call it 'whatever's in the back of my truck,'" he told her.

She reclined, squirming, and then pulling a wrench out from under her.

"Oops," he said, taking it and tossing it behind him. "I wasn't planning on company back here anytime soon."

"Thanks for inviting me anyhow," she said. "I needed to get away for a couple of hours."

"Me too, desperately. Are you just coming off of work?"

"No. I was heading in, and they canceled me. The floor's overstaffed tonight. I'm not complaining. I've slept about six hours in three days."

Jake thought of his own insomnia the last several nights. Memories occupied his every waking thought, so many that they wouldn't let him sleep. The instant he closed his eyes, he'd hear Maribelle or Petra. He'd get a flash of a picture show they watched in the asylum theatre or remember their muffled giggles when they sat for services in the large, eerie chapel.

"Get ready," he told her, pointing at the sky.

The lights from a 747 blinked in the distance. Within seconds they could hear it and then feel it as the wind rushed around the enormous jet.

It dropped lower and grew deafening as it hovered right above them. Jake imagined an alien landing might look something like it. The sound and sight seemed to swallow them.

He looked over to see Charlie's eyes, round and sparkling in the strobe lights. She glanced at him and as they gazed at one another, his breath seemed to expand for the first time in days.

When it was over, Charlie sat up. She grabbed a dark backpack and set it on his stomach.

"What's this?" he asked.

"I found it in the downstairs tunnel."

Jake unzipped the bag and reached inside.

"Here," Charlie said, turning on a flashlight and pointing it toward the bag.

He pulled out a stack of photos, swallowing thickly as he looked at the faces of his friends. The image of himself standing next to his mother brought no warmth. The woman had not loved him, not wanted him. He'd first found love and acceptance with Maribelle and Petra.

Jake unfolded the list and read the long-ago getaway plan that had gone terribly wrong.

"I wasn't sure if you'd want it," Charlie said, "but…"

He sighed and touched her hand. "Thanks. It's good and bad, which is the story of my life lately, emphasis on the bad."

She sat up and took a drink. "I spent eight years married to a complete narcissist, and I think the ghost who's haunting Wilder's Grove tried to strangle me."

"My mother put me in a mental institution when I was ten," he returned. "One of the girls who was there with me has been murdered and I'm pretty sure a guy I've been letting hypnotize me for the last two weeks is trying to frame me for her death."

Charlie's mouth fell open, and Jake waited for her to hop off the back of the truck, jump in her car and flee into the night. Instead she broke two more beers out of the plastic ring and handed him one. "Have a pocket knife?" she asked. "I think we need to shotgun these ones."

He sat up, rifled around in his tool box and came out with a flathead screwdriver. "Next best thing," he told her.

She jammed the screwdriver into the can and covered the opening with her thumb. He did the same and then, without counting, they both popped the tops and sucked the beer from the cans. A younger version of himself would have told her how hot it was. The man was just grateful she hadn't run away.

She dropped the can in a plastic grocery sack and took a big breath. "Well, if this is a 'whose life is more fucked up' contest, you're definitely winning. Though I dare say winning is not the right word. Why don't you tell me about it?"

And he did.

38

They had talked until two am. Mostly Jake had talked. He'd started with the day, two weeks gone, when Petra had walked into his office and reached deep into the marrow of his life and pulled it all loose. He'd ended with the hypnotist who'd tricked him into revealing his deepest secrets.

She'd listened quietly, peppering in a question here and there, but mostly deep in thought as if he'd offered a tricky riddle and if she considered it long enough the answer would reveal itself.

In the end, she'd simply said, "You've got to find Gus."

They'd parted ways without so much as a kiss, though every fiber in his being wanted to kiss her, wanted to wrap his arms around her and crush her against him, wanted to take her home and forget about Petra and Gus and Maribelle.

Instead, she'd hugged him, and he'd climbed into his truck and driven home alone.

Now, with the sun washing the world in its optimistic morning glow, Jake felt better than he had in days. He flipped the radio station from classic rock to oldies to country, hoping for some old-timer crooning about true love, but every damn channel had an advertisement for Kenny's Buick Sales or Squeaky-Clean Carwash.

As Dig Deep Excavating slid into view, he saw the flash of red and blue lights. Not one but a dozen police cars sat in the front and back parking lots.

He hit the gas and swung into the lot fast, slamming the brakes when the nose of his truck nearly shot through a stream of yellow crime scene tape that stretched across the driveway. He killed the engine and jumped out.

An officer held up a hand to block Jake's entrance. "This is a crime scene, sir. You'll have to—"

Jake barreled through him and stepped over the tape as Detective Bryant came around the building.

"What's happened? It's not Barbie? Did somebody get hurt?"

If his mind had been working properly, he would have realized that Barbie getting clonked in the head with an excavator scoop or Willis having a heart attack wouldn't have summoned Bryant. Such incidents called for an ambulance, not a dozen police cars.

"Just hold on right there," Bryant commanded, picking up a walkie-talkie when sound crackled through.

Jake spotted Barbie, Willis, Ricardo, and the Jones boys all standing by the skid steer. Barbie looked scared, fiddling with the buttons on her blouse. Ricardo and Willis talked in hushed voices, their heads close together. Their troubled gazes were locked on a high point in the hill that rose up behind the gravel pit where the forest took over. The Jones boys stood shoulder to shoulder. They too watched that distant rise with uncertainty.

"Hey." Jake waved and trotted over. "What the hell is going on?"

Barbie started to speak and instead burst into tears. Ricardo wrapped an arm around her shoulders and seemed unwilling or unable to meet Jake's eyes.

"Willis?" Jake asked.

The man who'd been his friend, Lennon's friend, for decades looked at him gravely, and Jake felt his stomach, which had been fluttery moments before, solidify into a boulder.

"What? Someone tell me what the fuck is happening."

Willis nodded toward the hill where men emerged from the trees. They were carrying something. A stretcher. Covered in a white sheet.

"Holy shit," he murmured. "What? Who? There's a body back there?"

The Jones boys glanced at him, a question in their eyes, and he understood. The realization hit him like the tip of a baseball bat into his guts. There was a dead body behind his shop and everyone thought he'd put it there.

"Ricardo found her," Willis said.

"Her?" Jake's eyes shot to Ricardo.

Ricardo patted Barbie's back and pulled himself up taller. "What's left of her. She was in bad shape. The animals probably..." He trailed off.

"Who? Who was it?" Jake demanded.

Ricardo shook his head. "I don't know, but... well, she wore something awful similar to the woman who showed up here, the one who went missing."

"Petra..." Jake whispered. How had he not instantly thought of her?

Ricardo screwed his eyes shut as if the name accompanied an image too horrific to see. And yet from his expression, he saw it anyway, seared on the backs of his eyelids or on the doorway into his mind.

Detective Bryant had returned his radio to the waistband of his pants. He walked toward Jake now with a cold expression and handcuffs in his right hand. "Jake Edwards, you have the right to remain silent. Anything you say—"

Jake gaped at him and took an involuntary step back. He half considered running and then the vision of what would come next flashed into his mind. He'd sprint across the dirt lot, dodging in and out of equipment, while a sea of blue-clad men, armed with guns and black batons, descended on him like angry hornets after he'd kicked their nest.

"Barbie," Jake said, ignoring Bryant as he continued his Miranda rights. "Barbie!" he said louder.

She dropped her hands away from her buttons and looked at him as if he seeing him for the first time.

"Please call Osmond Casper. He's in the Rolodex. Tell him what happened."

Bryant was on him now, roughly turning Jake around. "Hands behind you, Jake," he commanded.

Jake didn't extend them back. "Wait, where are you taking me? I need to know what police station I'll be at."

"Bay City," Bryant said.

"Call Casper," Jake told Barbie. "Tell him to get to the police station in Bay City as soon as he can."

"Okay, Jakey," she whispered, tears drawing grim mascara lines over her powdered cheeks.

"Do it now," he shouted, and she jumped.

Ricardo pulled her protectively closer, but Willis stepped forward. "Don't worry, Jake. We'll get in touch with Osmond now." Willis took Barbie's hand, and he and Ricardo led her toward the office.

"Good luck, boss," Allen Jones said. Though from their expressions, the Jones boys thought he'd need a helluva lot more than luck.

∽

CHARLIE SAT up on the couch, groggy, with the hint of a hangover needling her brain. She'd fallen asleep on the sofa after her evening with Jake, fully intending to wake up and go to bed once she caught the eleven o'clock news.

"Bones?" she called as she stood and stretched her arms overhead.

Her low back ached from the awkward sleeping position. As she ambled into the kitchen, Charlie searched for her kitty, but he didn't appear with his usual morning chatter.

Uneasy, she hurried to the window and peered at the bird feeder on the front lawn. No dead birds lay beneath it and no Bones.

Above her, something creaked.

"Come here kitty, kitty," she called, foregoing coffee for a few minutes to track down her cat.

As she walked up the stairs, icy fingers grasped her arm and tugged her backward. Charlie gasped and clutched the bannister. She twisted around, knowing before she'd turned that the stairway would lie empty below her.

"Leave me alone," she hissed, rubbing her arm where the cold sensation lingered.

At the top of the stairs, the hall stretched long and the rooms stood dark on either side.

"Bones?" she called, her voice wavering.

A muffled meow drifted behind her closed bedroom door. Charlie hurried over and grasped the knob, yanking her hand back when she registered the icy brass beneath her fingers.

The cat meowed again and scratched at the door.

Behind Charlie, a floorboard creaked and she froze. Her mind insisted it was the ghost, but her body sensed otherwise.

As she turned, the man stepped from a darkened doorway. He moved fast, and her brain had barely registered the need to run when the butt of his gun smashed into the side of her head.

∼

Hours passed in the claustrophobic little room with the sticky table and the too-bright overhead lights. A migraine flirted with the backs of Jake's eyes and he squeezed them shut, massaging the bridge of his nose. "I didn't kill her. How many ways can I say it? You need to get those idiots searching my house out looking for Trent Henderson or Gus or whatever the hell his name is."

Bryant's partner broke in. "You inserted yourself into this investigation from day one, Jake. You!" He jabbed a finger at him. "I think you're looking for fame, suffering from a guilty conscience or trying to make sure we're not onto you. But guess what, buddy? Your little plan has backfired. You put yourself right smack dab on the bullseye."

Bryant didn't interject. He watched Jake with shrewd, emotionless eyes.

"What about Adrian? Did you talk to Adrian? She was looking into the doctors. She knows Gus exists."

"Adrian didn't have any business meddling in this case," Bryant snapped. "And the only thing Adrian knows is that a man named Augustus Church once worked as a psychiatrist at the Northern Michigan Asylum. There is not a single shred of evidence he ever had any contact with Petra Collins."

Jake threw up his hands. "Where's my lawyer?"

"I'm sure he'll be here anytime," Bryant said. "But let's switch gears for a moment. I'd like you to tell us why you broke into Petra's home two days ago."

39

After eight hours of questioning, they released Jake. He left the station with Osmond Casper, who encouraged him to go home, talk to no one, and he'd be in touch soon.

When Jake walked into his house, the evidence of the search was everywhere. Drawers had been pulled out and left haphazardly on the floor. Every cupboard in the kitchen stood open. Streaks of fingerprint dust coated chair backs, light switches and door frames.

He sat heavily in his easy chair and stared numbly at the opposite wall. His lower back ached after hours sitting.

Norm had told them Jake had broken into Petra's house. Jake had been furious initially, but when he thought of Norm sitting beneath the hot fluorescent lights, the two detectives bearing down on him, he understood. Norm needed to shift the blame to anyone except himself. Jake was the next best thing.

Something lumpy poked his side and he reached down, finding the backpack Charlie had given him the night before. He pulled it out and opened it, looking into the dark interior where the photographs lay. He reached in and felt a jagged hole in the fabric. He peeled the bag open wider. In the bottom corner of the bag, the narrow, jagged hole marred the fabric.

As Jake poked a finger through the hole, a memory slowly swam up from the gloomy depths.

"The dagger! Where's the dagger?" The words had fled down the tunnel that night, mixed with Maribelle's screams. It had been Dr. Gus's voice Jake had heard thirty years ago as he dragged Maribelle into the darkness.

40

Wind whipped the trees, snatching their leaves and hurling them into the road.

Jake pressed the accelerator to the floor. If a cop saw him, he'd get a ticket or, worse, arrested for reckless driving, but it was too late to play it safe now.

He took the corner fast, tires squealing, the pickup lifting for an instant before the tread caught the pavement and rocked him back down.

He'd called Charlie first, calm as he listened to the ringing phone and left her a message. The second time he called, the phone rang and rang. The third time it emitted a busy signal. Maybe she was talking to her mother or a girlfriend. Jake didn't think so. He thought somewhere in Wilder's Grove a phone had been left off the hook.

The house came into focus at the same time as the green Honda Accord. Jake had seen the car before. It had been parked outside the office of Trent Henderson, who'd never been Trent Henderson at all.

He hit the curb and slammed on the brake. Leaving the truck running, parked half in the driveway and half on the sidewalk, he jumped out and ran up the porch. He pounded the front door. "Charlie!" he yelled. He tried the knob and found it locked.

He sprinted to the side of the house. The door by the laundry room was locked, as was the sliding glass door on the back porch. The wind howled, nearly muting the sound of the heavy planter he smashed against the slider. The glass cracked but didn't shatter. The planter broke in half. Black dirt and the tangled roots of the geranium fell to the wood deck. Jake kicked the crack in the glass and it exploded into the kitchen.

He burst in, the wind following and bringing leaves, driving the pebbles of glass across the floor and beneath the farmhouse table.

He registered a mug on the table lying on its side. Coffee pooled on the bench beneath it. "Charlie?" he shouted, running through the house, pounding up the stairs.

No response. The house was quiet—eerily quiet. He heard a sound, a tiny mewling, and swung around. He gazed at the closed bedroom door and noticed a speckling of something dark on the doorframe. He touched it and cringed at the red smear on his fingertips.

When he pushed open the door to Charlie's bedroom, her cat leapt out, racing down the hall and out of sight.

Jake's breath caught in his throat. What would he find in the room? What was the cat running away from?

He stepped inside and studied the made bed, the slippers near the door to the bathroom, a half-filled laundry basket in the corner. Jake pushed into the bathroom, caught his colorless reflection in the mirror, and tried not see the panic in his eyes. He ripped back the shower curtain and stared into the empty tub, sagging forward and bracing his hands on his knees.

Straightening up, he hurried unsteadily back down the stairs, pushing open doors and calling Charlie's name.

In the study, the phone hung off the hook. It dangled above

the thick gray carpeting. No blood or broken furniture accompanied the image, but it knocked the breath out of him just the same.

Beside the phone, he saw the hastily scribbled note.

Do you know what brings back memories, Jacob? Returning to the place where you made them. Meet me in the tunnel and we'll take a walk down memory lane. Oh, and don't forget to bring back what you stole.

The man hadn't signed his name. There was no mention of Charlie, but Jake knew what he had to do.

He found a trowel in Charlie's shed and walked across the yard. Despite the rushing wind, he heard it, felt it. The dagger he'd buried thirty years before throbbed beneath him.

Charlie had planted a bird feeder almost directly on top of it. Jake wrenched the feeder out and tossed it aside, dropping to his knees and plunging the shovel in. Almost immediately it hit steel. He pulled the dagger out, feeling the heat of it. Dirt filled the crevices in the decorative bronze hilt, but the ten-inch steel blade looked oddly clean despite decades in the ground.

As Jake climbed into his truck, a blur in an upstairs window caught his eye. He stared at the gray face of woman glaring down at him. Her dark eyes were furious and her mouth was open as if screaming at him to stop. He blinked and she was gone.

∼

THE NEARLY THREE-HOUR drive seemed endless and when Jake finally sped down the tree-lined road to the asylum, his entire body ached. Before he pulled into the parking lot, he jerked the truck to the curb and jumped out, running a canvas bag into the woods and shoving it beneath a bush. He took a mental picture of the trees surrounding it, so he could retrieve it when the time was right.

He parked and sprinted to the door at the stairwell leading to the steam tunnels. As he jerked it open, he heard the crunching of twigs.

He turned to see Trent, or Gus, standing at the edge of the woods, slightly concealed, though the gun in his right hand was apparent.

"Amazing the things we remember when death is on the line," Gus said. "Where's the dagger, Jake?"

"Where's Charlie? Take me to her, show me she's alive, and I'll take you to the dagger. I won't fight you. I'll lead you right to it."

Gus smirked and waved the gun. "Or I could shoot you in the leg or maybe the abdomen. I spent years working with the human body. I know all the places to aim for maximum pain, but minimal threat of death."

"How old are you, Gus? Seventy or close to it? Hands gotten shaky at all?"

"Would you stake your life on it?" Gus held the gun pointed at Jake. It didn't waver.

"Shoot me then. I won't give you the dagger until I see her."

Gus lifted his other hand to the gun and widened his stance. Jake didn't move. His breath slowed and stopped as he stared at the black barrel aimed at his forehead.

Seconds passed and then Gus lowered the gun. "You first," he said, gesturing toward the path behind him.

They walked through the thick growth of the forest following no discernible path. At the top of a hill, Gus stopped. "Down the hill," he said, pointing, but keeping the gun fixed on Jake's back.

Gus paused at a wall of vines and tangled brush.

"Go," he commanded.

Jake stared at the brush. "Where? Into the bush?"

Gus nodded. Jake held up his hands and pushed into the foliage. He stepped through, fighting back branches, and felt a wooden door beneath his palms. He pushed and stumbled forward into emptiness. He blinked, his eyes slow to adjust to the gloom. The walls were brick and rose into an arched hall with a dirt floor and the clammy wet smell of underground.

"What is this?" Jake muttered.

At the far end of the tunnel, he made out an orange glow. Stones crunched beneath him as he walked down the passage, breaking into a run when he saw Charlie curled on the floor.

The spherical brick room was lit by torches that hung in heavy black candelabras. Charlie lay on the stone floor, eyes closed, arms pushed behind her back where her hands were bound.

"Charlie?" Jake whispered, squatting beside her body, putting his fingers to her neck. He found her pulse, slow, rhythmic. She wasn't dead.

"There, you see. She's alive and well. Now take me to the dagger and you can have her."

It was a lie. Jake and Gus both knew it.

"I'll give it to you. But why? Why have you done all this? You killed Petra for an old dagger?"

The man before him looked nothing like the hypnotist he'd met two weeks before. This man had wild, despairing eyes. His cheeks were hollowed and when he spoke, his lips curled in a snarl. "You rotten little son of a bitch. I told the brotherhood. I told them thirty years ago that the seer prophesied your coming. You'd undo us all, she said, but no, no, we had to keep you alive. You could tell us things, they insisted. What spirits might you be able to see?" Gus laughed. "Her. You could see the goddamn witch!"

Jake tried to puzzle out the man's rantings, but they made absolutely no sense. Gus had clearly gone as insane as the patients he once claimed to heal. "Trent... Gus, I have no idea what you're talking about."

"And you never did."

"I was ten years old!"

Gus walked to a wooden podium and rested his hands on an enormous leather-bound book. "You dug that dagger up. Do you know how many of the brotherhood have died? Not just died, been murdered. My best friend was beaten to death in his own bed! And you wonder what I could possibly want with some old knife you dug out of the ground? If I could go back in time, I'd have killed you the first night we brought you into the chamber."

"Instead you killed Maribelle."

Gus didn't answer. He stared unblinking at the book, and then his head shot up as if he realized time was of the essence. He walked to Charlie and squatted, pressing the barrel of the gun into the back of her head. "Where's the dagger, Jake?"

～

JAKE LED Gus through the woods to the place he'd tucked the bag. He grabbed the dagger and held it out.

Gus leaned in and stared at it, studying the hilt, eyes roving over the blade. The dagger Jake had pulled from the earth all those years ago had been there a very long time. There was no way Gus could have ever laid eyes on it and yet...

Gus's face darkened and he slowly lifted the gun.

Jake cringed away, holding up his hands.

"You thought you were so smart," Gus growled. "Even back then. You were an arrogant little prick and Maribelle was so sure Daddy would always protect her." Gus spit in the dirt. "You have ten seconds to produce the real dagger. Ten, nine, eight, seven..."

Jake bit his teeth together and considered his options, most of which were dire.

"Four, three, two..." Gus continued, cocking the revolver.

"It's right there," Jake blurted. "In the bush."

Gus glanced at the bush, but kept the gun pointed at Jake's head. "Get it."

Jake walked to the bush and knelt, reaching in for a second canvas sack he'd dropped the dagger into. When he pulled it free, Gus's eyes blazed.

"You'd never know the power it contains," he whispered.

"What power is that?"

Gus stared at him with disgust. "I searched for thirty years for you," he muttered. "Some of the others believed you'd fled the country, that you were this brilliant kid intentionally thwarting us, and all the while you were skinning elbows on a baseball diamond like every other snot-nose in America. What I don't understand is why she protected you."

Jake blinked at him, trying to piece together the baffling story. "Maribelle?" he asked.

"Maribelle?" Gus mocked in a whiny voice. "Yes, your little sidekick." Gus's eyes widened and he suddenly perked up. "She knew. Somehow she discovered the power of the dagger. That's why. Her father said she wanted to ruin him. She must have wanted to ruin all of us."

"Is that why you killed her? Trying to make her talk?"

Gus sneered. "I didn't have to do a thing to her. Joseph Claude took care of that. Of course, he was supposed to get her damn secrets first, but..." Gus shrugged. "The line between torture and murder is not exactly in a textbook, now is it?"

"Her father killed her?"

Deeper in the trees, a twig snapped and Gus's eye twitched, but he held the gun steady. "Bury it. Now. You have to bury it in the same place you took it from."

Jake puzzled at the man's fearful expression and stared beyond him into the leaf-thick trees. The wind had not followed Jake north, but the sky revealed charcoal clouds on the horizon. Rain would come within the hour. "I don't have a shovel," Jake said.

"Go." Gus jerked the gun back the way they'd come. "There's one in the stone room."

As Jake walked, his eyes roved across the overgrown path. He searched for a fallen branch large enough to knock the gun from Gus's hand. Even as his mind sorted various scenarios to overpower the man, each ended with the likely outcome that Jake would get shot. He might survive, might wrestle the gun from the man's hand. Just as likely he might end up dead or bleeding out in the weedy forest.

"Who's there?" Gus hissed the words and Jake slowed, trying to cast a glance over his shoulder.

"Walk," the man shouted.

The gun butted him in the back of the head. Jake dropped into a crouch and Gus stumbled and swore. Jake swiped the man's legs out from under him, but Gus managed to hold onto the gun. Their eyes met for an instant and Gus tensed as he squeezed the trigger.

The bullet caught Jake high on the right side, ripping through his shoulder. The impact rocked him back and he spun, didn't go down. Jake ducked and zigzagged into the trees, branches snatching at his hair as he fled.

Two more shots rang out and he winced at each bang, expecting the searing pain once more, this time in his back, crippling him or tearing through some artery, leaving him to bleed out.

He stopped running when he nearly slammed into a wall of brush. Dazed, he backed away from it and turned in a terrified circle. He'd ended up back at the chamber.

As his eyes swiveled between the trees, he expected to see Gus, gun lifted, but the doctor hadn't followed him. Blood seeping from his shoulder and soaking the right half of his shirt, Jake used his left hand to reach through the brush and push against the wooden door. It swung in and he stepped into the cool tunnel, leaning on the clammy wall to catch his breath.

He hadn't lost enough blood to pass out, but eventually it would come to that. He hobbled down the hall to the chamber, moving slowly in case Gus awaited him inside.

Charlie no longer lay on her side. She sat up, looking disoriented. A mottled yellowing bruise covered the left side of her face where Gus had struck her with something.

When her eyes registered Jake, she gasped and struggled to her feet. "You're covered in blood," she whispered, searching the hall behind him.

"Yeah. We have to hurry. Here, turn around." With his left hand he fumbled to release her, but it was no use. Gus had bound her with zip ties. "Hold on," he muttered.

He'd slung the canvas bag over his shoulder before he'd tripped Gus in the woods. Now he clenched his teeth, eyes watering with pain as he shuffled the bag off of his injured arm and dropped it on the ground. The dagger felt hot to the touch when he pulled it from the bag.

"Hold really still." He sawed the dagger across the zip ties. Halfway through the second tie, his hand went numb and the dagger clattered to the floor.

"It's okay," she said as he bent to pick it up. She wriggled her arms and managed to pull her hands free.

Jake paused, flexing and unflexing his hand. It tingled but seemed uninjured.

"Where's the guy, Jake? With the gun?"

"I don't know. We have to go, but…" Jake ran to the book on the pedestal. The book was huge and he'd never be able to carry it with his bum shoulder. He grabbed the loose-leaf papers lying on top. "Put the dagger and these papers in my bag," he insisted, nodding at the dropped dagger.

Charlie, hands shaking, took the papers and pushed them into the bag. When she touched the dagger, she recoiled. "It moved."

"Here, hold the bag." He thrust the bag into her hands and as she held it open, he snatched the dagger from the ground and dropped it inside. He took the bag back and pushed the straps over his good shoulder, then thought better of it. "I've got to carry the dagger. It's our only weapon. If Gus comes back..."

"Who's Gus?" she murmured, eyes locked on the bag as he handed it back to her.

"The guy with the gun," he said. "You carry the bag."

He reached inside and extracted the dagger. As before, it felt hot to the touch and it seemed to throb in rhythm with his own pulse.

They ran down the tunnel and pushed into the woods. As they jogged through thick foliage thunder cracked in the distance.

Charlie skidded to a stop in front of him.

"What?" he blurted, stepping around her and expecting to see Gus in their path.

The tall grass and shiny leaves were splashed in red. Blood matted the ground and dripped from hanging branches. At the edge of some trampled grass, Jake spotted Gus's gun.

"What is this?" Charlie whimpered, shaking her head and walking backwards.

A hand pressed on Jake's arm and he turned to see Horace standing beside him.

Run, the spirit mouthed, though no sound emerged.

"The other way," Jake shouted. "Run, Charlie, just run!"

Charlie took off in front of him. As they raced into the trees, the rain began to fall.

EPILOGUE

Jake looked beyond Abe, who sat at his kitchen table reading the papers they'd taken from the stone chamber near the asylum.

In the sunroom that opened off the Levetts' kitchen, Charlie sat in a canvas director's chair, a sky-blue throw draped over her shoulders. Orla handed her a mug of tea and sat next to her in a matching chair.

Abe glanced up. "Man, I wish you'd grabbed that book," he muttered, shaking his head.

"I wasn't thinking straight," Jake admitted, scratching at his shoulder. It was immobilized with a sling that was attached by velcro to his chest. He hated the damn thing, but not quite as much as he hated the fiery spears that jammed through his shoulder if he so much as sneezed without the sling on.

"According to this…" Abe started, tapping the paper.

"Wait," Orla called. "I'd like to hear this."

"Me too," Charlie agreed.

Both women walked into the kitchen. Charlie touched Jake's good hand.

"Any pain?" she asked.

"Nah, I'm good. Thanks, Charlie."

She smiled and took a seat on the couch next to Orla.

Twain and Dickens jumped onto the couch, cramming themselves in the space between the two women. Charlie laughed as Twain licked her cheek.

"Honey," Orla spoke to Abe. "Can you put the Hounds of Hell out before you start?"

Abe gave her an exasperated look, but smiled. "Sure thing." He walked to the front door. "Twain, Dickens, come on, guys. Go water the plants."

The dogs jumped from the couch, tripping over each other in their run to freedom.

Abe returned to the table, but didn't sit down. He studied the pages as he walked around the room. "According to these, an alchemist visited the grounds of the Northern Michigan Asylum in 1872. He was summoned there by a group of men. A witch had been murdered and buried in the forest. Ever since, the land had become toxic. Not toxic to the plants, but the men and their families. If any of them stepped foot in the woods, they grew ill and died within days."

"A witch?" Orla puzzled.

Abe glared at the pages. "They called her a witch, but in those days any non-compliant woman might earn the label."

"But that doesn't explain the land becoming toxic," Charlie interjected.

"We can't know why they made those claims, at least not by reading this. This document explains that an alchemist, who is referred to as Pike, bound the curse to the dagger. As long as the dagger remained in the ground, the witch's curse could do no harm."

Jake frowned and shifted in his chair, wincing at the pain in his shoulder.

Abe looked at him, cocking his head. "How did you find it, Jake? This letter says that dagger was buried four feet deep."

Jake looked away and fixed his eyes on a glass orb resting as a bookend on a wall shelf. A misty blue glaze drifted in the glass ball and he recalled the day he'd felt the earth pulsing beneath him. Several of the kids had been playing hide and seek, and Jake had snuck into the woods, further than the children were permitted to go. The ground beneath him throbbed, and when he'd knelt and touched the earth, the woman's voice filled his head. "The witch told me," he said at last.

Charlie blinked at him, leaning forward as if she hadn't caught his words. He had no intention of repeating them.

"You could see her?" Orla asked. No hint of disbelief tinged her words.

Jake shook his head. "I found the place by accident. I felt the dagger. The ground above it had an energy, a beat. I wonder if she drew me to it somehow. I ran away, but then she reached out to me in the night. She wanted me to dig it up, but it wasn't four feet in. Maybe the ground eroded where it had been buried, but there's no way I dug that deep."

"She wanted you to break the binding," Orla murmured.

Jake nodded. "I didn't know it then. Horace warned me against it, but I did it anyway."

"Who's Horace?" Abe asked, drawing his eyebrows together.

"The ghost Jake saw as a boy," Charlie answered for him, giving Jake a tender look.

"This story is more complex than an Agatha Christie novel," Abe deadpanned.

"He was my father," Jake blurted, knowledge that had come to him in the forest as he'd gazed at the spirit's face and seen his own eyes looking back at him.

"Really?" Charlie breathed.

He nodded. "I realized it in the woods. I'd never known and then... and then I just did."

"You never knew your father?" Orla asked.

"No." Jake wrapped his good arm around Charlie, who'd

walked across the room. She rested her head against the left side of his chest.

"You dug up the dagger," Abe continued, "and then, if everything your cop friend found out is true, doctors at the asylum started dropping like flies."

"But you said they died in mysterious ways," Orla cut in. "They weren't going for a walk on cursed ground and keeling over dead. How could this curse reach into the world and kill them?"

"Maybe it was never the curse at all," Charlie said, pulling back from Jake. "Maybe someone wanted vengeance for all the horrible things they did."

"A vigilante?" Jake asked.

"Why not?" Abe agreed. "What's more plausible?"

"None of it," Orla said, "which means any of it."

"Do you want to try, honey?" Abe asked, nodding at the wooden box the dagger lay within.

Orla nodded and slid off her nude gloves. She walked to the box and reached a hand gingerly inside. Her eyes closed, her mouth turned into a tiny wrinkled bud and her forehead scrunched above her black eyebrows.

"A magic man," she whispered. "They... the men of that place, the grounds where the asylum was built... they did something horrible, not only to the witch." Orla shuddered. "To her child, I think. I can't see it, but I feel it. Even this magic man was... horrified. But they paid him and he provided a service. They were dying, these men, but the dagger"—her fingers lingered on the hilt—"the dagger captured the curse."

"And I set it free," Jake said.

Orla pulled her hand back and gazed at her fingertips as if they burned.

"What's my responsibility to this?" Jake asked, gesturing at the dagger laying on the table.

Abe crossed his arms across his chest and studied the dagger. Orla held her hands, gloves back on, tight in her lap.

Charlie spoke first. "Return it and maybe the doctors who did these terrible things live. Destroy it and maybe they all die."

"If there are any left alive, that is," Jake muttered.

"We can't tell you what to do with this, Jake," Abe said. "You were chosen."

"What would you do?" he asked.

"I'd toss it in the deepest, darkest lake I could find," Orla murmured.

∼

A MONTH HAD PASSED without a sighting of the mean-eyed lady. Charlie's coffee mugs sat unbroken on the kitchen table, the television stayed silent at night and no dead birds appeared on the lawn. Every now and then Charlie found herself hovering extra-long before the mirror, searching for the woman's face in the glass, but she never appeared.

Outside, she heard Jake's truck engine as he pulled into her driveway. A moment later, her front door opened.

"Knock, knock," he called.

"I'm in the kitchen."

Jake walked in with a large blue cooler and a plastic stick from which hung a string and several dangling feathers with a bell in their center.

"It's for Bones." He grinned and shook the cat toy, before pushing the cooler onto the counter and snaking an arm around Charlie's waist. He pulled her close and kissed her, lingering with his face in the crook of her neck. "Mmm, you smell like chocolate."

Charlie leaned into him, resting her cheek against the top of his head. "Double chocolate muffins for the road."

"Those are my favorite."

"I know," she whispered, kissing his temple.

A bell tinkled, and Charlie looked down to see Bones batting at the feathers on the string.

"I love that you bought him that stupid thing," she murmured.

He straightened up and kissed her nose. "Bones, get the birdie, come on kitty." Jake danced the feathers across the floor as Bones raced after them.

Charlie opened the cooler, already half full with sandwiches, bottled water, and beer. She added the muffins and a plastic container of watermelon.

"Jake, why do you think she was haunting Wilder's Grove?"

Jake frowned and paused with the cat toy in mid-air. Bones jumped and twisted sideways, snapping his jaws on a feather and pulling the toy from Jake's hand. He laughed. "Look at him go."

Bones marched triumphantly from the kitchen, the feathers poking from his mouth, and the stick dragging behind him.

"I think when I dug up the dagger, I became its keeper. She wanted me to stay with it and when I moved out... maybe she was trying to keep other people away just in case."

Charlie nodded. "She's gone. Not so much as a fluttering curtain since..."

A knock sounded on the door before she could finish.

"I'll get it," Jake told her, kissing her before he walked from the kitchen.

∼

Adrian Bryant stood on the porch in full police uniform.

"Are you here to arrest me?" he asked.

She smiled and shook her head. "I'm here to tell you they found DNA under Petra's fingernails. It went to the crime lab the day they found her and results just came back. They match Augustus Church."

"Where'd you get his DNA?"

"His apartment. He was renting a place less than a mile from Petra's duplex. Apparently, he'd only been living there for about three months. We've tracked him to more than twenty residences in the last three years. The guy was a total nut."

"Yeah, tell me about it." Jake smiled. "The uniform suits you, Miss Bryant."

She grinned. "You think so? I'm sorry, Jake. And even though he'll never say it out loud, my dad is sorry too. If they'd listened to you, they might have nailed the guy. Now who knows where he is?"

Jake thought of blood-splattered trees and swallowed back the bile surging in his throat.

"I doubt he got far," Jake said.

∼

JAKE RANG the doorbell at his childhood home in Alpena. His heart galloped in his chest and a trickle of cold sweat gathered at the back of his neck.

When the door opened, he let his breath out in a rush and took a step back.

A woman, much too young to be his mother, stared back at him.

"Hi," he stammered. "Does Margaret Dunn live here?"

The woman's face fell. She shook her head.

"I'm so sorry to tell you this, but Margaret passed two years ago."

"Okay." Jake nodded, a hollow feeling expanding out from his chest.

As he turned to walk back to his truck, the woman stopped him.

"Are you Jacob? Margaret's son, Jacob?"

Jake paused, the hollow space shrinking as he turned around. "Yes."

The woman's eyes widened, and she stepped onto the porch, extending her hands to grasp Jake's.

"I'm Courtney. Your mom was my aunt. I can't believe it's you. We all knew she had a son, but... well, you disappeared." Courtney shook her head slowly. "Please, come inside. We should talk."

Jake blinked at her, unsure how to respond.

"I didn't realize she had any siblings," he admitted.

"Come in. Will you? We can talk?"

Jake glanced at the truck where he saw Charlie watched them.

"Sure, okay. Let me grab my girlfriend."

∽

JAKE AND CHARLIE sat on an ugly floral-patterned brown couch. He remembered the couch. The same furnishings from his childhood filled the space. Drab and brown. The house was musty, colorless, and sad. He felt that most of all, the veil of grief that seemed to hover in the thick air.

Courtney, a small, diminutive woman, not quite thirty with a head of bushy blonde hair, had assembled a stack of photo albums on the coffee table before them.

"I'm in charge of your mom's estate," she explained. "But I live in Indiana, so I try to drive up every few weeks sift through things. Obviously, I've barely made a dent, but..." She studied Jake with curious brown eyes, "it's technically yours, Jake. Your mother's will named you as the beneficiary."

Jake shook his head. "No. I can't. I don't want it."

Charlie reached for him. She took his hand, smoothing her fingers over his palm.

Courtney frowned. "They put you in an institution. My mom told me that, but... nothing else. My mom was older than yours by about five years. She adopted me in her forties. Linda was her name."

"Linda?" Jake murmured. A vague memory of his grandparents speaking the name Linda surfaced, but he had no context.

"Can you tell us about them?" Charlie asked. "About Jake's family?"

"I don't remember much," Jake confessed, which wasn't entirely true. He remembered the loneliness of his life in his grandparents' house. He just didn't understand it.

Courtney nodded and leaned back in the stiff brown chair she sat in. "My mom left here when she was fifteen. She didn't get along with her parents. I never met them. I was twenty the first time I met Margaret. My mother had a stroke and Margaret drove to Indiana to visit us. A year later my mom died and Margaret called me and asked me to come here." Courtney looked around the sitting room.

"I understood why my mom had left. This place is-"

"Depressing," Jake offered.

"Yeah, exactly. Margaret was polite, but distant and rather cool. I spent a few days here. She gave me photographs from my mother's childhood and some of her things. My third night here, Margaret woke me up in the night. She said she needed to tell me the story of her life."

Jake realized he'd begun to squeeze Charlie's hand tightly. He gave her an apologetic smile, but she only squeezed back.

"When your mom was sixteen years old, she ran away from home," Courtney explained. "This was in the fifties. Our mothers were raised staunchly Catholic."

"Yeah," Jake murmured. The house had been largely cleared of décor, but crucifix-shaped silhouettes remained on every wall.

"It was very shameful for their parents. Both of their daughters ran away. My mom got married at sixteen and moved in with her husband's family in Indiana. When your mom ran away, she didn't have anywhere to go. She took a train to Detroit and got a job cleaning at the Stratmore Hotel. That's where she met Horace."

Jake's mouth went dry. He felt Charlie's eyes on him, but didn't turn to face her.

"Horace played piano in the hotel and around the city. Your mother told me they fell in love, but their joy lasted less than two months. Apparently, Horace tried to break up a fight at a club one night and he got stabbed. He died in a Detroit alley."

Jake allowed his eyes to drift shut. He thought of the spirit of the man who'd comforted him as a child, a man who'd bled to death in a dark alley.

"Your mother told me she called your parents to come get her. She was pregnant, poor and alone." Courtney watched him with despairing eyes. "They were angry with her. They tried to make her put you up for adoption, but she wouldn't."

"She should have," Jake muttered.

Again, he sensed Charlie's gaze, but he couldn't look at her.

Courtney leaned forward, clasping her hands on her knees. "She acknowledged that she emotionally abandoned you, Jake. She wanted me to know her story just in case you came back someday. She was so bitter and heartbroken. Even as an old woman," Courtney shook her head. "That night was the only time she warmed to me. The next morning, the Margaret I'd first met reappeared. Quiet, withdrawn and not all that nice. Two years ago, she died of a heart attack. She named me the executor of her estate, but you're the beneficiary. Technically, this house belongs to you."

Jake shook his head. "I don't want it. I don't want any of it."

LET HER REST

THEY DROVE IN SILENCE. Charlie considered the slope of Jake's clenched jaw, but allowed him time to process the words Courtney had told him.

He pulled into the parking lot for the Star Line Ferry to Mackinac Island. He turned off the truck and looked at Charlie.

"Are you okay?" she asked, searching his steady blue eyes.

He smiled, though two worry lines remained between his eyebrows. "I am. I will be. I needed to hear those things and now..." He shrugged. "Now I have a story. It doesn't make everything better, but it's a start."

∾

WHEN THEY STEPPED onto the ferry, only twenty other passengers boarded alongside Jake and Charlie. The day, which began sunny, had turned gray with heavy clouds obscuring the sky.

Halfway to the island, Jake stood. Charlie followed him to the back of the boat where they stopped at the rail. Slate-colored water frothed against the stern of the ferry.

Jake unzipped the blue backpack he'd taken the night he'd run from the asylum so many years before.

Charlie's mouth turned down when he reached for the dagger.

Jake didn't hesitate, but slipped the blade free and let it fall over the side of the boat.

It disappeared into the dark water.

Don't miss the final book in the Northern Michigan Asylum Series: Bitter Ground

ALSO BY J.R. ERICKSON

Read the Other Books in the Northern Michigan Asylum Series

Some Can See
Calling Back the Dead
Ashes Beneath Her
Dead Stream Curse
Rag Doll Bones
Dark Omen
Let Her Rest
Bitter Ground

Available in Ebook, Paperback and on Audible!

ACKNOWLEDGMENTS

Many thanks to the people who made this book possible. Thank you to Rena Hoberman of Cover Quill for the beautiful cover. Thank you to RJ Locksley for copy editing Let Her Rest. Many thanks to Will and Donamarie for beta reading the original manuscript. Thank you to my amazing Advanced Reader Team. Lastly, and most of all, thank you to my family and friends for always supporting and encouraging me on this journey.

ABOUT THE AUTHOR

J.R. Erickson, also known as Jacki Riegle, is an indie author who writes stories that weave together the threads of fantasy and reality. She is the author of the Northern Michigan Asylum Series as well the urban fantasy series: Born of Shadows. The Northern Michigan Asylum Series is inspired by the real Northern Michigan Asylum, a sprawling mental institution in Traverse City, Michigan that closed in 1989. Though the setting for her novel is real, the characters and story are very much fiction.

Jacki was born and raised near Mason, Michigan, but she wandered to the north in her mid-twenties, and she has never looked back. These days, Jacki passes the time in the Traverse City area with her excavator husband, her wild little boy, and her three kitties: Floki, Beast, and Mamoo.

To find out more about J.R. Erickson, visit her website at www.jrericksonauthor.com.

CPSIA information can be obtained
at www.ICGtesting.com
Printed in the USA
LVHW102036080123
736729LV00002B/200